HARDENED

ASHE BARKER

Published by Stormy Night Publications and Design, LLC.
www.StormyNightPublications.com

Cover design by Korey Mae Johnson
www.koreymaejohnson.com

Images by Shutterstock/Julia Gurevich and 123RF/rook76

1st Print Edition. May 2016

ISBN-13: 978-1533471048

ISBN-10: 1533471045

FOR AUDIENCES 18+ ONLY

This book is intended for adults only. Spanking and other sexual activities represented in this book are fantasies only, intended for adults.

CHAPTER ONE

Leeds, UK
June 2010

Tick. Tock. Tick. Tock. My cellmate's tiny alarm clock counts down the endless stream of empty, torturous seconds, the inexorable creep of time as I wait for nothing at all to happen.

By now I really should be better able to endure the crushing boredom, but it gets no easier. Twenty-five months, three weeks, and five days have crawled past since I heard the three words that marked the beginning of this mind-numbing existence.

Take him down. The Honourable Mister Justice Merryweather decided in his wisdom that five years' imprisonment was about right for my part in the bungled attempt to relieve an inner city sub-post office of its day's takings. That was fair enough, I suppose, even though my job on that fateful day amounted to no more than stealing a fast motor and making sure I was outside the post office at the right time, engine running.

The rest of the gang I had hooked up with for that one and only job took it into their heads to take shotguns along though. One warning shot brought down the post office ceiling, along with the full weight of the law, which landed full square on all our heads. No judge will stand for firearms. I appreciate that sentiment now, though my resentment was bitter and real enough at the time.

I was fucking furious to be picked up by the police two days later and identified by a woman who had pushed her pram past the post office that day and happened to spot me waiting in the souped-up BMW. I remembered her too, pretty enough in a harassed, mumsy sort of a way. I watched her arse all the way down the street while my cock throbbed in my jeans.

My arrest particularly rankled because I'd performed my part to perfection. It was the rest who screwed up and even then all they needed to do was keep their mouths shut about who had been outside in the car. Like most young hotheads I was convinced I was invincible, too clever to be caught. Maybe I wouldn't have been, at least not for a while, but for the dickhead who fired into the air, then topped it all off by letting his mask slip and was caught on the CCTV. We got away with over twenty thousand pounds in cash, but with the CCTV evidence it was only a matter of time before the plods rounded us up.

And speaking of time, I've had plenty of it since then, certainly more than enough to reconsider my priorities. My two-and-a-bit years older, wiser, and no doubt mellower self is now ready to acknowledge that his honour had a point when he described our gang as greedy, amoral, and a danger to society. I like to think I'm a reformed character these days, but that remains to be seen. The question will be settled more speedily if I'm successful in convincing the parole board to grant me early release on the grounds of good behaviour and a genuinely remorseful attitude. I've had to work on the latter, but I have my parole hearing in a month's time and I rather think I might pull it off. As for good behaviour, that's a matter of perspective but I lean toward the view that what the screws don't see the heart need not grieve over. I manage to stay out of trouble by and large, and give the biggest idiots in this place a wide berth.

So, I spend most of my time cooped up in my cell, as do all the inmates of HMP Leeds, better known to those of us more intimately acquainted with the establishment as Armley jail. It could be worse; I've managed to earn myself enhanced status. This means I get a slightly bigger cell and I'm allowed a radio, books, personal photographs, that sort of thing. Oh, and a proper toilet, although it doesn't have a door. We may live in virtual isolation, but prisoners get no privacy. This is one of the things I most miss about being on the outside, and it's the main reason that once I manage to get out I won't be back. Not ever.

I have plans, and they do not involve an eight by six foot room, bunk beds, and two cell mates who snore, fart, and generally make me want to punch the wall.

It could be worse. Johnny and Bako aren't that bad really, and we sort of get along as long as no one touches anyone else's stuff, which isn't easy in such a small space. But we manage. Johnny's doing three years for drug dealing, and Bako managed to con his employers out of a few thousand in trumped-up travel expenses. He's hoping to be sent to an open prison soon as his was a white-collar crime. He's non-violent and not considered a danger to the public.

I wouldn't describe myself as violent either, but armed robbery is armed robbery and the system sees it otherwise, so I've spent my entire sentence in a closed facility. Still, I'm up for parole soon, and meanwhile I manage to maintain my sanity by spending as much time as I can in the prison gym, and by checking out Officer MacBride's sweet little arse at every opportunity.

I'm not convinced of the wisdom of female prison officers working in a men's facility, though I understand the theory well enough. Females defuse situations, and are believed to have a calming effect on us rampant males. I suppose it works, up to a point, as there aren't that many men, even the hardened criminals who inhabit this place, who would attack a woman without a second thought. Still, it does depend somewhat on how you define calm. The delectable Miss MacBride has a distinctly unsettling effect on me, and I swear she does it on purpose. No woman can fill out a pair of trousers like that, or slink along the corridors oozing sex appeal, and not be aware of it. Can she?

In the past I would have been certain, but it's been over two years since I got laid, let alone had the chance to hone my spanking skills on a pretty heart-shaped bottom, so I'm rusty. And horny. And bored. This is always a combustible cocktail in my view, so I check Bako's travel alarm clock again to remind myself how much longer I have to wait before recreation time. I have an hour's gym session booked and I need it. It's been three days since I had a decent workout and I'm wound up tight as a spring. I need to work off some of this bloody frustration, get a sweat on and feel the burn or I'll go mad.

Ten minutes to go. I lay back on my bunk and stare at the underside of Johnny's mattress two feet from the end of my nose. I start to count.

I reach a steady six hundred and fifty, and check Bako's clock again. It's after two in the afternoon. I'm already eating into my session and no screw has arrived to escort me upstairs to the gym. I roll from my bunk to peer out the small peephole in the door. I only have a view of a couple of feet in any direction, but it's enough to know that there is no officer about to unlock the cell and let me out.

"Expecting someone?" Bako looks up from the newspaper he's reading on his own bunk.

"Gym session," I reply. "Should be up there by now."

Bako shrugs. "Probably short-staffed again. And there's been bother down on H wing."

"Not my fucking problem," I snap, and I kick the bottom of the door in my annoyance. I know better than to imagine I'll get time added on at the other end of my workout session to make up for what's lost now.

"Sit down, mate. They'll be here." Johnny is the more

placid among the three of us; I put it down to the lingering effects of all the weed he's smoked over the years. He's content to while away his entire sentence on his bunk and must have gained at least three stones while he's been in here. One of these days I'm convinced he's going to come crashing through that fucking bunk and smother me. I really should suggest we swap, but the bottom bunk is best. I had to wait a long time for mine and I'm not giving it up.

I kick the door again, and drop into the one chair we have between the three of us. "Bloody fucking hell, I hate this," I announce to no one in particular, and tunnel my fingers through my hair. The sooner I can get before that parole board the better. Meanwhile, I start my warm-ups, just in case the fucking screws do actually remember me.

It's twenty minutes before the rattle of keys in the lock signals some action. The door opens, and my mood lightens just fractionally. Miss MacBride stands in the entrance, beckons me out, then steps back to allow me to pass.

"About time too," I growl. I might have sworn and kicked up a fuss. I would have if one of the male officers had come along to escort me, but I'm not inclined to this time, not at Miss MacBride. I suppose the prison authorities must be right, she does have a calming effect.

She offers me an apologetic smile. "I'm sorry. I know it's way past your time, but we don't have enough officers on today and I got held up in the kitchen. You've still got half an hour though." She sets a cracking pace down the wing and I console myself by hanging back a little, just enough to get a decent view of her gorgeous bottom.

Shit, that pert little arse is just begging to be spanked. I swear my hand is twitching.

I shove the offending limb in my jeans pocket and follow Miss MacBride to the end of the wing where she pauses to manage the locks. We pass through and head up two flights of stairs, then she stops again to unlock the door to the gym.

"Is no one else here?" I ask, surprised.

"Not today. Privileges are withdrawn because of the

disturbances down on H wing."

"How come I'm allowed up here then?"

"You're on G wing, and I offered to do the extra escort duty."

"Why?"

"Because I felt like it. Are you going to do those bench presses or not?"

I'm at least a head taller than she is but she tilts her chin with a degree of belligerence, which causes my cock to harden. Christ, in different circumstances what I'd like to do to this tasty little piece. I glower at her, but step into the room and stride across the tiled floor to get started on my favourite bit of apparatus.

I love the weights, could spend all day here if that was permitted. I load up the correct resistances and lay back on the bench to start my workout.

I glance over at Miss MacBride, stationed by the door. "How long do I have?"

"I'm off duty at three. I'll stay until then, and escort you back to the wing."

"I had an hour booked."

"I know, sorry. There's no one else to take over though, and I need to be off."

"Something better to do?" I know I sound petulant, and this isn't her fault. Even so, I'm pissed off and she's the only one I can vent to.

"I'd stay if I could, but we've had some problems with staffing levels, and there's an overtime ban so—"

"Yeah, right." I return my attention to the weights and grasp the bar.

I spend the next thirty minutes pumping iron, conscious of Miss MacBride's quiet presence. She doesn't move from the edge of the room, nor does she do or say anything to disturb my concentration, at least not intentionally. The truth is, she and her hot little arse distract me just by fucking being there. I move from the bench press to the rowing machine to get some cardiovascular action, even though I know I'll hardly work up a sweat before it's time to go back down to the wing. Sure enough, I'm just getting into my rhythm when she calls out to me.

"Time's up. Could you start your cool-down now, North?"

I glance at the clock on the wall above her head. It's five minutes past three. Fair enough, I suppose, but still I don't hurry.

I slow my pace and after a few more seconds allow the rowing machine to come to a stop. I take a couple more minutes to complete my cool-down stretches, and to her credit Miss MacBride seems ready to wait even though I know she's already late and won't be getting paid for babysitting me.

I have a brief opportunity to peruse her. I wouldn't say she was a classic beauty, though it's hard to be sure under that shapeless prison service-issue jacket. I'd certainly give her the benefit of the doubt. Her short dark hair is neatly cut close in to her neck, and her build is one I would describe as elfin rather than slender, though I'm not quite sure where I dredged that word up from. It just seems to suit her. Miss MacBride's features are delicate: a finely shaped nose, deep blue eyes, small but full mouth with a slightly protruding lower lip that in my weaker moments I fantasise about nibbling. Her chin is pointed and all too ready to lift in a way I would describe as sassy if I were to meet her on the outside. In here, it's just her interpretation of authoritative, and she is trying for that look now as I saunter back across the gym toward her.

"Come on, we need to move it." She opens the door and waits for me to pass her.

I deliberately don't quicken my pace, just offer her a sardonic nod as I leave the room. She stops to lock it behind us as I continue along the austere, windowless corridor. One day, I promise myself, and soon, I'll be surrounded by light and fresh air. No more windowless anything for me, not once I'm out of here.

The sound of Miss MacBride's stout leather soles tapping on the floor echoes down the hallway, her footsteps rapid as she hurries to catch up with me. I have to wait at the top of the stairs in any case as she needs to unlock the door to allow me through. Resentful, I glare at her under my eyebrows, not quite ready to forgive her for this injustice, which is really none of her doing.

"I'm sorry, I'd let you stay longer if I could," she mumbles as she fiddles with her monster bunch of keys.

I'm inclined to believe her, but I'm still too pissed off to say so. We complete the short walk back to my cell in silence.

• • • • • • •

I'm late. Again. Andy's going to kick off. Again.

I close and lock the heavy steel door, fully aware that North is still glowering at me from inside his cell, then I sprint down the wing and through the double set of lockable gates to reach the octagon. That's what we call the eight-sided central area, the hub if you like from which branch out the spokes of the eight wings that make up this section of the prison. Armley jail is a traditional Victorian building, austere but very functional, I suppose. There are newer sections—for example the education block, the kitchens, and the gymnasium—but the inmates are mainly housed in the old wings. There are communal areas fitted out with snooker tables and a television room, and a chapel of course, but for the most part their time is spent locked up in their cells.

I was surprised to learn this when I joined the prison service eighteen months ago. I had an image of the prison as a place of rehabilitation, where offenders might learn new skills, become ready to re-join society. The truth is we just contain the men for the duration of their sentence, then the system turfs them out and hopes for the best. It rarely works out well; the rate of recidivism is horrendous.

It's not unusual for the men to spend twenty-three hours a day in their cells, and that can easily stretch to a complete lockdown if circumstances require it. Like now, for instance. We have staffing levels approaching crisis point, and the cutbacks are starting to really impact on the quality of life for the inmates. Education is curtailed, which means the men spend even more time locked up, free association rarely happens, and the gym is used more by off-duty prison staff than it is by the inmates. There is a constant undercurrent of discontent that has become worse recently, fuelled by long-running quarrels and jealousies that always simmer below the surface. It takes very little to ignite the tinderbox and frequent scuffles break out between prisoners, which is why the managers of the prison prefer to keep them locked up and separated. There have been several incidents of officers being threatened. Not me, at least not yet, but we're all extra vigilant and almost all nonessential contact between prisoners is avoided. The austere regime can't be helped, but I don't blame the men for being resentful and sooner or later it's inevitable that something will erupt.

There are days when I find it hard to remember what I found so attractive about this job, especially when I know that as soon as I get home I'm in for another round of complaining and criticism from Andy. My fiancé loathes my choice of career. He can't even start to understand what drew me to the prison service and why I stay, and there are times I can see his point. I'm under constant pressure from him to resign, to find something 'nice' to do—maybe join him in the finance section of the local council. I could, I suppose, I got an A level in mathematics, but the idea of working in an office leaves me cold.

I hand in my keys and radio and head for the staff cloakroom. I could take a shower—the facilities for officers here are excellent—but I don't. Andy will be tetchy enough because I'm going to be at least half an hour late and he wanted to go shopping. I knew I'd be pushed to get home in time so I suggested he go alone and I'd meet him in town, then maybe we could get something to eat together. He wouldn't hear of that and insisted I head home first.

So I do. I nip through the traffic, relieved to have missed the rush hour at least, and dash into the flat we share just forty minutes late.

Andy is seething, as I knew he would be. He grabs his car keys and stalks out without so much as a word of 'hello,' 'how was your day,' or anything. I follow, wishing I had time at least to change my clothes. All the way into the town centre Andy refuses to so much as speak to me and I wonder, not for the first time, what he would have done if I hadn't followed him out to the car. Would he have gone alone as I suggested to him? Or would he have stormed back in, demanding to know what I think I'm playing at?

One day, maybe, I'll find out.

I take advantage of the frosty silence to think back over my day.

Four officers phoned in sick, which meant we were spread even more thinly than usual. That, combined with the scuffles down on H wing meant that most of the inmates spent the day locked up while those of us who did show up for duty patrolled the parts of the prison where trouble seemed ready to kick off. The governor ordered that prisoners could only leave their cells for essential purposes—medical appointments, court appearances, some visits. Education was cancelled, as well as all association and recreation. That strategy might be enough to keep the lid on for now but makes for a bored, discontented wing, and prisoners with a grievance are a volatile bunch. In the long term the policy causes more trouble than it solves.

Still, I got my fix of Jared North today, though I had to bend the rules and piss off Andy to do it. North was down to miss his gym session, but I offered to escort him and not put in for overtime. The wing supervisor was happy enough to let me do it, so I got to ogle him on the bench press for half an hour.

It was not especially professional of me, I know that, but

I couldn't help it. There's something about that man, something I can't quite pin down but that makes my stomach clench and causes me to dampen my underwear. He's off limits, obviously, and I would never dream of making so much as a flirty remark to him, but I can look. And I can imagine.

My good sense screams at me to stay well away from G wing. Jared North, Prisoner Number KG8329 is an armed robber, for Christ's sake, doing five years. According to his prison record he's not been any real bother for the last year or so now and might have a shot at parole before much longer, but he's most definitely bad news, a man to be avoided.

So why, when I could have just clocked off on time and headed home, did I volunteer for unpaid overtime just to escort him to the gym? And having done that, why do I now feel so bloody guilty for having dragged him out of there early? He was lucky to get any time at all.

Tomorrow, if I get a chance, I'll drop by his cell and try to explain.

Any excuse…

• • • • • • •

I'm on the late shift today, two in the afternoon until ten at night. Andy always hates this, complains that I'm never at home and when I do get there I'm too tired to be decent company. I suppose he has a point, but mine isn't a nice nine-to-five job and he knew that when we started seeing each other. He's still sulking from yesterday and I was secretly quite glad to see the back of him this morning as he left for work. I had a few hours to myself so I got on with cleaning our flat and put something in the slow cooker for later. I was at the outer gate by quarter to two as it takes a while to get through security and onto the wing.

When I eventually get inside it's to learn that two of yesterday's absentees are still off sick and we have reliable intelligence to suggest there's contraband on the wing. Usually that means someone managed to smuggle drugs in, but this time apparently it's a mobile phone. The governor has ordered a cell search.

I'm paired with another officer and we're assigned to search the even numbered cells. My colleague, Jim, is an experienced old hand close to retirement. I like him well enough, but I know he's just working out his final months until he can draw his pension and he's looking for a quiet life. He'll be well and truly pissed off if we do find anything because the aftermath of that entails hours of reports and form-filling, and Jim just wants to clock off and go home to his Doris who's making a shepherd's pie this evening, I gather.

I find I have little interest in clocking off myself as it's only Andy waiting for me, with his sour face and unending complaints. I'll do any paperwork that might arise.

"Okay, everyone outside. Stand in the corridor." Jim unlocks cell number two and the occupants file out past us to lounge against the emulsioned brick wall opposite. Their expressions are sullen but resigned; this is a common enough occurrence.

Jim and I step into the narrow cell and start the search. We strip the beds, lift mattresses, drag the bedframes away from the walls, then do the same with the small items of other furniture. We open drawers, cupboards, even lift the lid on the cistern. All personal property is examined, then one by one Jim does a pat-down of each of the men themselves. As a female officer I'm not permitted to do that so I finish off the cell search by shaking out the laundry. I try not to make too much mess, but this is never a tidy business and the men are expected to clear up after we've finished.

We find nothing and move on to repeat it all in the next cell along.

The cell occupied by Jared North is the eighth on our list. He rolls from his bunk and files out with the other two inmates. As I start the bed search I can see him leaning against the doorframe, his back to me. He is chatting to his cellmates, seemingly unconcerned that his belongings are about to be heaped onto the floor for him to sort out later. There are days I hate this job, and today is one of them.

I leave the toilet to Jim and quickly strip the top bunk. I find nothing and move down to drag North's mattress from the metal frame. I might have missed it, but for the faint clunk as I pull the bed out. There's something lodged inside the mattress cover. I glance up to see that Jim is still occupied in the toilet cubicle. I open my mouth to call out to him, but I don't. Instead I run my fingers around the edges of the thin mattress to discover whatever it is that shouldn't be there.

A hard, flat shape meets my questing fingers. It could be the phone we're seeking. My heart sinks—North will end up on report for this, and probably find himself back on a basic wing. Bloody idiot, what was he thinking of?

I slip my hand inside the mattress cover to grasp the offending item, and I pull it out.

Not a phone. A camera. I turn it over in my hand. It's one of those tiny digital things, the sort you just point and press, and quite new I'd say. And definitely contraband. Without thinking through what I'm doing I slip it into the pocket of my uniform trousers and continue with the search.

I refuse to even look at North as Jim concludes our business with the obligatory pat-down, though the prisoner can't fail to have seen the mess I've made of his neat bed. He has to know what I found, but he's saying nothing. Even more inexplicable, neither am I.

• • • • • • •

The following day I clock on, the camera still tucked in my pocket. Needless to say, I checked the memory card at home after my shift. North seems to like to take pictures of prison life, though I'm relieved to see he's not particularly interested in photographing other prisoners. I would have to take issue with that; even hardened criminals are entitled to their privacy. The pictures on the card are of his cell, the wing, the laundry where he usually works. And there are several of me.

I resolve to ask him about those, though I'm not at all sure I want to know his answer.

I check the work rota, and find that North is in the laundry. I spend a couple of hours on paperwork and do my usual rounds of the cells and communal areas, then make my way along to the utility wing where our industrial-sized washing machines are housed.

North is occupied piling small bags of underwear into the huge dryer. Prisoners like to get the same underwear back from the wash as the alternative is to wear things that hundreds of other men might have worn before and of course no one likes that. Each man has a small cotton bag that they can mark with their name, and into that they place all their small, personal items of laundry. With luck, the bag will be returned to the wing with its contents still inside, but now freshly laundered. The system works, on the whole.

Another prisoner is here too, but I know that Pearson is due a visit later so he'll need to be making his way to the visitors' suite before long, for processing.

"Pearson, you're going to be late." He has plenty of time, but I want to talk to North alone.

"No, miss. I'm fine for a bit yet." Pearson seems quite content to continue shoving clothes into the steam press and slamming down the lid. I watch him for a couple of minutes before I try again.

"We're short-staffed today, everything takes longer. Better get a move on, Pearson."

"Is someone else coming, then?" Pearson switches off his laundry press and ambles over to where I'm stationed by the door. The regulations require at least two people to be present when the laundry is in use in case of accidents.

"Soon. I'll let you out then I'll stay with North until Jackson arrives."

It'll be at least half an hour before the next prisoner is detailed to come down and take over from Pearson, which should be ample time to ask Jared North about the camera. I precede the prisoner down to the gates at the end of the utility wing corridor and let him through. From there another officer will let Pearson back onto the wing, and onto the visitors' suite. I relock the security gate and return to the laundry room.

North is still occupied with his task, though he does glance at me over his shoulder as I re-enter the huge room, then he switches his attention back to his work.

"I want my property back." His curt remark is delivered without even looking at me. He straightens, flexes his muscles, and drags another wheeled bin of dirty laundry in the direction of an empty washing machine.

"You're not supposed to have a camera in here. You know that."

"Neither are you, Miss MacBride." Now he does turn to regard me fully, one hip propped on the edge of the bin, his expression inscrutable. "Care to explain?"

I don't. I don't care to explain at all. I have nothing even vaguely resembling an explanation to offer, either to North or to myself.

"Where did you get it?" I try to inject a note of authority into my question.

He simply shakes his head.

I try again, piling on the officiousness as best I can. "Someone brought it in for you. I want to know who that was."

More head-shaking.

"I could put you on report, you do realise that?"

Now he just chuckles. "But you won't. You can't."

"I—"

He continues as though I hadn't spoken. "Because if you do, you'll have to also explain why you didn't report it

15

yesterday. Why you hid it, and I assume took it home with you. And why you brought it back. I hope you *did* bring my camera back, Miss MacBride."

"Why did you take pictures of me?" I blurt out the question, homing in on the one aspect of all this that makes me most uncomfortable. And most exhilarated.

He smiles and meets my gaze, though he appears rather calmer than I am right now.

"Because I like looking at you."

"What do you mean? That's, that's…"

"You're prettier than Mr. Drummond."

"That's not saying much." Our wing supervisor is certainly no oil painting, I'm not sure I appreciate the comparison.

"Perhaps not. So, are you going to give it back to me?" He holds out his hand, one eyebrow raised in what could only be described as a direct challenge.

I tilt up my chin; assertiveness is everything in these confrontational situations between officers and prisoners. "No, North, I'm not. It's a contraband item and it's been confiscated."

He appears quite unruffled. "I see. Very well, I'll apply to the governor for it to be returned."

"No! No, you can't." I take a step toward him, then pause, uncertain how best to proceed.

"Can I not? Oh, I understand, because then you'll have to explain how it found its way into your pocket during the cell search. Yes, I can see that might be awkward. Still, that isn't really my problem." He starts to load the laundry into the machine. "Could you close the door as you leave, Miss MacBride?"

I stand, glaring at his muscled back, intensely aware of the camera nestling in my pocket. He has me, it's as simple as that. I have no choice.

"Okay, you can have it back. But you have to delete the pictures of me."

He turns to face me again. "Are you still here, Miss

16

MacBride?"

I retrieve the camera from my pocket and hold it out to him. "Delete the photographs of me and, and you need to promise you won't take any more."

"I don't need to promise you anything. Why didn't you delete the pictures if it matters so much to you? You had all night to do it."

Because they were yours. I scowl at him, reluctant to acknowledge the truth of the matter, even to myself. And perhaps because I was flattered by the attention, by the fact that this enigmatic, compelling man thought me interesting enough to want to take my picture. Even as I allow that ridiculous notion to crystallise, I quash it. He's a criminal, a prisoner. He is *not* someone whose opinion matters to me.

I press the on/off button on the top of the camera and squint at the menu of controls that appear in the small screen on the rear. I try to navigate through to select and delete the pictures of me, but I'm soon hopelessly lost. It was easy enough to find my way around the gadget last night in the privacy of my own kitchen, but here, under the harsh scrutiny of Jared North himself, I'm all thumbs.

"Shall I?" He holds out his hand again, and I pass the camera to him.

In just a couple of seconds he has selected the pictures of me and they are ready to be erased. He hands the camera back. "You do it, then you'll know for sure that they're gone."

I shake my head. "I trust you."

"Really? How touching, Miss MacBride." He hits 'delete' and the offending photographs disappear. "But can I trust you, I wonder?"

"I won't report the camera, if that's what you mean."

"It wasn't, but I'll settle for that. I should thank you, I suppose, for rescuing me in the cell search."

"Just… don't take pictures of people, okay? And make sure no one else finds it."

He pockets the camera, then leans back on the laundry

bin to regard me with undisguised interest. "So, why didn't you report me? That wasn't very officer-like of you."

"It's complicated. I suppose I believe people should have a chance, that's all."

"Bullshit. You know the rules. So do I. It's my job to break them, yours to enforce. So, why didn't you?"

I step back and start to turn away. "I have to go. Like I said before, we're short-staffed."

I march across the laundry, the sound of my stout leather boots echoing around the space.

"Wait, Miss MacBride."

Something in his tone stops me in my tracks. Halfway to the door I halt and turn to face him again.

"Come back here."

It's a command. Here. In this place, I issue instructions and prisoners obey. Somehow though, that seems not to apply between Jared North and myself. Putting one foot in front of the other, I make my way back to stand before him

"I meant it. Thank you for not reporting me. I do appreciate it. I'm curious about why you kept your mouth shut, but if you prefer not to say I can live with that." He smiles at me, and there's genuine warmth in his slate grey eyes. They're a beautiful colour, deep, rich, very dark. And very, very sexy.

Out of my depth now, totally at sea, I offer him a brief nod. "I really do need to be getting off." Even so, I make no move to leave.

"I know." He cups my chin in his hand, his touch gentle but confident. Something coils and clenches, deep in my stomach. My breath hitches as he lowers his face toward mine. "I meant it, you know. You really are a whole lot prettier than Drummond. Quite lovely, in fact."

"North, I—"

"Shhh," he whispers, then he brushes his lips across mine.

I gasp, but I don't pull away. Instead, I stand perfectly still, my lips parted, waiting.

North is unhurried. He rests his forehead against mine as he cradles my face between his hands, but still he does nothing to deepen the kiss, if it was even a kiss at all.

"What are you doing? You shouldn't..." My protest is whispered, breathy.

"No," agrees North. And still he doesn't release me. Neither does he back off.

Moments lengthen, time seems to stand still, but I'm the one who cracks first. Suddenly I can stand it no longer. I reach for him, looping my arms around his neck and I stretch up on my toes to slant my lips over his.

It's as though he was waiting for me to commit, to do something, anything. He responds instantly, plunging his tongue into my mouth to stroke and taste me. His fingers tangle in my hair, combing the cropped strands back from my face as he takes over to deepen the kiss.

I hang on to him, even as I berate myself for what I'm doing, what I'm allowing to happen. This is wrong, on so many levels. This is forbidden. I'm breaking every rule, every principle, all my values tossed up in the air. I hate myself even as I reach to tangle my fingers in his dark, silky hair to pull him closer.

Without breaking the kiss North starts to move, pushing, walking me backwards until I'm pressed up against one of the huge machines. He plants his left hand beside my head and continues to kiss me, as the other hand trails a leisurely path down my regulation-issue jacket to rest at my hip. He presses against me, the bulge of his erection unmistakeable against my lower abdomen. Without conscious thought I slide my hand between our bodies to reach for him, then stroke my fingers along the solid length of his cock.

"Ah, Miss MacBride, that feels good." His tone is low, a sensual murmur as he nuzzles my neck.

"Yes, I—"

"Anyone here? North? What are you up to?"

I am jolted back to my senses as Jackson's voice rings

out around the utility room. His footsteps sound as he marches toward where we are concealed behind the industrial washer. I stare up at North, desperate now. We can't be found here, together. We just can't.

North lays a finger over my lips to signal me to be quiet.

He calls out to the other man. "I'm here. Won't be a sec."

"Where's the stuff for C wing?" We hear the sound of wheeled bins being shunted around as Jackson searches for his first delivery of the afternoon.

"Over there, by the door." Jared steps away from me, and winks. He actually bloody well winks at me before he turns and strides off to help the other man. By the time I peer around the edge of the washing machine North is ushering Jackson out of the room. He glances back over his shoulder and lifts a hand to me as he follows the other prisoner, leaving me alone to make my escape.

• • • • • • •

My heart is in my mouth as I clock on for my next shift. I can't face North again after what happened yesterday, I just can't. I report to the poky, cluttered wing office to learn that staffing levels are a little better so the lockdown is relaxed. Education is reinstated, and some free association is permitted for prisoners with enhanced status.

I'm stationed on G wing as usual so I take up my normal position at the end of the recreation hall to keep an eye on things. Aside from my personal tribulations we're still on alert for potential disturbances. The cell search of a couple of days ago did nothing to calm the prisoners' mood and we all know that if there's going to be trouble, it will start out here.

Today though things seem unusually calm, and I spend an hour exchanging clipped pleasantries with the men who wander down toward my end. For the most part they are civil to me, and I find it works best if I return the courtesy.

We all get along better then. Not all officers see the point in engaging in conversation with prisoners, an attitude I find frankly baffling. My more experienced colleagues such as Jim insist I'll come around to their way of thinking eventually. I sincerely hope not.

"Go on, you can take your break now if you like." The wing supervisor, Mr. Drummond, has arrived to take over the watch. He's an officer with twenty years under his belt and he reckons he knows everything there is to know about incarcerating offenders. He's a great believer in keeping prisoners in line, showing them who's boss, in whatever way seems to work. Mr. Drummond has been on report for using 'excessive force' a number of times and actually brags about it. He makes me nervous, and the men loathe him. But he's in charge and I'm not, so I nod and move toward the outer gate.

Then I pause, look back over my shoulder. I know Jared North isn't in the recreation room because I'd have noticed—definitely. I escorted Bako, one of his cellmates, down to the education block earlier so he's not going to be back for a while yet, and yes, the third man is playing snooker. That means there's a reasonable chance I'll find Prisoner KG8329 alone in his cell. I can't avoid him so I might as well face the problem head on. At the very least I owe him an apology for my appalling behaviour yesterday, and I'm still uncomfortable about the way I curtailed his gym session earlier in the week. This might be an ideal time to talk to him, especially as I'm on my break so I can't be accused of time-wasting.

I turn on my heel and march back along the wing to the cells at the far end.

North's door is ajar, and I hear the low hum of the radio coming from inside. I halt at the entrance and peer round the door. All three bunks are empty. Disappointed, I start to withdraw.

"Something I can do for you, Miss MacBride?" The voice is drawling, not quite mocking me but not far from it.

There is something in North's tone that always causes my stomach to clench. Despite what happened between us yesterday I know he dislikes me, and I understand why. I'm a screw, it's in the nature of our relationship that he should distrust and despise me, but still his contempt hurts. That kiss yesterday confused things but I doubt anything has fundamentally changed. I wish the situation were different. I wish I could impress him, somehow manage to earn his approval, if only a little.

My apology for grabbing and groping him yesterday might help. I step right inside the cell. North is seated at the table behind the door, which had concealed him from my sight at first. He has a pen in his hand and a sheet of paper laid out in front of him.

"I'm glad I've caught you."

One dark, sardonic eyebrow lifts. "Oh, were you thinking I might have slipped out then? Gone down the pub, perhaps, or decided to catch the latest Bond movie? Leeds United are at home this afternoon, maybe you thought I'd be at the match."

I know better than to react. I take a deep breath and continue. "I just wanted to talk to you for a moment, that's all. But if I'm disturbing you, it can wait." I take step back, intending to leave him to whatever he's doing.

"Wait, Miss MacBride." His tone is stern and authoritative. I find myself obeying. Again. He lays his pen down on the table and smiles at me, his expression nothing short of dazzling. "That was uncalled for. I didn't mean to be rude. What was it you wanted to talk about?"

I step back inside and pull the door closed behind me to reduce the likelihood of being overheard. There is nothing wrong in an officer speaking to a prisoner one to one, but this conversation is private and I prefer to keep it between ourselves.

"I wanted to apologise, about yesterday. And about your gym session."

"Oh?" He lifts that eyebrow again but says nothing more

to help.

"Yes." I decide to concentrate on the gym; it's the less personal of the two incidents. "For cutting short your workout. I know how much you enjoy using the gym, so…"

He leans forward, his elbows resting on the table. "As I understood it, you were doing unpaid overtime just escorting me up there."

"I was, but you still had to finish early and I'm sorry. That's all, really."

"Was it your fault?"

"That's not the point. It wasn't your fault either, but you were the one to lose out."

"You didn't answer my question, Miss MacBride. I asked you if it was your fault."

I shake my head. "No."

"So, why are you here? Really?"

"I told you, to apologise."

"Why, if it was none of your doing? How were you responsible? Why do you think you owe me an apology?"

"Because I was late taking you up there, and I made you leave before your hour was up. I was already on overtime—"

"Unpaid overtime."

"Yes, unpaid, but I was there anyway, so I could have stayed longer. I should have. I could tell you were angry, so I thought…" I run out of words. This was a bad idea, I should never have started this conversation.

"And yesterday?"

"I should never have done—that. It was unprofessional."

"Which bit?"

"What do you mean?"

"Well, was it unprofessional to hide my camera from the cell search? Or to take it home with you, then bring it back in here for me? Or maybe it was the kiss that's bothering you, although that was the bit I preferred the most."

"All of it," I confirm, utterly miserable. "I can't even

23

start to think what got into me. Or what you must think. I don't normally leap on prisoners like that."

"No? That's a pity." He pauses, cocking his head to one side as he peruses me with interest. "Is that it? Have you covered everything now? All your sins laid bare?"

"It's enough. You'd be within your rights to report me for sexual harassment."

His eyes widen, then he laughs out loud. "Miss MacBride, you really are full of surprises. You thought I was angry with you? Offended even?"

"Yes, of course. Or you should be. I behaved like a, a…"

"A slut?"

"What? No!"

"No?"

"Well, yes. Perhaps. I'm not like that, though, not really."

"And that bothers you?"

"Yes. A little."

"A little?"

His expression of disbelief suggests I'm not fooling him at all. He's right. Under his questioning I find myself wanting to admit that his displeasure over the last couple of days bothers me a lot. Much more than I at first realised.

"More than a little," I agree. "I'll try to make it up to you?"

"I see. And how do you intend to do this, Miss MacBride? Extra visiting privileges, perhaps? Or maybe some more money to spend? Do you have money for me, Miss MacBride?"

"Of course not." I am indignant at the suggestion. I might have something of a temporary crush on this particular prisoner, which has led to some serious lapses in judgement, but a bent officer I am not. "I just wanted to make it right, that's all, and if you think I'm going to let you use this as an excuse to get extra privileges then you can think again. It's not happening." I turn to leave.

"Wait." The single word drips with authority. It's another command; he expects me to obey.

I turn to face him, my hand still on the door. "Yes?"

"I accept your apology, Miss MacBride, but if you were in the wrong over all these matters, and you clearly believe that you were, then that deserves a punishment, does it not? Isn't that how these things work?"

"Is it?"

"I think so. And so do you. That's why you're here."

"I have no idea what you mean."

"You came here to be punished."

"No, I didn't."

I tip up my chin as he gets to his feet to pace to the far end of the cell. He leans on the wall eight feet from where I stand and he watches me. His arms are folded across his chest, and just like yesterday he is quite still, quite calm, which is more than can be said for me. My heart is thumping, my breathing rapid. I dread to think what is happening to my blood pressure under that cool, hard scrutiny.

At last, he speaks. "Miss MacBride, you deserve a spanking. A good, hard spanking and I'm more than happy to oblige you."

"That's ridiculous!" I can't believe he actually said something so outrageous.

"Is it? Okay then. You can close the door on your way out." He makes no move toward me, nor does he return to his bunk. For myself, I am rooted to the spot.

His gaze is unwavering, assured. The corner of his lip quirks. He watches as I struggle to find my next words. He is patient, leisurely almost, allowing me all the time I need to process his shocking and wholly inappropriate suggestion. My voice when it emerges is a strangled squeak.

"All right. Thank you."

"Is that 'all right, thank you, I'm leaving now'? Or 'all right, thank you, please spank me'?"

My eyes must be like saucers. I can barely comprehend what he is proposing. "What, here? Now?"

"Here and now is where we find ourselves, so yes, I think

that would be best."

"Will it hurt?" *Jesus, where did that come from?*

"Oh, yes. Would you want it any other way?"

Probably not. My pussy is moistening as I anticipate what's to come, despite the impossible situation. For heaven's sake, anyone might walk in.

"You have keys, Miss MacBride. If you're worried we might be disturbed you could always lock the door."

I gape at him. Did I really voice my only objection out loud?

He smiles at me again and holds out his hand. "Let me, Miss MacBride. The keys, please?"

And—I do it. I actually hand over my keys to one of the prison inmates. It's the cardinal sin among officers, and I've committed it without a murmur of protest. North steps around me to pull the door closed and uses my key to lock it. He then hands the heavy bunch back to me.

"You need to keep these safe, Miss MacBride." He murmurs the advice, then drops a light kiss on my forehead.

Beyond amazed, I take the keys and shove them back in the pocket of my uniform trousers. Then I stand and stare at him, totally at a loss for what to do next. North helps me out of my predicament by sitting down again on the chair where he was seated when I entered. He leans back, his expression serious though not threatening in any sense. He hasn't said so, but I have no doubt that if I chose to I could just unlock the door and walk out of here and he wouldn't lift a finger to prevent me leaving.

"I'll be spanking your bare bottom, so if you would be so good as to lower your trousers to your knees, then you can lie across my lap."

"I… I…"

"Do not keep me waiting, Miss MacBride."

"My name's Molly." I blurt it out. It seems important to me that if I'm to accept a spanking from this man, and it seems that I am doing just that, then he should at least know my name.

"Molly? That's pretty. It suits you. I'm Jared, though I imagine you already knew that."

I nod. I checked his records, though we never use other than last name and number to address a prisoner. "Jared," I repeat. "I knew someone at school called Jared."

"Did you?" He pauses for a few moments, his head cocked to one side. "Are you playing for time, Molly?"

"No, of course not." I take a step toward him.

"Good, because even though we're locked in here it won't be long before someone comes looking for you. We wouldn't want to be disturbed, would we?"

"No. I'm on my break, I have half an hour…"

"I see. That should be enough time. Shall we get on, then?"

"Yes, of course." I move to stand beside him, wondering how to proceed. What is the protocol for this? Is there even such a thing?

"Your trousers, Molly. Bare bottom, remember. Perhaps you'd like to take off your jacket, too."

I chew on my lower lip, every professional instinct, every shred of modesty I ever possessed screaming at me to turn now and run. I do none of that though. Instead, my fingers are shaking as I unbutton my uniform jacket and take it off. I lay it across the bunk I know to be Jared North's then I unfasten the front of my trousers and lower the zip.

"Push them down, please." He is implacable and not letting me off any of this. I have no choice but to do as he says. At this moment I have no notion where this craving to be spanked came from, even less where it has been lurking all these years. But once he shone his spotlight on my suppressed desire, I was somehow caught in the beam, unable to step away. And now, if I'm to receive the spanking I apparently crave, he will require me to prepare myself for it. I must bare my bottom, and submit to him.

It's time to embrace the inevitable. I hook my thumbs over the waistband of my loosened trousers and I shove them down.

CHAPTER TWO

I let out my breath, though I'm careful not to let her know I was holding it. Right up to the moment Molly dropped her pants for me, I expected her to bolt for the door. Usually so confident and assertive, the delectable Miss MacBride is completely vulnerable as she stands before me with her trousers around her knees. She hasn't said as much, but I can read her well enough to be certain this is new to her, her first spanking. I consider myself a lucky man, and I have no intention of blowing this now.

"Would you turn up the volume of the radio?" I tilt my chin toward the TV sitting on the small chest of drawers beside my bunk. Molly obeys me, adjusting the sound to a level likely to at least mask any noise we might make.

I pat my lap, urging her to lay herself across my thighs. Having brought her to this point it's best to move this on briskly now, not least because we have limited time and I have no intention of rushing at the end. Also in my experience a new submissive requires direction and firm control to get her past the initial shyness and insecurity. From the way she's trembling in front of me it's clear that Molly MacBride is painfully shy about what's going to happen to her and is racked with nerves.

"You don't have to do this, you do know that? Yesterday's over and done with, there'll be no hard feelings." She's scared, but it's taken courage and determination to get this far. I doubt she'll back out now, but I have to ask.

"I know that. I… I want this. I want you to do this. Please, be quick." She throws herself forward to dangle across my lap, her stomach on my thighs and her head just off the floor. She grabs hold of my ankle to steady herself. Her trousers are down, but her crisp white cotton shirt is quite long at the back and covers her bottom. I leave that for now as I arrange her more securely. It would never do for her to fall. I lift my knee a little to elevate her bottom— I prefer her pretty little cheeks to be nice and high for what I have in mind.

My cock has been stiffening since she first uttered the words 'I'm sorry,' and is rock solid now. She can't but be aware of my monster boner nudging her waist as I pull her in close and slide my leg over both of hers to trap her in position. I'm not really expecting a struggle, and if she asks me to I'll let her up anyway, but a firm approach usually pays dividends. No woman wants to be spanked by a man who doesn't seem to mean business. Well, that's been my observation anyway. Sure enough, almost as soon as I take charge she settles and her body relaxes.

I take hold of the hem of her shirt between my fingers. "May I?"

She nods, and tenses again. I lift her shirt to reveal her perfect, round bottom, still covered in her pristine white, sheer lace knickers. It's all I can do to not shoot my load right here and now. I have never seen anything quite so fucking beautiful in my life. Who would have dreamed such a treat lay beneath those serviceable prison-issue trousers? If this little adventure means I end up spending the remainder of my sentence in solitary with the sex offenders and violent psychopaths, it'll have been worth it. Pity about the parole though.

I shove that unwelcome thought aside. "This is a bare-bottom spanking. Molly. Nothing else counts. I love your taste in underwear, but we need to lose the knickers too." I hook my fingers into the elastic at the top of her panties, and though my words are issued as a statement, we both know I'm seeking permission.

She nods again, and I slide the lace over her buttocks to settle around her knees with the trousers, then take a moment to admire the peachy loveliness of her heart-shaped bottom.

I cup the lower curve of one cheek in my hand, comparing the pale tone of her skin to the darker shade of mine. Her arse is smooth, unblemished, the flesh firm to my touch. Her muscles contract under my hand as she clenches. I squeeze and caress her curves, first one cheek then the other, and I wait from her to soften again. Several moments pass as I caress her trembling buttocks, then she seems to simply sag across my lap as she sinks into this.

Fucking perfect.

"Ready?"

"Yes." Her reply is breathy but unequivocal.

"If you need me to stop, just say so. Okay?"

"Don't I need a safeword?"

Ah, not a complete novice then. "If you like, though I'll hear you if you just say you've had enough. Or if I think you've reached your limit."

"Okay."

I'm touched by her trust in me and oddly humbled by it. If I were a less sex-starved and rather nobler man, I'd probably not lay a hand on her at all. Perhaps it's better for both of us that I'm a selfish bastard and though I take my responsibilities as a dom seriously enough, I'm no saint and I'll take submission where I can find it. Here, for example, draped across my knees, waiting.

I deliver the first slap, not especially hard, and I follow it with a firm rub to soothe the pain away. Molly lets out a soft sigh, her buttocks clench hard, then she relaxes under my hand. I repeat, this time on the other side, then pick up the tempo a little as I drop light spanks over both cheeks. Her firm bottom quivers with each spank, and quickly blushes to a pale rosiness followed by a deeper pink. As I build the pressure and make the slaps harder she starts to squeak and squeal, wriggling a little but never trying to avoid my hand.

Her buttocks are a bright, flaming crimson by the time I pause, but Molly makes no attempt to get up.

"Do you want more?" Christ, I hope so, but for her first time this has already been quite an introduction to the not-so-gentle art of kink.

"Yes. Please."

Her voice is shaky but clear enough. I'm happy to continue if she is. I intend to push her to her limit or as close as I can get. She'll leave here sore, a bit confused probably, but still craving more.

"I'd like to use my belt. Is that all right?"

"Oh, I'm not sure..."

"Yes, you are. Remember, I'll stop whenever you tell me you've had enough."

"Okay then, just for a bit..."

I don't bother to correct that. In truth, I'll be the one deciding how much she needs, unless she calls a full stop to the proceedings, but I think that's unlikely. I've never had a subbie safeword on me yet. I ease her forward slightly so I can reach the buckle of my belt. I slide it from the loops of my jeans and fold it into a double thickness, clasping the buckle within my hand.

"Ten strokes with the belt, okay? You can count them if you like."

Her response is a breathy squeak, and she grabs my ankle again. I pull back my arm and take the first swing.

Molly lets out a yelp and her entire body jerks. I watch as the darker crimson line of the belt blooms across her right buttock, pausing to allow her to process the sensation and to settle again. It takes several seconds, then when she becomes still I drop the next stroke across her left cheek.

Molly flinches, but there is no sound this time. Neither is she counting, at least not out loud. I wait for a few moments, then deliver two more strokes in quick succession. This does elicit a sharp cry, and I half expect her to ask me to stop. She's shuddering, and her grip tightens on my leg, but as the seconds pass there are no words of defeat or surrender from her. I allow her ample time to call a halt if she wants to, then I repeat the two strokes.

Molly manages to stifle a squeal, for which I am grateful. I suspect we are both mindful of the men milling about just on the other side of the cell door and neither of us wants to attract attention. Had I had longer in which to plan this scene I would have certainly opted for a more secluded setting, but we are where we are. Next time, perhaps…

I apply two more strokes with my belt, gathering in intensity now. Molly is absorbing the pain well, riding it like a natural. She is tense, still rigid across my lap, but if anything, she has lifted her cute bottom up for me to spank. I can only guess at what else might be going on in her head, but I know without a shadow of a doubt that she's loving what I'm doing to her.

"These will be the last two. They're going to be across the backs of your thighs and they'll really hurt. If you think you might scream tell me now and I'll find you a gag."

"No, thank you. I'll be quiet, I promise."

"Good girl." I spend a few moments stroking her flaming buttocks, the heat radiating up into my palm. Molly makes a sound deep in her throat, which I swear sounds like a purr to me. I continue the sensual caress, pressing my hand into her punished skin to better drive home the experience, to draw out for her that heady mix of pain and pleasure that will set the endorphins coursing freely through her system. This is why I didn't want to rush.

"Are you ready?" I murmur.

"Yes," she replies, pressing her bottom into my hand.

I draw my palm lower, down over the curve to stroke the backs of her legs, the crease where her bottom meets her thighs. This is the sweet spot I am about to thrash. I rub her there as I lean to my right, just enough to get a decent view of her pussy lips peeking out from between her legs. She is swollen, glistening, the moisture betraying her arousal. I trail my thumb along the length of her slit, ready to withdraw at the slightest protest from her. She submitted to a spanking, no more, and I won't push her.

Molly gasps, but doesn't pull away from me. Encouraged but still cautious I angle my hand so I can push my thumb between her folds to reach her clit. She parts her legs and lifts her bottom up. I require no further urging. Her clit is plump, swollen with her arousal. I take it between my finger and thumb and squeeze, gentle at first then firming up the pressure.

Molly is squirming on my lap, wriggling and writhing as she seeks to direct the touch to her sensitive tip. I know just what she needs, and have no intention of allowing her to set the pace now. I trail my fingertips around her clit, then flick the end. I swipe it from side to side, then from the bottom to the top. She is panting, thrusting her hips back, wordlessly begging me for her release.

She is there, right at the top, hovering at the edge of the precipice. I tease her for several moments, bringing her almost to the point of no return, then allowing her to slide back down. Her breath has been transformed into soft, sobbing gulps and her thighs are spread wide. When I am convinced she can take no more, I lift my hand from her.

"Close your legs, Molly." I issue the command and wait for her to comply. She's reluctant, but gloriously obedient even so. I transfer my belt back into my right hand ready for the final two strokes.

I thrash her across both thighs.

"Aagh!" Despite her good intentions Molly lets out a scream. I expected this, but even so, she did promise me that she would be quiet.

"Molly, I can still gag you."

"I'm sorry, Jared, truly. I won't make a sound next time."

She sounds so contrite I can't help but smile.

"Good. Make sure you don't or I'll add on more strokes to help you learn that I mean what I say." I keep my tone cool and clipped and the words stern because that's what she needs. Molly MacBride is a natural submissive and she craves my authority and rigid control right now.

I drop the final stroke across her thighs, just below the first. She spasms hard, her entire body convulsing as she fights to absorb the pain. She shudders, her muscles softening as she lets it seep through her and away.

Even before she has finished processing the sensation I slide my hand back between her legs and rub her engorged clit. Her orgasm is instant, racking her body as I squeeze and tug on her sensitive nub. Her shudders, violent at first, subside but she is still trembling as I lift her from my lap and cradle her in my arms. She reaches up and locks her arms around my neck, her face buried in the dark grey fabric of my prison-issue T shirt.

I pull her in close and hold her. She is sobbing, her tears dampening my clothes. I rub my palm between her shoulder blades and kiss her short, sleek hair. It smells of apples, and something else. Cinnamon perhaps?

"You're okay, I have you."

She grasps me tighter for a few moments, then relaxes her grip. She lifts her face to look up at me.

Her eyelashes are spiky with tears, her cheeks flushed though nowhere nearer as pink as her bottom. Her trousers and those glorious scraps of lace that pass for knickers are still around her knees and as I shift my legs her sore buttocks are pressed against my jeans. Awareness of her discomfort flares in her eyes, though she does not protest. She gives a little shake of her head, as though recovering her senses and remembering where she is.

"I should go. My break…"

I glance at the clock. "You have a few minutes yet. How do you feel?"

Confusion flutters across her features. She grimaces.

"Good. Bad. Christ, I shouldn't have done that."

Here we go. I smile at her. "But you did. And you enjoyed it, yes?"

She shakes her head, denial etched across her face. She opens her mouth to refute my conclusion but I lay a finger across her lips.

"Think carefully, and only say it if it's true. Don't lie to me, or to yourself, Molly. So, did you enjoy what we just did?"

She hesitates, then flattens her lips and nods. It's brief, but the gesture is acknowledgement enough. I leave it there.

"Do you want to go?"

"I should. Really."

She makes to get up from my lap but I hold her in place. "Not so fast. Just take a moment to let your head clear before you try to stand." Molly would not be the first subbie whose knees gave out as soon as I let go of her. I prefer not to have to pick her up from the floor of my cell if I can help it.

She accepts my advice and we sit in something close to companionable silence for a couple of minutes. It is Molly who speaks first.

"I really do need to be getting back on the wing. Mr. Drummond will be looking for me soon."

She's right, sadly. I help her to her feet and pull her pants back up for her, then I fasten them. It's an effort but I try not to grin too much when she hisses with pain as the sturdy, serviceable fabric of her uniform rubs against her tender skin.

I lean across her to retrieve her jacket from my bunk and pass it to her, just as all hell breaks loose outside.

· · · · · · ·

Jesus, what's all that din? There's a horrendous crash right outside the cell, followed by shouts and the pounding of running feet. I thrust my arms into my jacket as I rush for the cell door. It doesn't budge

"It's locked. Give me your keys." Jared holds out his hand, clearly expecting my compliance.

I shake my head, my prison officer sense of duty coming back to the fore with a vengeance now. "No, there's trouble on the wing, I need to—"

"Give me the fucking keys, Molly." His tone is harsh, demanding obedience.

I swallow and hand over the keys, then step back away from him. Gone is the gentle, almost lover-like persona of moments ago. The man now confronting me looks nothing short of deadly

"You stay there. Don't move and don't make a fucking sound." He unlocks the door and opens it just a few inches then leans through to check outside. A moment later he hurls himself back inside the cell and slams the door shut. He turns the key in the lock, then pockets it.

"What's going on? You have to let me out." I dart back to the door to rattle the handle uselessly. "Give me my keys back. Now, or I'll put you on report." My head is filled with all manner of nightmare scenarios, the worst of which is the dawning belief that Jared North somehow duped me into staying in with him here whilst goodness knows what was happening outside. I am mortified, and more than a little terrified. My only weapon is bravado, and I pile it on thick as I advance on him. "Don't make this any worse. Let me out now and we can say nothing more about this."

North's handsome mouth twists into parody of a smile. "Sweetheart, you won't be in any position to say anything to anyone, ever again, if I let you go out there right now. There's a full-blown riot kicking off, and if you blunder into the middle of it, you're dead."

"What?" I whirl to gape at the locked door, processing the shouts and crashes from the other side. The din is getting louder, the sound of splintering wood and breaking glass gaining ground over the raised voices. I leap back in shock when something big and heavy collides with the cell door. It rattles within the frame, but holds firm.

Jared pushes past me to press his ear up against the door. He turns back to me, his expression grim. "Just an accident, I think, probably a couple of dickheads trying to kill each other. Doesn't sound as though they're trying to batter their way in here. Yet."

"Why would they?" I'm baffled, bewildered, desperately searching my recollections of basic training for any instructions on how to respond to this sort of eventuality. My mind's a blank.

"If they realise there's a screw trapped on the wing, they'll use you as a hostage. If you're lucky."

"And if I'm not?"

He shakes his head. "Molly, don't go there."

His meaning is clear. I'm a woman, trapped among a bunch of violent, angry, resentful men, convicted criminals all of them, who make their contempt for the prison authorities evident at every opportunity. Jared's right. I'm in a lot of trouble.

"No one but me knows you're in here, and it's best that lot doesn't find out. We need to get you out, and quick."

"The other officers will come looking for me. They'll know I'm unaccounted for."

"Probably, but they'll have to get through that set of mad sods to find you. It's more likely the screws'll wait it out, see what happens when the food in here starts to run out or the lunatics get bored of smashing this place up."

"But—that could be days."

He nods, his expression grim. "I can't see a locked cell door being ignored for that long, can you?"

"No, but—"

"I'll get you out of here, but it'll be better if we wait until everything calms down a bit."

"How? How do you intend on doing that?"

"I have an idea. First though, we need to let the other screws know you're safe, at least for now. You have a radio, right?"

"Yes." I pull the receiver from the breast pocket of my jacket.

"Right. Get on it and tell whoever's out there and listening that you're safe and unhurt."

"I'll tell them I'm not hurt. I don't feel exactly safe though."

My companion gives a sardonic chuckle, then silently unlocks the door again. This time he opens it just the merest crack, but spends a few seconds carefully scanning the scene outside. He closes and locks it again then turns to me. He gestures to the radio, still silent in my hand. His meaning clear. Do as I say.

I keep my voice low as I speak into the microphone. "MacBride to control. Can anyone hear me?"

There's crackle of static, then a voice booms out. "MacBride? Where the fuck are you? We need you up here. Now!"

I adjust the volume to quiet the voice, then turn to Jared. "It's Drummond," I hiss. I could add that he sounds pissed off, but that would be superfluous.

"Right, just tell him you're still trapped on the wing and to wait for more information."

I get back on the radio and relay that message. It is met by a barrage of expletives from Drummond; the gist of his outburst being that I should know better than to get myself into a hostage situation, he's not about to endanger other officers by trying to rescue me, and that I need to hang on until reinforcements can be drafted in.

His attitude rankles, but I seek to reassure him. "Sir, I'm fine, for now. And I'm not a hostage." At least I hope I'm not. I glance at Jared for confirmation.

He smiles at me as he slides a finger across the front of his throat, signalling me to end the conversation with Drummond. I do so, and replace the radio in my pocket.

"So, what happens now?" I ask, my voice creditably steady, considering.

"I always had Drummond down as a prick. I was right."

He lies down on his bunk, his hands behind his head. "So now, we wait. I can offer you coffee, or a digestive biscuit. Or another orgasm if you prefer."

Heat floods my face as the extent of my predicament sinks in. How could I have been so weak, so stupid? Am I really so bloody needy that I put myself in this situation? My career is in tatters, even assuming I do manage to escape this God-awful mess with my life. I turn away from Jared's knowing expression, fervently wishing I had never set eyes on the man.

"Oh, come on now, Molly, it wasn't that bad." His tone is lighter now, almost mocking. "Come and put your feet up for a while. I reckon we have a couple of hours to kill before it'll be safe to try and make a run for it."

"Go to hell," I mutter.

Now he has the gall to bloody laugh out loud. "I daresay I will, eventually. Meanwhile though, I suggest we both try to stay calm and try not to attract any attention. At least sit down. My coffee's not that bad."

I perch on the bunk opposite Jared's and lean forward, my head in my hands. I'm shaking, absolutely bloody terrified, an abject failure as an officer, and all this fool can do is take the piss.

"Are you crying?" His voice is gentler now. He actually sounds concerned. "I told I'd get you out of here, and I will."

"I don't see how."

"Take off your jacket. And your shirt."

"What?" I sit bolt upright. "Are you mad? If you lay a hand on me, I'll—"

"Keep your voice down or I might have to spank you again." He glances at his belt, still lying across the one small chair in the cell. "And do as you're told."

He rolls from the bunk and stands in front of me. Jared North is easily over six feet tall and towers over me. My slender grip on any remaining shreds of courage slips away. I shrink back from him. "Please, don't…"

"For fuck's sake, Molly, what do you think I am? You've been locked in here with me for the last half hour. If I was going to attack you, don't you think I'd have done it by now? Get your imagination under control and your stuff off, then do as I tell you."

He turns and makes the two strides it takes to cross the tiny cell. The muscles in his back and shoulders flex as he bends to drag open the drawer of his bedside locker and pulls out another prison-issue grey T shirt, this one neatly folded. He grins back at me. "You're lucky. This was for after the gym later today. I'm guessing that little expedition's off now so you get the fresh laundry."

"You want me to wear your T shirt? It won't fit." That muscular frame, honed by countless hours spent in the gym, is still very much in my thoughts.

"So roll up the sleeves. I just want to make sure you blend in a little, enough to not attract attention immediately when you walk out of here. It's lucky you have short hair, one less thing to worry about, and I don't have a hat to lend you."

"Walk out? You mean to disguise me as an inmate?"

He nods. "It should work. You only need to get as far as the gate—"

"This is Supervising Officer Drummond. All men are to return to their cells immediately." The synthetic voice rings out over the loudspeaker system, piped from the safety of the central control room. There is a brief pause, then the voice booms out again. "You will allow Officer MacBride to leave the wing unharmed. Any violence against an officer will be dealt with severely."

"What the...? Is that man actually a fucking moron?" Jared glares at the door, his expression thunderous. "Now they all fucking know you're in here."

"I asked him to wait until I contacted him again. You heard me say that?"

Jared nods, his expression grim now. "Right, but thanks to that dickhead time just ran out. Get that T shirt on."

It no longer occurs to me to argue. I slip my jacket off and dump it on the bunk, then I unbutton my shirt. I reach for the T shirt, intending to somehow manage to shimmy into it without giving Jared the benefit of a free show.

"I don't think so, Molly. Under other circumstances I'd be delighted in your choice of underwear, all that sexy uplift, defying the laws of nature, but it's not quite the look we're going for here. Lose the bra too, please."

"Why? What's wrong with it?" My uniform is hardly the most flattering outfit, but I like to jolly things up with some nice underwear. Normally it's just for me, although today Jared North has had ample opportunity to admire my choice of foundation garments. My lacy, balcony style bra cost me nearly thirty quid at *La Sensa* and I'm very proud of it. The matching lacy knickers spent enough time around my knees; he can't have failed to notice them.

He steps toward me and tips my chin up with his fingertips. "Nothing's wrong with it. It's lovely. Too lovely, because it accentuates your curves. The T shirt won't fool anyone for long, but it doesn't have to. Just the few seconds it will take to get to the gate at the end of the wing will be enough. But we do need those few seconds, and I'm worried that we may not get them. It'd only take one glance your way, and we might be in trouble. So do as I ask. Please."

"Do you promise not to look?"

"No."

I huff out an exasperated sigh, but at heart I know he's right. *La Sensa* doesn't go out of their way to blend into the crowd. I reach behind me to unhook the fastener and allow the cups to fall away. I turn to take the shirt that he holds out to me and I pull it over my head.

"Won't that attract attention too?" I straighten my new outfit, then tilt my chin to acknowledge the impressive erection that stretches the front of his jeans.

"Ah, yes, probably. But I'm only human, Miss MacBride. Could you take off your shoes too, and put these on?" He bends to pick up a battered pair of training shoes. "Not the nicest, I know, and Johnny will be sorry to lose them, but our need is greater."

I view the offered footwear with distaste. "Is this absolutely necessary?"

He grins. "No prisoner I've ever seen in here wears polished black leather boots. We need those few seconds, Molly."

I crouch to change my shoes, then straighten up. "Okay. I'm ready."

"Right, I need you to get back on that radio and tell the screws to have someone stationed by the gate into the octagon but don't tell them what we intend to do. I wouldn't put it past that idiot Drummond to broadcast our plan to the whole fucking wing. We can use your keys to get you through the gate, but if this turns to rat-shit we might need help to get you out."

"What do you mean, rat-shit?"

"It's a mob out there, especially after your muppet of a boss just announced that there's an officer still on the wing. They'll be looking for you, and men can do stupid things when they're running on pure testosterone…"

My stomach clenches. He's right. "What about you? Won't you be in danger too?"

He grins. "I'll survive. Just worry about yourself and make sure you get out of here. So when I give the word we walk out of the cell, no rushing, just a normal pace. Keep your head down and stick close to me. You stay by the wall and I'll shield you from view as best I can. If I tell you to run, you fucking do it. Fast. Head straight for the gate. Make sure you have the keys in your hand, ready, because you won't have long. If no one spots us, that'd be good and you can just slip through and away. If it gets nasty, I'll do what I can to make sure you get to the gate, but that could be where your mates come in. Right?"

"Right." I dig in the pocket of my discarded jacket for my radio. "MacBride to Control. Can someone come to the gate, please? Oh, and no more announcements over the loudspeaker, if that's not too much trouble." I'm past caring about Supervising Officer Drummond's professional sensibilities—the man's a liability.

"Understood." I think I recognise the governor's voice, which heartens me a little. Mr. Henderson has his head screwed on right. This might just work out after all.

"We'll give them a couple of minutes, then we go. Yes?"

I nod. "Yes. And... thank you. For everything."

"Thank me after, when all this is over." He unlocks the door and cracks it open again. As he surveys the situation out on the wing he places his finger over his lips, indicating that I should be quiet, then he beckons me forward. "I can see screws at the far end of the wing, beyond the gates. The men are starting a cell by cell search so it's now or never. Here are your keys. So, are we ready then?"

"I think so."

He winks at me. "It's been an exciting afternoon, Miss MacBride. You've brightened my day. Please feel free to drop in for another spanking, if you're passing."

"I should never have..."

"Hush, not now. We'll talk about it. Later. Come on."

He doesn't wait for my responses, just opens the door wide and steps out of the cell. My heart is thumping as I scuttle after him.

I slip between Jared and the wall, though we have to make frequent detours to navigate the chaos of broken furniture, upturned tables, and the wreckage of what was G wing's recreation area. The snooker table has been dragged up against the gate to prevent easy access from outside, but as the gate actually opens outwards I should be all right if I can just clamber over it.

The men are so pumped up I can almost smell their agitation. They are for the most part just milling around, scuffling with each other and hurling abuse at the prison officers huddled beyond the gate. A group who appears marginally more organised emerges from a cell across the corridor and barges into the one next door. Presumably, this is the search party looking for me.

"Don't look up, don't make eye contact. We're halfway there." Jared's tone is low as he leads the way forward.

We almost make it. We're within ten yards of the snooker table before we're rumbled.

"There! That's the screw bitch." The harsh snarl comes from Prisoner YC3471, a vile individual known as Grouch, doing seven years for grievous bodily harm, with intent. I'll be his next victim if he has his way.

"Run!" Jared shoves me in the middle of the back, propelling me forward as he spins to face our attackers. "Don't stop, just fucking run."

And I do it. I sprint hard for the snooker table and the gates beyond, pulling my keys from my pocket as I go. I don't need them, the gates swing open as I approach and I hurl myself over the torn green baize to land in an untidy sprawl at the feet of the prison governor.

The gates clang shut behind me. I stagger to my feet and turn back to look. My last sight of Jared North is his broad shoulders disappearing back down the wing in the direction of the toilets and showers. He is surrounded by other inmates, and even from this distance I can tell there's some furious gesturing going on. Someone swings a punch, Jared returns it, and disappears in a hail of fists and flying feet.

"Miss MacBride? Debriefing this way." Numb, I follow the governor in the direction of the waiting police officers.

CHAPTER THREE

2015

Northern Lights—copyright Jared North, 2014. I flick through the glossy volume of landscape images, each one depicting a wild, untamed vista, evocative scenery, dripping with atmosphere and mystery. It was the cover art that first captured my attention—a rugged, timeless moorland broken only by the stark silhouette of a wind farm perched upon the distant horizon. I picked up the book in a second-hand shop in Soho. It reminded me of my home in Yorkshire, so I bought it on impulse. It was only when I leafed through the pages later that I spotted the photographer's name—Jared North.

It's not a common name. It could be the same man. It must be…

The last time I saw Jared North, he was brawling with a mob of rioting prisoners in a disturbance at HMP Leeds. I narrowly escaped that skirmish unharmed but I was badly shaken, my confidence shattered. I never returned to my job as a prison officer.

That was five years ago, and so much has happened in my life since then. There have been major changes, massive upheaval. I've learned a lot, about me and perhaps about him. Or should that be, I now know much more about men *like* Jared North, or I think I do. I hardly know *him* at all, not really.

As I leaf through his beautiful pictures, my memories of the man himself flood back, unleashing powerful emotions, secret desires, and above all an overwhelming sense of loss. I am sobbing, tears streaming unchecked down my face though I could not really say why.

One thing I do know though, with absolute certainty— I have unfinished business with Jared North.

• • • • • • •

Many hours spent on the Internet have gained me little in the way of firm information about the man now. I am able to find no pictures of the photographer, Jared North, no personal details. He's published numerous collections of his work, mainly landscapes but also some wildlife photography and a few portraits. His pictures are stark, gritty, lots of light and shade, creative angles, intriguing close-up shots. His company has a registered office in Leeds, which is a clue of sorts, I suppose, though further investigations show it to simply be a firm of accountants. Needless to say, enquiries about the identity of their client yielded nothing.

He has a blog and a Facebook page, and I stalk him there, of course. If those were less public arenas I might attempt to make contact, but that would be unthinkable. What I need to say to him, to ask him, is private, and very personal.

Weeks after first purchasing his book my efforts have drawn a blank. I am no nearer to making contact with Jared now than when we parted on G wing at Armley jail five years ago, yet with every day that passes my craving to meet this man again grows stronger.

• • • • • • •

I have had a breakthrough. An announcement on his Facebook page tells me that the elusive Jared North is opening an exhibition of his latest collection of landscapes at a gallery in Yorkshire. It's to take place the week after next. A converted mill at Saltaire, usually home to a collection of Hockney paintings, is hosting the event. There is to be a reception, a chance to meet the artist himself and to buy original pieces of his work. I gulp at the prices; even just to get my hands on a ticket will cost me fifty pounds. I reach for my credit card.

I travel up to Yorkshire the day before the exhibition and I check into my hotel. It's one of those smart but impersonal places, out of town, surrounded by lawns and acres of car parking. Not my usual scene, but really, none of this is. I would not usually dream of presenting myself before a near-perfect stranger in the hope he might remember spanking me once upon a time. But for Jared North I am making an exception.

The event is scheduled to start at six o'clock. There are cocktails, an opportunity to view the exhibition, a few nibbles, and the speeches themselves will start at around seven. I have a new outfit just for the occasion, a smart, knee-length dress in navy with matching white shoes and a clutch bag. I even invested in new lingerie, because I know how much Jared appreciates lacy underwear. Not that I expect him to be seeing mine. Chance would be a fine thing, but it's the thought that counts.

I arrive just as the doors open at six and wander aimlessly around the near-deserted venue. The exhibits are stunning, but I've seen many of them already on Jared's blog. One or two have small sticky red dots attached to their title signage indicating that they are already sold. There is nothing here priced at under two thousand pounds, many cost much more than that. I can only conclude that Jared North has done all right for himself.

The rooms fill up during the course of the next hour, and by seven the place is heaving. I find a secluded alcove and slip into the shadows to wait and to watch.

It isn't long before the gallery owner steps up onto a small podium and coughs into the microphone, the polite signal calling for silence. A hush descends on the room. We all wait, expectant.

"Thank you, ladies and gentlemen, and may I welcome you to the Titus Salt Gallery, here in historic Saltaire. This evening we are delighted to honour a true local talent. Jared North was born and grew up not ten miles from where we now stand. Since then he has travelled the world, capturing every continent on film, but it is his native Yorkshire that is the subject of this evening's showing. You will have seen examples of his work already and there will be ample opportunity to enjoy it further as the evening progresses. For now though, please join me in welcoming the man himself, Jared North."

There's a round of enthusiastic clapping as a man shoulders his way from the back of the room, through the throng of assembled admirers, heading for the podium. His progress takes him right past my alcove, he passes not three feet from me. My Jared.

He has changed. The prison haircut and austere T shirt and jeans have given way to expensive styling. His almost-black hair is longer now, though so is mine. His suit is well cut, and looks to be a designer label though I couldn't say which one. His features appear less harsh here in the muted lighting of the art gallery than they did in his cell at Armley, though they could not be described as soft even so. His eyes are the colour of dark slate, a shade I've remembered with pinpoint accuracy across the years. His jaw is square, his lips full. He reaches the podium and smiles at the crowd surrounding him, displaying even white teeth. It has only been five years, but he doesn't seem to have aged at all. His tanned face is striking, many would describe him as handsome. To me, he is quite simply breath-taking.

I shrink back into my alcove as he starts to speak.

Jared's words dwell upon how pleasant it is to be back in Yorkshire, where his roots run deep. He is appreciative of the accolades, the support of those who buy his work, the critics who admire his efforts and recommend his art. He goes on to applaud the Titus Salt Gallery, and the local creative scene, as well as the wider landscape of moors and hills that provides him with a wealth of raw materials.

I hear every other word, no more. My attention is riveted on the man himself—his tall, ripped body, his sensual, mobile features, his smile, his laugh. I never heard him laugh before, but I do now as he responds to a comment from the gallery owner beside him. All too soon, he is done, stepping down from the podium to greet the guests closest to him as the owner exhorts everyone to mingle, to eat and drink, to view the collection and to talk to the gallery staff if they wish to make a purchase.

I creep from my hidey hole and follow Jared around the collection, always remaining a discreet distance away, careful not to attract attention. He is constantly in demand, stopping to chat to groups of people, answering questions, offering advice or observations when asked. He's at ease, sure of himself. In command.

I suppose he always was.

By about eight-thirty most of the pictures are sporting little red dots. It has been a successful event and the gallery owner is beaming. Many guests are drifting off, and I know I need to leave soon if I hope to remain unnoticed. I still want to talk to Jared, but not here, not in public. I sidle over to the reception desk close to the entrance to pick up a handful of leaflets and his business card, in the hope I might at last be able to get his contact details.

"Are you a buyer?"

The soft, feminine voice comes from behind me. I turn to find myself eye to eye with a petite woman, her long dark hair caught up in a loose swirl on the top of her head. She is wearing a bright fuchsia cocktail dress and a navy jacket, which she is removing as she speaks to me. I haven't seen her before now, so I assume she has just arrived. She's very chic and stylish. My own more sober-coloured outfit that I had considered smart and understated now just appears dowdy beside hers. The new arrival is smiling at me though, and it would be rude not to be pleasant back.

"Oh, no. I would if I could afford them, but I'm just looking this evening." True enough, I suppose.

"Me too, though we do have several of Jared's pictures on the walls at home."

"Oh, you're a collector then? And a fan of Jared North?"

She laughs at that. "Among other things, I suppose I am a fan. Tonight I'm just his taxi driver though, come to pick him up and drive him home." She extends her hand to me. "I'm Rachel North."

I take the offered hand and shake it. I'm in a daze. *Rachel North. Drive Jared home.* Christ, I'm here talking to his bloody wife!

"Have you seen him anywhere? We should be getting off really…" She cranes her neck to peer around the room.

"Er, in the long gallery, I think. He was talking to some people…"

"Ah, well, that sounds about right. Always talking, that's Jared… Would you excuse me, I need to—" She breaks off. "Oh, there he is. Jared? Jared!"

He has just emerged from the gallery next door and turns to face us as my companion calls out to him. He lifts a hand, waves, then glances at me. Our eyes meet, and I could swear there's flicker of recognition, then it's gone. His features betray nothing more as he crosses the room to reach us. He bends to kiss Rachel on the cheek.

"Thank you for coming. I'll make it up to you, I promise."

"You'd better. You're on washing up duty for a week. And you can do the school run too." She turns to me. "It was nice meeting you, Miss…?"

"It's Mrs. Mrs. Mary Whitkirk. It was nice meeting you

50

too. And you, Mr. North." I'm backing away, desperately working to avoid eye contact. As if a wife lurking in the wings wasn't terminal enough, he has children too, and a school run to do. I just want to get out of here and I know I'm acting like a total muppet, but I can't help it. Rachel furrows her perfect brow in puzzlement, but makes no more of it. Linking her arm through Jared's, she tugs him in the direction of the door. I take my chance and do a quick sideways shuffle, then dive into the ladies' toilets.

When I emerge fifteen minutes later, it is to find the exhibition near enough deserted. A few stragglers are conducting their final bits of business with the gallery. Jared and his wife are long gone. Satisfied that the coast's clear I head for the door.

"Mrs. Whitkirk, do you have a moment?"

I halt and look around. The gallery owner is hurrying toward me.

"I'm glad I caught you, Jared North asked me to give you this." He thrusts a card into my hand then turns on his heel and scuttles back to his waiting customer.

I glance at the card, one of Jared's from the front desk. I turn it over. There's a mobile number scrawled on the back, and three words.

Molly? Call me.

I won't, of course. I can't, not now. Not after all this time.

Back in the safety of my anonymous hotel room I try to remember what I knew of Jared North when he was Prisoner Number KG8329. Was he married back then? I don't recall any visitors, and no mention of it on his file. Surely I would have spotted that. If I'd known I would never have… I couldn't have…

But I did, and the consequences were awesome. They still are.

He saw me. He recognised me, and he wants to talk. He

must want to, he gave me his number. And I need to talk to him. There are things I need to say, questions I must ask someone and he could help me to understand. It wouldn't need to have anything to do with his marriage, it's not as though I want to sleep with him.

Liar. Who am I trying to kid? But what I want and what I actually intend to do are two different things.

I pick up the card again though I don't need to. The number is now etched in my memory. I have only to dial it, and I'll hear his voice. Or I could text him. Maybe that would be easier. And then, he'd have my number too. I draw my lower lip between my teeth and tap a short message into the phone.

This is Molly. I'm at the Radisson Blu. Could we meet?

I press send before I can change my mind.
His reply arrives less than three minutes later.

I'll be in the lounge at your hotel tomorrow morning. 10 a.m.

• • • • • • •

I'm awake before six. By the time I've showered, dressed, and packed my belongings ready to check out after breakfast I still have two hours to kill. I lay on my bed watching breakfast television news and taking none of it in. I reach for the small pad of notepaper and the hotel issue pencil on the side table and start to jot down questions I might like to ask Jared.

Why did you spank me?
How did you know I'd like it?
Do all men who spank, spank like that?
Do you spank your wife?

I cross out that last one. Too personal.

Would you spank me again?

I start to cross that out too, but decide to leave it. That is, after all, my burning question.

I'm not sure I'll have the courage to ask any of this stuff, let alone the last question. But the spanking isn't where I should start anyway. Before I can get to any of that, I owe him an apology. Another one.

• • • • • • •

I'm in the hotel lounge at five to ten, my overnight bag stowed safe behind the check-in desk. My train to London leaves at noon, but I have no idea if I'll be on it or not. I take a seat at a table by the French window overlooking the gardens. I can see the canopy over the main entrance from here, so I'll know when he arrives. I order coffee, then call the waiter back and, ever the optimist, I ask for a pot for two.

"Molly?" The familiar tone behind me takes me by surprise. I whirl in my seat. Jared has somehow managed to enter the hotel without me spotting him. He inclines his head and takes the sofa opposite me. His long legs stretch across the space between us as he leans back and regards me, his expression a mix of amusement and interest. "It's good to see you, Molly, but to what do I owe this? I assumed you left the area."

"I did. I've been living in London. My train back leaves in a couple of hours."

"Oh, just a flying visit then? Lucky we ran into each other last night." He leans forward, his elbows on the table. "Or was it?"

"What do you mean?"

"You're a long way from home by the sound of it. Was it luck, or did you come looking for me?"

I open my mouth to trot out some trite denial, but it dies

on my lips. His eyes are cool, his expression hard. He expects the truth.

"Yes. I've been trying to find you. I bought a ticket for the gallery, and…"

"You came all the way from London? Especially for my showing last night?"

I nod. "Needed to see you. I hoped…" I fall silent, no longer certain what it is I hoped for, but it wasn't this. I remember a warm, vibrant man, a man who excited and terrified me in equal measure, and who saved my life when circumstances called for it. The man sitting opposite me now looks as though he'd like to throttle me.

My fragile courage deserts me. "I don't want to cause any trouble. I'll just go." I reach for my handbag, just as the waiter arrives with our coffee. He arranges the mugs, the jug of milk and the cafatière, and I remain in my seat intending to sign for the order, but the waiter hands the bill to Jared. He scribbles his name and hands it back.

He returns his attention to me. "And what trouble might that be, Molly? It is still Molly, I take it?"

I nod. "Mary's my real name, but everyone calls me Molly."

"And Mrs. Whitkirk? What's that about?"

"That's my married name."

"I see. Congratulations. Shall I pour?" He reaches for the cafatière and presses the filter down, his gaze never leaving mine.

"I offered you coffee once before I seem to recall. You declined."

I am unable to tear my gaze from his. "I remember," I murmur.

"So, you were saying, you don't want to cause me any trouble?" He pushes a cup of black coffee across the table toward me. "What did you mean by that, Molly? Help yourself to cream and sugar."

I add a generous portion of both to my cup, using the excuse to play for a few extra seconds in which to think. It doesn't help much. "I meant trouble between you and your wife. Rachel. She's very nice, by the way."

He nods as he helps himself from the cafatière. "She is. But Rachel's my sister, not my wife."

"Oh." I splash my coffee onto the polished table. "Oh, I see."

"Even if Rachel was my wife, I don't see how an old acquaintance being in the area could cause me a problem. What am I missing here, Molly?"

I'm at a loss, quite unable to articulate anything remotely sensible. Is that how he remembers me? As an old acquaintance, nothing more? How many crazy assumptions have I made about the attraction between us? It was clearly all one-sided. I've spent years fantasising about having kinky sex with a man who barely remembers me.

"I'm sorry, this was a bad idea." Mortified with embarrassment, I reach for my bag again. "I really do need to go. I have to get to the station, my train…"

"I'll give you a lift. I'll drive you all the way back to bloody London if I have to but I want an answer. What's this about, Molly? Why are you really here?"

I stare at him, feeling rather like a rabbit caught in headlamps. I want to be anywhere but here, but I can't move. At last I find my voice and I blurt out what's on my mind. "I wanted to see you. I keep thinking about what happened, that afternoon. I can't get it out of my head, and it confuses me. I don't understand."

"I'm not surprised you keep thinking about it—a prison riot's a memorable event. What exactly is it you don't understand, Molly?"

"It's not the riot. I meant I keep thinking about before that, just you and me, and that… that thing… that happened."

"Okay. The spanking. Is that it?"

I nod, as heat prickles up my face.

"Right then. If you want me to help you, I need to know what the problem is." His tone is gentler now, his gaze less intense.

I start to relax, just a little. "You'd help me? Really?"

"Why would I not?" He appears genuinely surprised at my question.

"Because of what I did. I got you into trouble, lost you privileges."

He laughs out loud. "Molly, I think it's fair to say I got myself into trouble that day. I did what I wanted to do, and later, when the riot started, I did what I had to do to get you out safely. None of it was your fault."

I bristle somewhat. "I was in charge. I was an officer."

"Molly, you were so not in charge." His voice is low, and he leans forward to look at me under his eyebrows. "You did as you were told, and you did it beautifully."

"What do you mean?" I detect some greater significance to his words, something I'm just not grasping.

"You were a submissive. I'm a dom, and I recognised the signs. I pressed a few of your buttons, and off you went."

"You manipulated me? Is that what you're saying?"

"Yes, that's about it."

"But, you were a prisoner. I was an officer, I took advantage of you. It was unprofessional."

He flashes me his dazzling, lopsided grin. "It might have been unprofessional, I leave that for you to decide, but you most certainly didn't take advantage of me."

"My managers didn't see it that way."

"You told them?"

I shake my head. "Not all of it. Not the spanking bit. But they knew I was in your cell. There were cameras on the wing and they obviously went over all the footage with a fine-tooth comb to gather evidence about how the riot started, ringleaders, all that stuff. I couldn't come up with a convincing explanation for what I was doing in your cell, and there were other questions too. For instance why were my clothes left behind in there? And why did I not come out when the furniture started flying and try to restore order?"

"You'd have been torn to bits."

"I should have tried."

"Fuck that. We did the right thing. We both survived, and none of the prisoners ended up on charges for murder or assault. And as for the clothes, we needed to make you as inconspicuous as possible, so you changed your officer's shirt for prison issue."

"You made me take off my bra too."

He smiles, his eyes twinkling. "Ah, yes, perhaps not strictly necessary but I've never been one to pass up an opportunity. Did they pick up on that?"

I nod, mortified just by the memory of trying to explain everything that happened that afternoon to a far from sympathetic management enquiry. Time to change the subject.

"Were you hurt? In the fight with the other men, I mean. I saw you, before they hustled me away."

"Bruised ribs and a broken finger, that's all. Nothing much. I was shipped off to Strangeways jail in Manchester and put back on basic though, which pissed me off. I liked my radio and proper toilet and I had to do without all those luxuries for months. My parole board was postponed too. I served an extra year for my part in the riot."

"But that wasn't fair, you had no part in it."

"Ah, Molly, such faith in the system. There's not a lot happens in prisons that I'd really describe as fair, but it's in the past now. I've moved on." He smiles at me and picks up the cafatière. "More coffee?"

I nod, and wait in silence as he pours. He sips his coffee, black I note, and fixes me with that stern look again.

"So, we've established that you believe you were a crap officer, though I think you're being rather hard on yourself. As screws go, I'd say you were decent enough. And we've dealt with Rachel. Now shall we discuss Mr. Whitkirk?"

"Who?"

"Your husband. I take it he isn't with you?"

"Oh, no. No, we're divorced. Well, nearly."

He makes no comment on that, just watches me, waiting for more.

"It was a mistake. I got married because I felt I had to. I had to do something, after what happened between us. Andy was there and he just sort of bulldozed me into it."

"You surprise me, Molly." He doesn't say it, but I sense I disappoint him too. That hurts.

"I surprised myself. But as you say, it's in the past and I've moved on."

"Have you? In that case, why are you back here, looking for me and wanting to discuss spanking? And why did you feel you had to do something?"

I draw in a deep breath and meet his gaze. His expression isn't hostile or accusing, just interested. And determined.

"Okay. Andy always hated my job, and after the riot he never got his head around how I came to spend forty minutes locked in a cell with prisoner. I told him nothing happened but he didn't believe me." Jared's lip quirks at that, and I shrug. I did what I did, and there's no undoing it all now. "He was jealous, angry, insecure, and I was fragile in the aftermath of it all. I was weak, and I wanted some peace and quiet. It just seemed—easier. So I handed in my notice and married him."

"I'm getting the impression this wasn't a love match."

"Not really, as it turns out. We were engaged though, and living together, so it was a natural step. Or it seemed like that at the time."

"You had a live-in fiancé, and you still let me spank you?"

"I know. I just got caught up in it, and you were…" I hesitate, try to find the right word. "You were very compelling. I did as you told me. I wanted to, but it was wrong, I see that now. I saw it then, straight after. I felt guilty, and stupid, and very confused. I needed someone to take charge, and I thought Andy could perhaps replace you."

"You were looking for a dom, even then?" He doesn't even pretend not to understand.

I nod. "I didn't know it at the time, but I do now. And I mistook Andy for that. It was unfair really, and not his fault. He was strict, and demanding. He told me what to do, and I obeyed him."

"So, what happened?" He is leaning forward, his expression gentle. He reaches for me and cups my face in his hand, and it is only then that I realise tears are streaming down my face.

"He wasn't kind. I think he was a bully, probably. He never spanked me, never laid a hand on me at all, but he was always angry, always critical of the things I did, anything I said." I stop to gulp in a few much-needed breaths. "He used to call me names, really horrible things, and each time it felt like a punch in the gut. I'm glad he wasn't into spanking, I would never have felt safe with him. He didn't seem to like me that much, not really."

"So you left him?"

I nod. "I was a coward about even that, though. I was too demoralised to tell him to his face, so one day I went to work and just didn't go home. I took a room in a bed and breakfast and texted him to say I wasn't coming back. And do you know what? He didn't even care. He just replied to say 'fair enough,' and to let him have a forwarding address for his lawyer to be in touch."

"Heartless bastard. It sounds to me as though you did the right thing."

I manage a watery smile. In my heart I know I was right to end my marriage, but Jared is the first person to actually say it. He wipes away some of my tears with his thumb as I ramble on with my tale. "My family was incredulous when I told them what I'd done. My older sister couldn't understand why I dumped a decent husband and a good provider like Andy. He hadn't even been unfaithful, and we'd only just had a new driveway laid. My mother refused to let me move back in with her, and is still fond of reminding me that I made my bed and really should have laid in it."

"A new driveway, eh? That is a big deal, I suppose…"

"Oh, shut up." He frowns, so on impulse I grab his wrist and squeeze it. "I'm sorry, I just…"

"I know. Don't worry. I won't spank you for telling me to shut up."

I gaze at him, my bottom clenching. I wish he would. I so wish he would. I really ought to leave before I blurt out something very unwise.

"So, what would it take then? To get you to spank me?"

Too late.

CHAPTER FOUR

She's every bit as beguiling as I remember, but more vulnerable somehow, without the prison officer's uniform to serve as her armour. She holds onto my wrist, her grip tightening as though she expects me to pull away and abandon her. It's fair enough, I suppose. I did it before.

I should never have started that scene at Armley jail. It was wrong on so many levels, not least the fact that I was in no position to offer Molly the aftercare she needed. I knew it, I knew back then how our encounter was likely to end even without factoring a fucking prison riot into the equation, but I didn't let that stop me. I was horny, I needed an outlet, and she was there.

I did her a huge disservice, and it's not a mistake I'm about to repeat. I like to think I'm more in control now and less led by my dick. My dom instincts are if anything more powerful now than they were then, but so are my ethics, so woefully lacking in the past.

I shake my head. "I'd love to oblige you, Molly, but now's neither the time, nor the place. We've both moved on since that day—"

She blushes crimson, and drops her hold on my wrist. "Of course. I'm so sorry. I can't believe I actually said that.

I've embarrassed you, and myself. Look, I'll just go."

"No, Molly, I didn't mean—"

"Just forget it. Please." She reaches for her small bag again, and this time she manages to grab it and get to her feet. I stand too.

"Molly, don't rush off. I'd like to continue this…"

"No, no, we've said all we need to say. Too much, probably. Now if you'll excuse me I need to collect my luggage from reception and ask them to call me a taxi to the station, so …"

"I'll drive you." It seems to be the only way I'm going to be able to remain in her company for a little longer, hopefully enough time to drag my foot out of my mouth and explain what I really meant.

"That's okay, really. I can get a cab." She's already heading for the double doors that lead into the hotel reception area. I catch up with her and manage to steer her past the desk and out through the main doors without manhandling her too much—certainly not enough to attract the attention of the concierge. I nod to him as we pass. "Mrs. Whitkirk has to be off. I wonder, would you be so kind as to bring her luggage, please? It's with the receptionist."

"Of course, sir." The liveried attendant bustles off to do as I ask, leaving me to convince Molly of my good—well, not entirely bad—intentions.

"My car's over here. I'll drive you to the station."

She's still insisting she can make her own way even as I'm shepherding her across the acres of car parking in the direction of my dark grey Audi. The automatic locks open as we approach so I only have to open the passenger door and usher her inside. The matter is settled when the doorman arrives with her small suitcase and pops that in the boot. I slip him a crisp five-pound note and he leaves happy. I slide into the driver's side and start the engine.

"Jared, I'm not sure… Please, let me out."

She sounds scared. I curse inwardly and turn to face her.

"The doors aren't locked. I swear to you, I'm not about to abduct you or do you any harm. My days as an armed robber are behind me."

Her eyebrows shoot up under her wavy fringe and she shakes her head. "Oh, no, I didn't mean that. It's just—I'm embarrassed, that's all. I made a fool of myself, coming on to you like that and you were right to slap me down."

I manage a wry chuckle at her choice of words. "Sweetheart, you of all people should know that if I decide to start slapping it won't be in the public setting of hotel lounge. Like I said, there's a time and a place. If you want to make time, I can provide the place."

Her mouth makes a delightful little 'o' and she is speechless. I decide to treat her stunned silence as a point to me, and put the car in gear. There is no further protest from Molly as we exit the car park and join the Friday morning traffic.

The journey to the station is short, and neither of us speaks. I pull up in the short stay parking area and kill the engine. Molly makes no move to get out.

"What time's your train?"

She fishes in her bag for her purse, and extracts a ticket. "Five past twelve. It gets into Kings Cross at three-fifteen this afternoon."

"Do you have work later? Things to do… in London?"

She shakes her head. "Not really. Well, I do have work, when I get back, but I'm self-employed these days so I set my own hours. I make jewellery, and sell it on eBay."

"Ah, a fellow artist then?"

"Hardly." She lets out a derisive snort. "My stuff's not in your league. I'm lucky to get ten quid for one of my pieces."

"Do you make enough to live on?"

"On a good month. The rest of the time I turn down the heating and manage to get by."

"If you live off what you earn that makes you a fellow artist. Wait here."

"Why? Where are you going?"

"Wait." I offer no more explanation, and get out of the car. At the station entrance I glance back. She is still seated exactly where I left her, her obedience gratifying and more than a little encouraging. A plan is starting to form in my mind, and I need her compliance if it's to work.

Five minutes later I emerge from the station to find her still in the passenger seat, though looking somewhat anxious. I slide back into the car beside her.

"Give me your ticket, please."

It's still in her hand. She passes it to me. I tear it in half, then in half again. I drop the pieces in the tray in front of my gear lever.

"Why did you do that?" She looks from the pile of torn card to me and back again. "That cost me forty pounds."

"Here, have this one." I reach into my jacket pocket for the first-class open ticket I just purchased and hand it to her. "It's valid for three months. Now, you have plenty of time."

"What? I can't. I mean—"

"You had a train to catch, now you don't. You can go back to London whenever you like, but there's no immediate hurry. We need time, to talk. Now we have it."

"But, my hotel—"

"You can stay with Rachel. She owns a pub and has rooms to let."

"Oh." Her expression suggests surprise, and just possibly disappointment. I decide to try my luck.

"Or, you could stay at my place. It's a bit further away— that's why I was staying over with Rachel last night—but there's plenty of room and I think you'd like it there."

"But you don't know me. And you could hardly say we're friends."

"I know you well enough. The question is, do you trust me? Ex-con and all that?"

She holds my gaze for several seconds. I hold my breath.

"I do. Trust you. I always did."

"My place then?"

She inclines her head. "Thank you. It's just for a night or two, while we talk, and…" She doesn't elaborate, and neither do I.

"Right." I start the engine and offer her a smile, hoping I manage to inject sufficient warmth to provide the reassurance she needs. I've picked up enough in the way of signals from her to be reasonably certain that my chequered past is not so much the issue, but hers—riddled with guilt, doubt, and self-recrimination—most certainly is.

• • • • • • •

I'm fond of my place, though I don't entertain there very often. Privacy means a lot to me, which is why I decided to buy and convert Cote House Barn about a mile from Summerbridge in Nidderdale, North Yorkshire. When I acquired the property a year ago, it was a semi-derelict pile of rubble set in the middle of a field occupied by a bunch of not especially curious sheep. The Yorkshire stone walls and roof were intact though, more or less, and the structure basically sound. It took six months to renovate and convert the wreck of a building into the isolated country house I now like to call home. The sheep still amble around outside and we manage to ignore each other pretty much as I rattle around among my four bedrooms, dining room, lounge, kitchen, and study. The views are stunning, inspirational as far as I'm concerned, but the main reason I adore this place is the studio I installed in the roof space. Natural light pours through the skylights and the huge room serves as both workspace and viewing gallery.

Molly says very little during the drive out here, just gazing out of the window at the scenery of the Dales National Park. As we reach Nidderdale and the road starts to climb, leaving behind the last shreds of what might pass for civilisation around here, she peers from side to side, her expression intent. I have the uneasy sense she might bolt at the first provocation. I need to tread carefully, since I have every intention of disturbing her equilibrium—eventually.

I smile to myself as I turn into the long, cobbled driveway leading to the forecourt in front of my house as I wonder what Molly will make of the exhibits in my personal gallery.

I park the car and get out, then walk around to open Molly's door. "We're here. Come on, I'll give you the guided tour." I retrieve her case from the boot of the car and lead the way up the two steps to my front door. Molly stands beside the car, rooted to the spot.

"Are you okay?" I call.

She turns at the sound of my voice. "Oh, yes. It's just— wow! Look at this." She turns three hundred and sixty degrees and gestures to the world at large, swinging her arm around in a wide arc. "It's so ... huge. And empty. There's nothing for miles around."

I grin. Factually, that's not correct. I'm surrounded by moorland, huge rock formations that attract tourists and geology students in about equal measure, and there's even a Ministry of Defence communications station a couple of miles to the south. The massive 'golf ball' installations can be seen for miles. But I know what she means, and vast emptiness is why I'm here.

"Yes, it seems so. I enjoy the solitude, the peace and quiet, the space. I don't much appreciate being closed in— I'm sure you'll understand why."

"Don't you get lonely, up here all on your own?"

I shake my head. "Not really. I've lived in overcrowded conditions, and believe me, this is better. In any case, most of the time I'm working, or out on location somewhere. It's rare that I get to spend more than few days at a time here. I wish I did."

"I'm sorry." She stands at the foot of the steps looking up at me, her face betraying her discomfort.

I deposit the case on the top step and go back down. She drops her gaze immediately. I cup her chin in my palm, realising this is only the second time I've really touched her since we slipped out of my cell at Armley. I tilt her face back up so she has to meet my eyes.

"Why are you sorry, Molly?"

"I locked you up."

"It was your job."

"I know, but—"

"You did what you were paid to do. If I was minded to blame anyone else, it might be the judge who sentenced me, or the dickheads I used to hang around with who couldn't organise a piss up in a brewery let alone a half decent post office robbery. But I don't. I take responsibility for what I did and for what happened to me back then, just as I do now."

"What do you mean, now? Are you still—?"

I shake my head. "No, definitely no. I'm a reformed character." *Well, that's true, more or less.*

"But, how did you manage it? I mean, this is some transformation… all of this."

I lower my head to kiss her forehead. Her eyelids droop in silent acceptance. My cock springs to attention. Time to move this on.

"Come inside. I'll give you the tour, then explain my meteoric rise to fame and fortune." I step away and hold out my hand. She laces her fingers through mine and follows me up the steps.

The tour of the downstairs rooms doesn't take long. I fling open the dining room door for Molly to peer through, then the lounge. I've not lived here long enough to accumulate much so I'm still rather minimalist in my decor. It probably looks somewhat austere to Molly, though she's too polite to say so. She seems impressed by my kitchen, which pleases me. Next to my studio this is probably the room I spend the most time in when I'm here. I enjoy cooking, it appeals to my creative urges. And I appreciate decent food—another legacy from my prison days, I suppose. I put on a pot of fresh coffee then lead Molly upstairs.

Two of my bedrooms are unfurnished. I'll get round to sorting that at some stage, but the trip to Ikea can wait. I show her into the guest bedroom.

"You can use this one, while you're here."

She glances at me, surprised. "Oh… right. I assumed…" She blushes again, quite beautifully.

I enjoy a fleeting image of that same peachy redness splashed across her rather gorgeous buttocks and the blood drains straight to my cock. "Or not. We'll see how it goes, shall we?"

I know exactly how the sleeping arrangements are going to pan out, but if those endless months and years spent cooling my heels in Armley taught me anything at all, it was patience. She'll share my bed, but I'll wait until she's ready to ask me for that privilege. "Shall we move on?"

I lead the way along the upstairs hallway to my room, the biggest and by far the most comfortable. My emperor-size bed dominates the space, set in the centre of the room, facing floor-to-ceiling windows that open onto a stunning view of Brimham Rocks. I seldom watch television in here—the natural view is so much more entertaining—so the wall-mounted screen is modest in comparison to the fifty-odd inch monster in my lounge downstairs. I do appreciate atmosphere and mood though, so I have a state-of-the-art sound system. There are other subtle concessions to my personal preferences, but I see no point in drawing Molly's attention to the slotted head and footboards, so convenient for tying a submissive to my bed, or to the various hooks in the beams above our heads. There'll be time enough for all of that later, if she responds as I hope she will to the images in my personal photo gallery.

"I love this room," breathes Molly, walking across to stand before the picture window and gaze at the vista beyond.

I move to stand close behind her. "Me too." I lift her hair from her shoulders and kiss the nape of her neck. "Your hair used to be shorter."

She angles her head to allow me better access. "I know. Andy didn't like it so I let it grow."

I comb my fingers through the wavy locks. "This is nice, but I liked the sassy cropped look too."

"So did I, but…"

"How long has it been? Since you separated?"

"Just a couple of months."

"Long enough not to be trying to please him anymore."

She turns to smile at me, the first genuine smile I think I've seen since we met at the hotel. "You're right. I'm making an appointment at a hairdresser first thing on Monday."

I wink at her. "Go, girl. So, shall I show you the rest now?"

"There's more?"

"Upstairs. My studio. This house is my workplace as well as my home."

"It's a fabulous place to work."

"I think so, and the short commute is another advantage. Come on." I step away and offer her my hand again. She takes it and I lead her from the room.

The flight of wooden stairs leading to my artistic domain is at the end of the hallway. Molly follows me up and we enter. I'm still holding her hand as I step back to allow her an uninterrupted view of the space. She gasps and her grip on my fingers tightens as she takes in her new surroundings.

"Oh. Oh, my goodness. Are all these yours?"

"Yes," I murmur. "I originally produced the collection as commission for a club in New York, but I liked them, so I had a set printed for here too."

"I… see." She lets go of my hand and steps forward to stand before the first of my black and white images, a picture of a beautiful blond submissive kneeling, bound and naked before a man in an Armani suit. His head is deliberately cropped off; the woman is the focus of the work. Her posture screams surrender, obedience, compliance. It's powerful, seductive, elegant, and erotic, even if I do say so myself.

"Do you like it?" I ask, my tone deliberately low.

She nods, gnawing at her lower lip as she considers her response. "Yes. I do. It's very—expressive. Who is she?"

"Her name's Naomi. That's her dom she's kneeling in front of. What does the image express, would you say, Molly?"

She turns to look at me, ignoring my question. "They're not just models, then?"

I shake my head slowly. "No, they're friends of mine and their lifestyle is real enough. What does the image say to you, Molly?"

"She loves him. Does she? She looks as though she might."

"I'm sure she does, and he adores her. Is that what you see? Love?"

"Yes, and trust. He could do anything to her, and she's powerless. Vulnerable."

"Okay. What about that one?" I direct her to the next image a few metres along the wall. In this scene Naomi is photographed in the centre of a large, empty room. She is naked, of course, suspended from the ceiling, her arms above her head and her toes just touching the floor. She is looking straight into the camera, her eyes brimming with fat, shiny tears.

Molly eyes the picture critically before announcing her judgement. "It's a beautiful image. She's very lovely."

"She is. Do you like this picture, Molly?"

She hesitates, then, "No, not as much as the other one. She looks sad. Scared perhaps."

"How does it make *you* feel?"

"It makes me feel … apprehensive. As though something unpleasant is about to happen."

"Maybe it already happened."

"No. She's waiting, anticipating." She turns to me suddenly, her eyes wide. "It's because she's alone! That's why she's so unhappy. She's waiting for *him*."

I maintain a neutral expression, though inside I'm singing. Molly gets it. She fucking knows. "Let's look at a few more."

I guide her along the gallery, pausing before each picture. Naomi is not featured in all of them. The collection made use of a range of models, some male, some female, but all submissives. They are mostly naked, invariably bound, some gagged. All are captured by my camera, suspended in a permanent state of sub euphoria.

Each image evokes a different response from Molly—awe, anticipation, uncertainty, joy, disappointment. She describes her feelings as we stand before each canvas, occasionally asking me a question but for the most part she is captivated by the scenes depicted in the collection. As we reach the last one she turns to regard me.

"This is you, isn't it? It's your lifestyle too."

I incline my head, never breaking her gaze. "Yes. I'm a dom."

"And you were back then, at Armley. That was why I was so… so drawn to you. I didn't want to be, I tried to keep my distance, but you were like a magnet to me and I kept coming back."

"I know. I was very aware of you too."

"Were you? I thought you despised me. I was an officer, a screw."

"You were, but it didn't seem to matter. Not then, not now."

"Now? Are you still…?" Her words trail away and I'm not entirely certain what it was she wanted to ask. I need to know.

"Am I still what? A dom? Or aware of you?"

Her response comes in a whisper. "Both."

I nod again, slowly, watching the myriad emotions flitting across her expressive face. "Yes. Both."

She swallows, twisting her fingers together in front of her waist. Her hands are shaking, I note, but she makes no attempt to step back from me. Neither does she lower her gaze. I take that as a sign she is interested in exploring this aspect of my nature—and hers—a little more, so I press my advantage.

"You want me to control you? To take charge of what happens next?"

"I don't know. I…" She pauses, straightens her shoulders and lets her hands drop to her sides. "Yes. I'd like that. I want to know how it would be, how it would feel."

"Why?"

"Excuse me?"

"Why do you want to know? Can you not imagine it?"

She tilts her chin up, just a fraction, but enough to let me know she means it. "It's not the same. I want to… to actually *feel* it. I want it to happen… to me. Again."

"Again?"

"I want to feel the way I did that other time, in your cell. But without the distractions, the stuff in the way. My uniform, my job…"

"…a hundred rioting prisoners on the other side of the door?" I smile at the recollection. A little grim humour never goes amiss.

She flattens her lips in response. "That too. I was terrified."

"You hid it well. I have to say, you look more frightened now than you did that day." I reach out to cup her chin in my palm "Are you frightened of me, Molly?"

"Yes. No." She chews on her lower lip for a few moments, as though considering what to say to me next. "I think nervous and a little scared would be a better description. And… hopeful."

I smile, my carefully cultivated dom smile, which I hope conveys mastery in abundance but also enough warmth to offer the comfort she needs. Despite our earlier encounter I have no doubt that this is to be Molly's first real experience of submission, and it's my responsibility to make it work for her. I can only guess at what fumbling attempts to seek out the fulfilment she needs might have been made during her ill-fated marriage, but this is to be different.

"You came here looking for me. That doesn't seem like the action of a woman who's scared. You could have explored your submissive side with someone else, a dom who isn't an armed robber for a start. Why me?"

"I know you. And I trust you." She hesitates again, then, "Are you still… involved in any of that stuff? I mean… I assumed…" She gestures to the gallery surrounding us, my studio.

I shake my head. "No. I'm a photographer these days, nothing more. I've been successful and I make enough from that not to have any wish to risk it all by getting involved in anything criminal." I lean in to murmur in her ear. "I'm a reformed character, Molly."

She shivers. Actually fucking trembles. It's time to move this back downstairs, to my bedroom.

I tilt my head back to meet her gaze once more. Her eyes are a deep shade of azure, the pupils already dilating. "Molly, I want you in my bed. No, scratch that. I want you on my bed, tied to it. I'll lay you bare, spread you out, and play with you for hours. I'll pleasure you and I'll hurt you, and I'll make you scream from both. Is that what you want, too, little Molly?"

Her mouth opens. No words emerge. She clears her throat and tries again.

"Yes, sir. Yes, please."

CHAPTER FIVE

Wordless, he leads me from the gallery. I follow him back down the short flight of stairs to the landing below, then along the carpeted hallway toward his bedroom. I walk a couple of paces behind Jared and can't help but be aware of the powerful set of his shoulders, the muscles that ripple beneath the soft, silky shirt. He was always a powerfully built man, no doubt honed by those hours spent in the prison gym, but now he is simply magnificent. Jared removed his jacket when we arrived at the house and now I watch him roll up his sleeves as he precedes me. I gulp, at the same time as my pussy contracts in helpless arousal. My underwear is already moist, has been since he first took me into his studio to show me his artwork.

The gallery held such sensuous, evocative pictures, each one totally arousing though in different ways. Every image spoke to me. No, they sang to me. They awoke dormant emotions within me, revealing yearnings and desires I have suppressed or been too afraid to allow to surface. But it seems my inner submissive is finally to see the light of day.

I'm so far out of my comfort zone I could easily bolt for the door.

But I won't. I came here for a purpose and I will see it

through. I'd never forgive myself if I didn't seize this opportunity. I have to know. I have to understand what I am. Who I am. This voyage of discovery was a goal I hardly articulated, even to myself, but Jared recognises something in me, just as I did in him five years ago. He understands me even when I can't fathom myself. He can help my inner submissive to emerge. I had agonised over how I might persuade him to help me. I had only to ask.

Now, I have only to trust him, and everything will be all right.

He gestures me through the bedroom door ahead of him, then closes it behind us with a soft click.

I stand in the centre of the room at the foot of his enormous bed and I turn to face him.

"Do you have questions for me, Molly? Anything you need to ask me now, before we start?"

His voice is low, steady, with a rich, seductive timbre that causes something really weird to happen low down in my belly. My pussy spasms, becomes wetter. In contrast my mouth is dry. I run my tongue across my lips and try to come up with an intelligent response. I can only manage the obvious.

"I just want to know what you intend to do."

He smiles, a not entirely pleasant expression. "I bet you do. Or perhaps not. I think you might turn and run right now if I were to describe exactly what I intend to do to your lush little body."

I shift back a fraction as he advances. He stops.

"Don't do that. You have no need to back away from me. I'm only going to touch you with your permission. There'll be no shocks, nothing sudden or unexpected. We'll talk about what's happening and you can tell me if it's too much."

"You'll stop?"

"Of course."

"Will I have a safeword?"

"Ah, Molly, you've done your homework. Yes, you will.

Do you have one in mind?"

"What about 'jailbird'?"

He grins again, this time in genuine amusement I think. "Very apt. We'll go with that then. That can be your 'all stop' but we also need a mercy word, one that means 'slow down, I need to talk,' or that you're struggling. Any ideas?"

I try to think but my mind's a blank. I shake my head.

"How about 'cooler'? That seems to fit."

This time it's my turn to nod. Jared seems satisfied. He strolls across the room to take a seat beside the huge picture window. He stretches out his long, denim-clad legs and leans back to regard me in silence for several moments.

"Okay, we start with some basics. I want you to undress. Remove all your clothes, fold them neatly, and place them on the chest over there." He tips his chin in the direction of a low chest of drawers on the opposite wall. "Then you'll come and stand in front of me with your feet shoulder width apart and your hands clasped behind your head. Can you manage that?"

We both know he is not enquiring about my physical ability to complete the task, and it's a good question. The honest answer is… I don't know.

I stand, rooted to the spot. This is it. The moment. Submission starts here.

Natural modesty, rampant curiosity, and hot desire war within me. Jared lifts one eyebrow, watching me as I try to process his instruction. I play for time.

"Everything? You mean me to be naked?"

"Was any part of 'remove all your clothes' unclear?"

I shake my head and reach for the top button of my blouse.

"Molly, we need to agree to some ground rules and we might as well start now. When I ask you a question I expect you to answer me with words. A nod or a head shake won't do. And you'll call me sir."

His tone has hardened, cooled. He sounds stern and demanding and implacable. I stop, my hands still on the collar of my blouse, and I look at him. His expression doesn't waver, but I swear his eyebrow lifts a fraction more, as though daring me to defy him.

There is no way I'm even considering that for a moment. "No, sir. Your instruction was clear. I just wanted to... check."

"Checking's good. Please always feel free to check or to clarify. That's better than earning yourself a punishment for not doing exactly as I ask. If you have further questions, you can ask me them whilst you undress."

That's my cue to get on with it. I take a deep breath and finish working my way down the buttons at the front of my blouse.

It's actually a lot easier than I anticipated to get naked in front of Jared North. His appreciative gaze encourages me, and the huge erection stretching his tight-fitting jeans leaves no room for doubt. He's enjoying the show.

I remove my blouse first, then I toe off my lace-up pumps before unfastening the loose-fitting cotton pants I chose in anticipation of the train journey back to London. I let them drop to the floor and step out of them. Wearing just my underwear, I'm glad of the instinctive impulse that drove me to wear a matching set again today, and one I consider particularly attractive at that. Cream-coloured low-cut cups edged with lace the colour of a rich caramel latte cradle and lift my breasts as though presenting them for scrutiny. The matching briefs are delicate and barely decent, exactly the look I want now. I sneak a quick glance at Jared's crotch and I'm gratified to note the bulge is even bigger. He doesn't look at all comfortable, which I consider mission accomplished.

I gather up the discarded clothing and fold each item. Then I undo my pretty, gravity-defying bra. I'm tempted to turn my back, but that would be futile, and in any case, this is what I want. I allow the lacy cups to tip forward to reveal my breasts, and offer up thanks that I am at least reasonably well-endowed in that department. My breasts are generously proportioned, and fairly perky though my nipples seem a little on the large side. Especially right now.

I sneak a look at him. His expression betrays nothing but patience.

I hook my thumbs in the elastic around the waist of my high-cut knickers and shove them down to reveal my neatly clipped mound. I seem to recall reading somewhere that dominant men often prefer no pubic hair at all, probably the same choice of literature that familiarised me with safewords. Andy preferred my pussy to be smooth too, but I defied him. I doubt if Jared would let me get away with that. I doubt I would want to.

I retrieve my underwear from the floor and drop the briefs on top of the rest of my clothes, then I go to place them on the chest as instructed. I turn and make my way over to Jared, my heart thumping. My legs are turning to jelly, but I get to the spot a yard or so in front of his feet and stop. I lift my hands and link my fingers together at the back of my head.

"Open your eyes. Look at me." His voice is soft, but no less compelling for that.

I hadn't even realised I had closed my eyes, but I raise my eyelids and meet his gaze. Jared is leaning forward now, his elbows resting on his thighs and his hands loosely clasped before him. He beckons me forward, to stand between his legs, then rakes me with his long, slow scrutiny. As I watch the top of his head he allows his gaze to drift down my body, as though taking careful note of every contour and hollow, no detail escaping his close examination. I hope he likes what he sees, though the bulge behind the zip of his jeans seems to confirm that he does. I expect he's becoming seriously uncomfortable now, and I take perverse pleasure in that.

"Turn around, please, and bend over."

"What?" My voice has transformed into a high-pitched squeak.

"I think you heard me, but I'm happy to clarify so that

you know exactly what I expect from you. Turn around, bend at the waist, and grip your ankles. I'd like you to arch your back as much as you're able then widen your stance a bit more. You're showing me how wet your pussy is, so offer me the best view you can. I want to see your juices glistening on your pussy lips and thighs."

Oh. My. God. I stare at him, mortified. I know I'm wet, and I knew he'd find that out before much longer, but the prospect of calmly displaying my decadent arousal for him to look at is more than I can handle.

"Sir, I... I... can't..."

"Can't? Do you mean you're not able to bend, or keep your balance? I'm happy to let you lean on something this first time, if that helps."

"It's not that, sir."

"So, what's stopping you? I've asked you to show me your wet pussy. What's the problem? You *are* wet, I take it?"

I forget his ground rules, and I nod miserably. I thought I could do this. I genuinely believed I was about to find what I was seeking, experience the thrill of submission, and with a dom who knew what he was doing and who could teach me. But I was wrong. All I'm ready to do is collapse in a heap at the first hurdle.

"Molly, use words. Either tell me what the problem is, or do as I ask."

"I'm embarrassed. You'll think I'm ..."

"A slut?" He helpfully finishes my sentence for me. "I know you're a slut. You wouldn't be standing in front of me naked if you weren't. But Molly, understand this. I *like* sluts. Sluts are honest about what they want and how they feel. Sluts turn me on. Sluts make me hard. Needy, wet little sluts make me so horny I want to spank them, and fuck them, then probably do it all again for good measure. Is that what you want too, Molly?"

Oh, Lord! "Yes, sir," I whisper.

"And is that the sort of slut you are? Needy and wet?"

"Yes, sir. Oh, God..."

"God isn't here, only me. But I'll try my best. In that case, my wet and needy and quite breathtakingly beautiful little slut, you know what you need to do."

"Yes, sir," I murmur, already starting to turn.

I bend over as instructed and grasp my lower calves, then I shuffle my feet a bit further apart.

"Wider, Molly." A sharp tap on my inner thigh indicates what's required. I shift my feet again.

"Good. Now lift your bottom up a bit more, please. Ah, yes, that's better. Are you comfortable?"

"Not exactly."

"Not exactly, *sir.*" He delivers a not-too-gentle slap to my upturned bottom. "I'm assuming you don't object to me touching you, but if you do, now's the time to say so."

"I… I don't object, sir." *Christ, if he doesn't touch me soon I think I might go up in flames.*

"If you want me to touch you, you have only to ask."

How does he know? How does he know just what I'm thinking every time?

"Please, sir, would you touch me?" I think I'm getting the hang of this.

His palm is on my buttock, his caress casual yet achingly accurate. His fingertips brush the very edges of my pussy, but no more. I groan and attempt to angle my hips to catch his wandering fingers.

He chuckles and slaps my bottom again. "Nice try, Molly. As soon as I do touch your delightfully wet cunt, I suspect you're going to come like the pretty little fuck-slut we both know you are. Am I right?"

"Yes, sir. Without a doubt." My pussy is quivering, positively throbbing with need.

"Shall we get that over with then?"

Oh, sweet Jesus!

"Molly? Did you say something?"

"No, sir. Just, please…"

"Is this what you want?" He swipes the flat of his hand slowly across my pussy from clit to arse, and my knees almost give way under me.

"Oh! Oh, yes. *Yes!*"

He repeats the caress once more, then again. I edge back toward him, seeking to increase the pressure. He stops stroking me, casually flicks the tip of my clit, then uses his thumbs to part the lips of my pussy.

"You'll have my cock inside you soon, but for now I'm thinking two fingers. Or perhaps three. How many would you like, little Molly?"

"Three, please," I mutter. "I'm a needy slut, remember."

"Ah, yes, of course you are. And I hate to disappoint." Even as he speaks he is sliding three fingers into me. He takes it slow, but still it feels tight, my entrance stretching to accept the intrusion. "Is that enough for you, my slut?"

I'm rocking back and forth on my heels to create the friction I crave. Jared snakes his free arm around the front of my thighs to pull me closer to him and hold me still. "Allow me, sweetheart."

He withdraws his fingers, then plunges them deep again. He continues to finger-fuck me, picking up a faster tempo as I writhe against his arm. He twists his free hand a little to lay the pad of his middle finger over my clit, and he rubs from side to side.

My orgasm surges up from almost nowhere to send me careering out of control. If he were not holding me up, I'm sure I would crumple into a boneless heap at his feet as my inner muscles convulse and my legs give way. I squeeze tight around his fingers as waves of pure delight flood through me, every nerve ending tingling, my nipples hardening into swollen pebbles of need. He takes my clit between his finger and thumb and squeezes it, not hard, but the pressure is enough to create never-ending spirals of lust that snake out from my core to reach my fingers, my toes, the very ends of my hair.

He continues to stroke, to tease, to rub, drawing the last shuddering sensations from me, taking my weight entirely now as he holds me in place. Eventually the waves of pleasure subside, the frantic quivering in my pussy diminishes to a mere tremor, and I manage to remember my name again. And his.

"Jared? Sir…?"

In a moment he has straightened my body to bring me upright, risen to his feet, and swept me up in his arms. Two strides later I am lying on the bed, on my back, gazing up at him as he bends over me.

He sweeps a lock of hair back from my face. "You all right?" He looks concerned.

"Yes. Yes, of course."

"Okay, so far so good. Now that we've started to deal with your inhibitions, and taken the edge off that rampant lust of yours, we can have some fun. I'm going to tie you to the bed. Is that okay with you?"

"You don't need to. I promise not to move."

"I won't restrain you if you prefer me not to, but I'd like you to try it."

"I see. Okay then." I'm not quite ready to say so yet, but the idea of being bound, unable to move, arouses me in ways I'd struggle to describe, even to Jared.

He drops a light kiss onto my forehead, then reaches past me to open the drawer beside the bed. He produces a pair of leather wristbands with metal clips attached, which he shows to me, that expressive eyebrow raised once more.

"No metal handcuffs?" I manage a smile and hold out my wrists to him.

"These are more comfortable, believe me." He fastens a cuff around each wrist, then attaches them to the headboard by the clips. My arms are stretched above my head, but I can still move. I'm surprised. I suppose I expected him to immobilise me completely.

He gives me that lopsided grin again, his dom antennae working on overdrive. "Baby steps, little Molly. Next time we might fasten your ankles to the bed too. This is enough, for now."

Relieved, and becoming more relaxed by the second, I

offer him another smile, a real one this time. "What happens now?"

"Now, we try out a few sensations, see what you like."

"And what I don't like?" I haven't quite shrugged off my trepidation.

He pauses to drag his admiring gaze the length of my body and back up to my face again. "Maybe, but I'm thinking you'll probably enjoy this. Shall we see? I have some toys we could play with."

"Toys? Not...?" I'm not sure what the correct collective term is for paddles and whips.

"Yes. Toys. So, now I have you tied to my bed, do you trust me enough to let me blindfold you?"

"Why? Why do you need to do that?"

"I don't need to. We can play perfectly well without, but I think you'd find the whole experience more exciting. Again, I'd like you to try it." He reaches back into the drawer and this time produces a dark red scarf, which he folds across the diagonal, then again to make a blindfold. He holds it before my face, but makes no move to cover my eyes.

I give a sharp nod. In for a penny, and all that.

"Tell me, Molly. I need to hear the words, to be sure."

"Yes, okay then. A blindfold. But no gags. I don't want you to gag me, definitely."

"Agreed. In any case I enjoy hearing my subs squeal too much for that, and while we're getting to know each other I need you to be able to tell me what you're feeling, what you like, what you want from me."

"I see. Yes..."

He winks at me, then lays the blindfold over my eyes and ties it at the back of my head. Immediately my sight is cut off. I sink back against the pillow propped behind my shoulders, relaxing into this thing we're doing. Jared was right, the whole effect is heightened by my helplessness. It is as though being bound affords me permission to abandon all responsibility and just let things happen as they will, all the while knowing I have only to say one of my safewords and it ends.

"Comfortable?" Jared speaks to me from close by. I turn my head toward the sound of his voice.

"Yes. I think so."

"Good. Tell me if you get a cramp, or any tingling in your fingers."

"What about tingling anywhere else?"

He chuckles. "Tell me about that too."

CHAPTER SIX

She is truly gorgeous, a feast, a blank canvas spread before me, just waiting for me to paint my dark designs all over her lush body.

I straighten, step back from the bed to survey the vision that is Molly MacBride. So many times back there in my stark little cell I imagined her like this, but the reality is beyond anything I could conjure up. It wouldn't be true exactly to say I've yearned for Molly in the years since we parted, though she has crossed my mind more than a few times. I can hardly believe she sought me out after all this time, but I've always been good at seizing my opportunities when they come my way. She's here now, and I intend to make this a memorable occasion for both of us.

She's aroused, but nervous. I can see it. I watch as she gnaws on her lower lip, one of her tells. I reach out to lay a fingertip across her lush little mouth and the unconscious chewing ceases. Instead she pokes out the tip of her tongue to lick my finger. My cock lurches painfully inside my jeans. I have to get naked soon, and now seems as good a time as any.

It takes me just a few moments to be rid of my clothes, during which time Molly squirms on my bed, her face turning from one side to the other as she listens to every movement, searching for clues. I sit beside her and she goes still.

"Jared? Sir…?"

"I'm here. I was just getting undressed."

"I want to see."

"Soon. For now, I want you to simply feel."

I trail my fingers down her chest, the length of her sternum, then back up again to rest my hand across her throat. I apply no pressure, I have no need to. She lies perfectly still, her breath coming in short little gasps. Her nipples are erect, hard, swollen buds, a dark, rosy pink and achingly tempting. I lean over to take one between my lips, and she lets out a startled yelp before arching her back to press the pebbled nub further into my mouth.

So eager. So fucking lovely.

I suck hard and use my tongue to press the tip against the roof of my mouth. It crosses my mind that clamps might be nice, and I have a delightful pair of clovers that would be perfect for Molly but I dismiss that idea. For now.

Instead I reach for her other breast and squeeze that nipple between my finger and thumb, tugging slightly to make sure I have her attention. It seems I do. Moaning softly, Molly writhes under me as I ramp up the pressure. I continue until she is bucking hard, her grunts and squeals near frantic, then I release her without warning and step away.

"Sir?" She swivels her head as though watching an invisible tennis match, seeking me out in her darkened world. I move to the foot of the bed and open the blanket box I keep there. Inside are my collection of toys. The floggers, paddles, and spanking crops are mostly well-used, items I know well and can wield with accurate and exquisite effect. Other toys such as vibrators and dildos, and, of course, butt plugs, are new. I like to keep things fresh.

Molly hears the sound of the chest opening and cranes her neck as though she might spot what I'm up to. I ignore her for now and make my selections.

A flogger first, I think, something delicate and sensuous. I pick up one of my personal favourites made of a soft, grey suede, and I move around the bed to stand beside her, the fronds trailing against my thigh and knees. I dangle the implement over her body so that just the tips of the lashes are in contact with her skin. Again, she goes stock still, rigid almost, but for her chest heaving.

I trail the flogger across her breasts, ensuring the feather-light tails tease and torment her swollen nipples, wrapping them around then dragging them across the sensitised nubs.

Molly is arching and rocking within the restraints, twisting her body as the flogger makes contact, seeking more from it, more from me, but ultimately she is helpless. I am the one in control.

I lift the flogger and bring it down over her breasts, leaving a faint smudge of a slightly deeper pink across her skin. She gasps, and continues to wriggle in her restraints. I was right to tie her up; she would never manage to remain still for this otherwise.

I lift the flogger again and continue to drop light strokes all over her chest and stomach, alternating the sharper blows with gently trailing the soft fronds over her pinkening skin. She likes it, I can tell. Molly arches her back, her moans becoming louder as I build the sensation little by little. She is murmuring something. I lean in a little to hear her incoherent half-sentences of want and need and growing desperation.

I move around the bed, whipping her from every angle until I sense she is on the verge of another orgasm. I slow it down, less of the sharp slapping and more trailing of soft suede across the curves of her breasts and belly. She is quivering, chewing on that lip again, though this time her response is driven by arousal and need.

"Spread your thighs for me, Molly."

She obeys, her reaction immediate, bending her knees and opening her legs wide. So fucking gorgeous. I resist the urge to simply fuck her then and there, and instead apply the flogger to her inner thighs. Finally I drop one last stroke right across her drenched pussy.

Molly squeals and slams her legs shut. It is exactly the reaction I expected, but I need to be stern, to make her understand that she must never close her body to me.

"Open them, Molly. Now."

"But it hurts."

"No, it doesn't. And in any case, you have your safewords." I pause to allow her time to process this, but not for long. I *will* have her obedience. "Now, Molly. Unless you prefer to stop. Do you want me to stop? You have only to ask and I'll untie you."

"I know. I just… it was a surprise." She starts to part her thighs once more. I wait until her legs are spread wide again, then I reach for my next toy of choice.

I flick the switch on a small bullet vibrator and without further preamble press it against her clit. Her hips thrust upwards and she cries out. I lift the toy away and wait for her to quieten again.

"I don't want you to come just yet. Try to control yourself."

"But I can't. It's so… so… I just can't."

"You know I'm going to spank you, whatever happens. The only question is, will it be a punishment spanking or an arousing one. The choice is yours, Molly."

"I'll try, sir. I will. I am."

I cup her cheek in my palm and stroke her damp hair back from her face. With an inexperienced submissive there's a time for sternness, and a time for comfort and reassurance. "I know, and I know it's hard but I'll tell you when to come and I'll make sure it's good for you. Your orgasm will be your reward for waiting, for doing as you're told. Okay?"

"Okay. Yes, I understand."

"Do you? Do you really understand that orgasms have to be earned now? That I'm in charge and you can please me by obeying? Is all that becoming clear to you?"

"Yes, sir," she whispers. "I think I get it now."

Perhaps she does, at least some of it. But she's a newbie and there's only so far I can push her. I reapply the vibe to her swollen clit and roll it over the thrumming nub a couple of times, then I press the switch to turn up the intensity before slipping it inside her pussy.

"Oh! Jared, sir!" Molly is pumping her hips up and down, seeking the friction she craves. I press her knees a little further apart and lean over her to blow on her clit, then I take it between my lips and I suck.

She doesn't yet have my permission to orgasm, but my poor little novice subbie never stands a chance. She erupts like a volcano, her entire body convulsing as I hollow my cheeks and increase the pressure on the sensitive bundle of nerves between my lips.

It's to be a punishment spanking after all then, though I think I can make the experience one she will remember with a degree of fondness. I draw out the pleasure for as long as possible, sucking, nibbling, tracing the outline of her labia with the tip of my tongue. I slide my fingers through her folds to reach her tight little puckered anus and I press there. I won't penetrate her arse today, I prefer to talk to her before taking that step, but she responds beautifully by lifting her bottom up to offer herself to me. Maybe she's not an anal virgin after all.

Ah, Molly mine, we'll have such a lot of fun together. I have some delightful plans for you.

As her climax ebbs away I slide the vibe from her pussy and replace it with two fingers, then add a third. She's tight and hot and wet. Above all, she's ready. I roll on a condom then position myself above her and place the head of my cock at her entrance.

"Now, I fuck you." She knows, but I prefer to say it. And hear her response.

"Yes, sir. I want…"

I lean down to whisper in her ear. "Tell me what you

want, Molly."

"I want you to fuck me. Please."

"Why? Would it be because you're a slut?"

"Yes, sir, I think it must be."

"How do you want to be fucked, Molly?"

"Sir…?" Her voice is a breathy, needy whisper.

"Do you want it hard, fast? Do you want me to ram my cock into you so deep you'll feel it in your tonsils? Is that the way you like to be fucked?"

"Yes! Yes, sir, deep and hard, but do it now. Please."

"That will be my absolute pleasure, little slut."

I drive my cock deep into her in one long, slow stroke. It's a snug fit; the walls of her channel grip and cling to my dick creating a friction so fucking tight I groan with the sheer delight of it. I'm balls deep in her before I stop, hold my position, allow both of us to adjust and gather our wits. Or what might be left of them. She is stretching around me, her cunt quivering, squeezing me hard. My weight is on my elbows, but I lower my face to brush my lips across hers.

"Christ, you're tight. And hot. And so fucking wet. Such a sloppy little slut—tell me how much you need this."

"I need it, sir. I need you—"

"How much, Molly?"

"More than anything, sir. Please, don't—"

"I'm going to fuck you until you scream for me to stop. Or to never stop. Which will it be?"

"I—"

I pull back and slam into her again, hard enough to drag a whimper from her as her cunt spasms around my cock.

"Is this how you want to be fucked, Molly? Is this how you like it? Are you going to come all over my cock like the hot little slut you are?"

She flexes her thighs and manages to thrust her hips up toward me, whether in demand or surrender I'm not certain but the signals are clear enough. My Molly likes me to talk dirty to her while my cock's buried in her cunt. She opens her mouth, but before she can speak again, I plunge my tongue inside to dance and play with hers. She tastes so sweet, and I wonder if she can detect her own musky flavours still on my tongue.

Should I release her from her restraints? She's responding to my rough handling so I decide against it, for now, and withdraw my cock almost pulling right out of her. My next stroke is hard and fast, just as she told me she wanted it, and as deep as before. Molly makes a strangled sound in her throat and arches up to meet me. I tear my mouth from hers and rear up above her, then pound my cock into her like this for a minute or so. Her response builds with each thrust. She's climbing, seeking, convulsing hard around my dick and I know neither of us will last much longer.

I slow down, just giving her short, shallow strokes now, teasing her entrance but not driving deep. She goes wild beneath me, bucking her hips up as though I might allow her to take over the rhythm, wanting me to pick up the pace again.

I *don't* think so.

"Be still, Molly," I growl.

She tries to do as I say, but can't remain motionless for more than the next few strokes. This time I stop altogether even though the effort is killing me, and I watch as she wriggles against the mattress. When she finally gives up and lies still I plunge my cock right in, filling her entirely.

Molly screams, her pussy convulses. My cock jerks hard, my balls contract, and my semen surges to fill the condom. Molly is sobbing her release and I collapse over her as I succumb to mine, though I do manage to roll to one side so as not to crush her. She continues to shudder for several more seconds. I reach over to release her wrists, then tug the blindfold up over her head. I always like to look into my sub's eyes as a scene ends because that's when she's at her most unguarded, her most vulnerable. I need to know what's in her head.

Molly's eyes are closed but I cup her chin and turn her

face toward me.

"Look at me," I command.

Her eyelids flutter and she raises them slowly. Her pupils are dilated, her eyes dark with arousal, with sated lust. She curls her mouth is a small, hesitant smile, which causes my softening cock to have a change of heart.

"Was that okay? Did I do all right?" she asks, then waits, trusting, for my affirmation. Or otherwise.

"Yes, love. You were perfect. Do you feel good?"

She nods, then collects herself. "Sorry, I mean… yes. I feel wonderful."

"And being tied up? How was that?"

"A bit overwhelming at first, but in a good way. The blindfold too…"

"Would you do it again?"

"What? Now?"

"Are you sore?" *Christ, I hope not. My dick's already twitching to start over.*

"No, sir. I don't think so."

"Right then. Just give me a moment to grab a fresh condom, then I'll see what I can do about that. By the time you leave this room you'll struggle to remember your own name, but you'll be able to feel me in every nerve ending you possess."

She lifts her hand to caress my cheek. "Is that a promise, sir?"

It was, and I hope I made good on it. By the time I've fucked Molly twice more, once from behind and then again with her bouncing on top of me, her gorgeous tits jiggling in front of my nose, I'm not sure either one of us can recall our names. We both collapse into an exhausted heap—a tangle of limbs, sticky, panting bodies, matted hair. Molly falls asleep almost immediately, and I doze for a few minutes. When I open my eyes she's still spark out so I peel myself away from her and roll from the bed. I need caffeine, food perhaps, and a breath of fresh air without a doubt. I pull the duvet up around her and gather up my clothes from the floor, then pad barefoot from the room.

Molly follows me an hour later. She finds me outside, my third cup of coffee in my hand, leaning on the dry stone wall that marks the edge of my patio.

This is one of my favourite places, the view from here nothing short of breath-taking. Combined with the potential I saw in the loft space, this spectacular vista was one of the main reasons I had to have this place. The dramatic landscape of Brimham Rocks is spread out before me, the bizarre mushroom-shaped lumps of millstone grit reaching as high as thirty or forty feet, balancing precariously one on top of the other, their weird contours carved out by aeons of wind, glacial, and rain erosion. The surrounding moorland that wraps around my house in all directions is now a kaleidoscopic riot of autumnal colours, the heathers and gorse shining in purples, golds, vivid greens, and flashes of brown as the bracken darkens to its winter hue. This magical place is a geologist's dream. Tourists flock here, as do climbers and all manner of outdoors enthusiasts, but for a jailbird turned honest photographer, it's quite simply home.

I glance over my shoulder as Molly approaches. "Coffee?" I offer her my cup.

"Thank you." She accepts and takes a sip, then wrinkles her nose. "No sugar or cream."

I drape an arm across her shoulders. "There's plenty inside. Come on."

I settle her at the kitchen table, place a fresh cup of steaming coffee, complete with two sugars and some cream, in front of her. "Are you hungry?"

"A little, but I'm fine for now." She looks up at me. "Can we talk?"

I take the seat opposite her. "You have questions." She must; it's inevitable.

"Yes. Lots."

"About what happened upstairs?"

She shakes her head. "Not that, well, not only that. It

93

was you I was wondering about actually." She casts her gaze around the spacious kitchen. "This, all of this, it's so different from anything I imagined."

"Not what you expected from a convicted armed robber, is that it?"

She reddens, but nods. "I'm sorry, I don't mean to be rude. But—yes. This has been quite a transformation. How did you...?"

"I was lucky, to an extent. But I worked hard too, and took my opportunities when they presented themselves."

"When did you decide to take up photography?"

"I always liked to take pictures, you must remember that. It almost got me in trouble." I glance at her, one eyebrow raised as I recall those few minutes we spent together in the prison laundry. She flushes, then smiles at me as she nods. "Right. I enjoyed messing about with my camera, even as a child, but I sort of lost sight of it for a while. I got caught up in all that bollocks you know about. Crime was sort of the family business. My dad spent more time inside than out while I was a kid."

I pause, wondering how much of my sordid past to share. She sits opposite me, still, silent, just watching me, and waiting. And she's interested, genuinely wanting to know my story. I decide to press on.

"I grew up in East Leeds. Robbing things was just that thing we did and I never thought of being any different. I saw prison as an occupational hazard and I served my apprenticeship in youth detention centres since I was about twelve years old. The closest I got to a positive role model was the guy who coached down at the boxing club where I liked to hang out, but I lost touch with him after one of my spells away. From there I roamed around the streets with my mates, collected an ASBO or two, became good at stealing motors, and eventually gravitated toward driving getaway cars for anyone needing the service. It was lucrative work, and I enjoyed it."

"But you got caught."

"I did, and had my first taste of prison. It was so much tougher than the juvenile facilities I was used to and I hated it. The closed-in feeling made me physically sick. Can you even start to imagine how that felt, compared to this…?"

"Is that why you own a place like this? The wide openness?"

I shrug. "Maybe, I'm not sure. Probably. But even if I hadn't been able to afford to move out here, I sure as hell wasn't going back inside. Once was more than enough. I did my time and eventually managed to convince the parole board to let me out."

"You said you got time added on, for the riot."

"Yes. An extra year, but I was a model prisoner from then on and perhaps I caught the parole board on a good day. They let me off two thirds of my remaining sentence so I was out by the end of 2011. I went to Rachel's to spend Christmas there, and just sort of stayed on."

"Your sister."

"Yeah. She'd just split from Brad, her husband, and she appreciated the extra help with the kids. She had two under five back then, and a stepdaughter who Brad seemed happy enough to leave with her. She was licensee of a dingy little pub in Morley. I moved in, did the heavy work in the cellar, and kept order in the bar. The arrangement suited us fine. Meanwhile, I was a hobby photographer again and I'd forgotten how much I missed it. I preferred landscapes and I had an eye for those, used to send my favourite pictures in to the television. You know, the ones they show on the weather bulletins—fog over Filey, the snow-capped hills of Skipton, that sort of thing?"

She is gazing at me, silent. But she nods slowly, seems to understand. So far so good.

"I entered an amateur photography competition. It was an impulse. I'd just pulled off a really dramatic shot of the Leeds skyline at dusk that I was particularly proud of, and I spotted an advert in the *Yorkshire Evening Post* inviting readers to send in their photos of the city. So I did. I won, and got a contract to provide more local pictures for the paper. They were picked up by a gallery, I got a corner in an exhibition, sold a couple of pictures, and I went from there. My big breakthrough came a year or so later when I came third in an international show and on the back of that I was offered an exhibition of my own in Brussels. From there on I was a photographer full time, the commissions rolled in, and I was earning good money."

"So you left the pub and bought this place?"

"No, not for a few years, though by then I was travelling a lot and spent less and less time with Rachel. I helped her to buy The Eagle in Baildon—that's the pub she owns now, a free house catering to real ale enthusiasts. I had a room there for when I was in the UK. I worked like a demon for the next couple of years, had a fair bit of my material published, built my reputation, and made sure I stayed well clear of my old haunts in East Leeds. When I had enough for the deposit I made an offer on this place. There was a lot of work to do though to make it habitable, so I only moved in a few months ago."

"So, no more life of crime, then. None at all?"

I shake my head. "None. I'm rehabilitated, a success story for the judicial system."

"I doubt the system could claim much of a hand in it."

"Oh, but it could. Prison worked as a deterrent in my case, but like I said, there was an element of luck. Rachel, for example, giving me a place to stay, a job, of sorts. That competition coming up just when it did, the exhibition in Brussels. But I was determined too. I'd have stayed as Rachel's cellar man if that was the best I could manage, but as it happened…"

"You're very talented."

"Thank you."

"As a photographer, and…"

I wait. No prompting from me, not on this.

"…and as a dom."

I doubt she's really qualified to say, but I accept her

comment at face value. "No regrets then, about what I did to you?"

She shakes her head, emphatic. "It was awesome, everything I ever imagined. More perhaps…"

That was what I hoped to hear. "Good. You'd do it again then?"

"With you?"

"Well, I'd like to hope so. Why, would you prefer to try another dom?"

More emphatic head shaking. "It was you I wanted. Ever since, well, ever since that other time. I'm glad I managed to find you again, and that you weren't married or—" She stops, meets my gaze, her brow furrowing. "You're not in a relationship, are you? I mean, Christ, I never even asked."

I grin at her and reach for her hand. "No, no other relationship. I like to play, but there's no regular little subbie waiting for me anywhere."

"I was waiting. Somewhere."

"Yes."

"When you say you like to play…?"

"Clubs, fetish meet-ups. Casual stuff mainly."

"Mainly?"

"I did have an exclusive relationship up until a few months ago but we agreed to go our separate ways. We wanted different things."

"I… I have no idea what I want…"

She's lying, or fooling herself. Molly knows full well what she came here in search of. I decide to name the beast.

"Apart from a chance to explore your submissive sexuality?"

She nods, relief flooding her features. I knew I was right. "Yes, exactly that." She looks doubtful suddenly. "Is that all right? I mean, if you don't want—"

"I *do* want. That suits me fine." *For now.*

"How long can I stay here with you?"

"How long do you want to stay?"

"I should go back soon. I have work, things to do.

Things to settle." *A solicitor to instruct, for one thing.* "It's time I got my divorce started."

"Sounds like the start of a plan. I have a trip to Paris planned for later in the week, but I'll only be away a few days. You're welcome to come back here whenever you want, and you have my mobile number."

"Is it okay to call you, then? If I need to talk, or… anything?"

"Of course. I'll take your call any time. And you have to take mine. Agreed?"

She nods. "Of course. So, we're agreed, it's just sex then. You'll show me things, help me to understand this weird stuff I feel inside, the things I want to do?"

"Ah, Molly, we're going to have such a lot of fun together. But understand this, when you're here with me it might be just sex but it's sex on my terms. That means you do as you're told. You have your safewords, but unless you want to use those I expect no arguments, no procrastinating. Obedience, Molly girl. Can you manage that, do you think?"

She inclines her head, though I have no real illusion that she has the first idea what she's letting herself in for. She'll start to learn soon enough.

I harden my tone deliberately. "You can start by losing the T shirt."

"What? Here?"

I get to my feet to loom over her. A little intimidation can go a long way, especially at this stage in the proceedings, and discipline needs to be both swift and decisive to make the point. I harden my gaze; the time for exchanging confidences is past. "What did I just say about arguing and procrastinating? You've already earned your first spanking. Now, for the avoidance of doubt, after your spanking I'm going to feed you, and I prefer you to undress for dinner. Then I intend to fuck you right here on my kitchen table. Do you have any objections, Molly? Are you ready, now, to do as I say?"

She lowers her gaze and grasps the hem of the borrowed

T shirt. "Yes, sir," she murmurs as she pulls it over her head and drops it onto the chair next to her. Then she gets to her feet to stand before me. "Do you want me to bend over your knee again, sir?"

"Not this time. I want you to go back up to my bedroom and bring me a spanking paddle. You'll find several in the chest at the foot of the bed but the one I want is made of pale coloured wood and has holes drilled in it. You'll bring it back here to me, then you can lean over the table, rest your elbows on the top, and lift your arse up as high as you can." I tip up her chin with the tips of my fingers. "You have a lesson to learn, so this is going to smart, little wannabe sub."

CHAPTER SEVEN

My heart is pounding as I sprint up the stairs and back into Jared's bedroom. He didn't tell me to hurry, but I get the impression he expects me to look smart. I don't want to attract further punishment, even though my pussy is creaming already at the prospect of what's to come in the next few minutes.

I crouch before the blanket chest and throw open the lid, then manage not to gasp at the array of sexy paraphernalia inside. Although I didn't actually see the toys he used on me earlier, I know there was a vibrator involved, and something that seemed a bit like a soft whip. He used it to wrap my body in a cloak of sensual tingling. It did hurt, though I would not exactly describe the experience that way. The entire adventure was exhilarating, a sharp burst of pain followed by a deep sensation of pleasure that seeped into my muscles and bones.

I don't expect the paddle to evoke the same response.

The implement he described comes readily to hand and I set it to one side. I take a few moments to peruse some of the remaining items, and imagine him utilising each and every one of them on me over time. My pussy clenches, spasming wildly as I start to imagine at least some of the sensations. There are whips, more spanking crops than I can count without extracting each one and laying them out on the carpet, several leather cuffs in various sizes and colours, metal handcuffs, leather straps, a formidable collection of paddles and canes. I suspect meting out discipline won't present a problem to Jared North.

I'm not entirely sure I can say the same for myself, but we shall see. Exciting times ahead. And challenging.

I close the lid, pick up the required paddle, and head back down to the kitchen.

Jared is leaning against the worktop, his arms folded across his chest. He narrows his eyes as I enter.

"Something held you up?" He tilts his head to one side as he regards me, his expression difficult to decipher.

"No, sir. I was just looking at the other things. In the blanket chest, I mean."

"I see. Did anything take your fancy?"

"Yes… I mean, no, not especially. Everything…" I falter, uncertain what the correct response might be. Will he object to me poking around in his belongings? He did send me up there, after all.

"Everything? What a brave little sub! Or maybe a foolhardy one. Don't worry, you'll get to try everything, if you want. And more besides. My collection's pretty extensive but there are lots more toys out there, once we know what you enjoy."

"What about things I don't enjoy?"

He shrugs. "Some of those I'll use for discipline, probably, such as now with that paddle you're cradling there. It's okay to say no though, if you really don't fancy something."

"Even if it's punishment? Like now? Can I just refuse to let you spank me?"

He nods. "Of course you can. I'm not about to drag you across the room, screaming and fighting, then strap you down while I whip you. This is all about consent. By submitting to me you accept my right to punish you, and you *will* bend over and present your bottom to be spanked. Won't you?"

He waits, unmoving except for one eyebrow, which he raises as he watches my response.

I shuffle before his calm, knowing scrutiny, the recollection of that day in his cell both powerful and very immediate. It's as though I'm catapulted right back there, the doubt, the nervousness, the unexpected longing I experienced every bit as real to me now as they were then. He just waited for me that time, too, while I made up my mind.

I meet his quiet gaze. "Yes, sir. Now?"

"Please." He nods in the direction of the table as he extends his hand to take the paddle from me. "Lean on your elbows, shoulders down, bum up, feet about shoulder width apart."

I move into position, the warmth of the polished oak oddly comforting. Turning my head to face him, I lay my cheek on the smooth wood. He quirks the edge of his mouth in a slight smile, which both comforts and reassures me. He steps forward, the paddle dangling from his right hand as he pauses behind me.

"How do you feel right now, Molly?" He lays his palm over my left buttock and caresses the trembling flesh.

"Scared, sir."

"Okay, I get that. We'll be quick then. How many strokes do you think would be fair for questioning my very clear instructions?"

I have no frame of reference for this, and had not anticipated being consulted in any case. I take a stab in the dark. "Ten?"

"Ten? That's ambitious. I'm impressed."

"Oh." My heart sinks a little. I want to impress him, but if Jared thinks ten is a lot… shit.

Jared chuckles. "Baby steps, Molly. We stop at six, less if I decide you've had enough." I'm still processing that when he speaks again. "I can warm you up first with a hand spanking if you like. I do advise that, though these strokes won't count against the six." He rubs large circles across my bottom as he speaks, his palm pressing hard, massaging me into relaxed acquiescence.

"Yes, sir. Thank you."

My body is sinking into the table as the tension I had been feeling dissipates. That state of relaxed well-being evaporates in a moment when he starts to spank me.

"Ooh! Ow! Sir, please…!"

Jared ignores my protests as he rains rapid slaps down on both my buttocks. I twist against the table, seeking to avoid the blows. He stops and steps away from me.

"When you're being punished I expect you to keep still and remain in position. You can make as much noise as you like—this time—but no moving."

"Yes, sir. Sorry…"

"Get back in position then." I shift to comply. "Good. Just lift your bottom a little higher, please. You need to offer me the best angle possible for maximum impact. I want to teach you a lesson with this spanking, a memorable one. And you want to learn it, right?"

"Right. I understand." And it's true, I do. More or less. I *need* this to hurt in order to anchor it firmly in my subconscious, along with the required obedience that will be attached to the pain he is about to inflict. With that in mind, I raise my bum an extra inch or two, acutely conscious of my smarting cheeks now fully exposed and vulnerable.

"Good girl, Molly." Jared starts spanking again, a series of rapid, sharp slaps on both cheeks, then shifting his attention down onto the backs of my thighs. I'm especially tender there, and can't contain my squeals of pain. By the time he pauses to pick up the paddle from the table alongside me, my entire bottom is burning. "Lift up again, please. And don't move until I tell you that you can."

I manage a tight little nod and do as I'm told.

Jared's arm swings, there's a brief rush of air, then a sharp crack as the paddle connects with my bottom.

"Aagh! Christ," I mutter. The first stroke lands in the centre of my right buttock and it hurts. It bloody well hurts a lot, more than I ever imagined. The burst of agony brings me right up onto my toes, my fingers clawing at the unyielding wood of the table top.

"One," announces Jared, shifting his stance slightly.

He swings again, and the second stroke sears my left buttock. I yelp, my breath catching in my throat, but I remain still.

"Two. Better." Jared pivots on his heel slightly, readying himself for the next stroke. It lands swiftly, a burst of pain exploding on my right side, just above the first.

"Jesus," I gasp, drawing comfort from the fact that I'm halfway through my punishment now and not reduced to a quivering wreck. Yet.

"Nearly there." Jared confirms my count as he lines up the next stroke. "Four."

I let out a startled scream. For some reason I'd expected this one to land on my left side, in a spot to mirror the last one. Jared is ringing the changes though and drops this on the back of my right thigh, just where it meets the lower curve of my buttock. It's absolute fucking agony and I'm starting to cry.

I'm angry with myself. I never imagined he'd actually hurt me so much I'd break down in tears. What an idiot I am. How naïve could I be?

"Molly? Remember, you have your safewords." Sensitive to my shifting reactions, Jared has paused. "You have two more to go, but we can take a time out. There's no rush."

I want this to be over. I want to know I weathered my first—well, second—spanking and survived it. I want him to cuddle me and praise me and fuck me until all of this is in the past and I'm his obedient little subbie once more. So, there *is* a rush.

"Now. Do it now, please. Finish it... sir."

"You sure?"

I nod, frantic that he should just deliver the final two

spanks, then tell me it's over.

Jared does not disappoint me.

"Five." That one lands on the upper curve of my left cheek and takes my breath away. I am chewing on my lower lip, panting. My entire bottom feels to be ablaze. But I remain motionless, just as instructed. Almost finished. So close. So. Fucking. Close.

"Six." The paddle connects with my smarting flesh one last time, this stroke blistering across my left upper thigh. I'm up on my toes again, grasping at the far edge of the table for support or I might crumple to the floor.

There's a clatter as the paddle lands on the table, then Jared's palm between my shoulder blades both grounds and reassures me. He moves to stand behind me, and I wince as the fabric of his jeans brushes the burning skin on my buttocks and thighs. He leans over, his hands planted on the table on either side of my shoulders, his lips close to my ear.

"Breathe in, Molly, then out. Slowly."

I manage to do as he says, though my breaths are ragged and uneven. Tears stream down my cheeks, but at Jared's insistence I concentrate on dragging in gulps of fresh air, then exhaling.

"In. Out. In. Out." Jared controls and regulates until I am steady once more. Then he straightens. "I promised to fuck you over this table. I am a man of my word, Molly. Spread your legs. Wide."

Yes! Despite my lingering tears my lips curve in a satisfied smile. I was punished, and I suppose I did deserve it though it was horrible while it was going on. But now I've earned this. I widen my stance.

Not enough it would seem, as Jared nudges my ankles a little further apart. I start to push myself up from the table.

"No. Stay there." The command is quiet, but delivered in a tone that brooks no debate. I remain in place, but twist my neck to watch him over my shoulder.

Jared toes off his trainers then pulls his T shirt over his head and drops it onto the tiles beneath our feet. His jeans soon follow. He is wearing nothing underneath. He bends to produce a condom from the back pocket of his discarded denims, then meets my gaze. His eyes are dark, the grey deepened to almost black, the shade matching his short-cropped hair. Even as a convicted prisoner Jared North carried an aura of power, a certain presence that drew me to him. Here, in his own environment, his dominant persona in full sway, he is larger than life and utterly compelling. I blink, momentarily overwhelmed.

"Molly? Are you okay?" He frowns and pauses in the act of snapping the foil surrounding the condom.

"Yes, sir, I just… You can be very intimidating, do you realise that?"

He inclines his head. "It goes with the territory. But you can say no to me, I've told you that already."

In theory, yes. In practice, I find that prospect hard to visualise. And nothing could be further from my mind.

"I don't want to say no."

"I'm relieved." He smiles at me. "What do you want right now, Molly?"

"I'm not sure. I feel a bit shaky, that's all. It'll pass." Unbelievably, out of nowhere, I start to cry. Great heaving sobs, I cover my face, hope that he won't press on with fucking me until I've had a moment to collect myself.

Jared mutters a curse, then scoops me up from the table and strides across the room. He carries me from the kitchen and up the stairs, back into the huge bedroom. In moments I am lying on the bed, my nose pressed against the muscled plane of his shoulder, my breasts flattened against his wide chest as Jared wraps his arms around me and holds me against him. I'm shaking, sore, and I feel utterly worthless, a grown woman allowing herself to be spanked like a little girl. I cling to Jared, trusting him to make this all okay again, to resurrect my fragile self-respect.

Jared grabs the duvet and wraps it around the pair of us. He's warm, solid, so sure of himself, and of me. His quiet strength and utter confidence somehow seep into me, bolstering my shattered self-esteem as he continues to hold me until my sobs subside. He is murmuring soft, soothing words, words of approval, praise, reassurance, his palm tracing large, slow circles between my shoulder blades. When my gulping breaths finally reduce to an occasional sniffle, he sits up and rummages in the bedside drawer for a moment, and manages to produce a small bar of chocolate.

"Open your mouth, Molly," he commands, then he pops a lump of the sweet stuff on my tongue. It tastes divine, the sugar rush calming me quickly as the chocolate softens in my mouth.

"Can I have some more?" I peer up at him, hopeful.

"As much as you like." He grins at me. "Is there anything else you'd like? A drink?"

"Not unless you can rustle up a one-shot latte."

"I have coffee."

I shake my head. Coffee needs making, and the apparatus is downstairs. What I need most right now is for Jared to remain where he is, holding me. And more chocolate, naturally. I part my lips to accept another piece.

"I'm sorry, that was my fault." He kisses my hair as he shifts us both into a sitting position. "I know now, though, that you're a snuggler after you've been punished. Feeling steadier now?"

"Yes, thank you. I don't know what happened; one moment I was fine, then the next I was suddenly so miserable and I felt like a fool."

"Sub-drop. It's common enough, a reaction to the rush of endorphins. I moved on too fast. Next time I'll take better care of you."

"Next time?" I don't even want to think about being spanked again, ever.

"Yes, next time. You're sure to slip up and I'm a stern dom, so it's inevitable that your bottom will bear the consequences. But you got through it just now, and you will again. And you'll learn each time. Just as important, so will I, and I'll provide the aftercare you need—cuddles, chocolate, a one-shot latte, time to cry if you need to, or to talk. You can trust me on that."

"I know." I brush my lips across his. "I don't want to talk right now though, if that's all right."

"Okay. So…?"

"I'd really like it if you'd fuck me now. Does that still count as aftercare?"

He flips me onto my back and props himself up on one elbow to grin down at me as I wince in pain. My bottom is decidedly tender and shows no sign of easing any time soon. "Whatever gets the job done, sweetheart. I reckon you'll prefer to be on all fours though, right?"

"Right, sir."

He kneels up and gestures for me to roll over. I need no further encouragement and quickly shift into position.

I'm delighted that Jared had the presence of mind to keep the condom in his hand as he carried me up here. He snaps the foil and sheathes himself, then moves behind me.

"Such lovely marks, Molly. Your arse is bright red, with pale circles where the holes on the paddle were."

"Is that why it had holes in it then? To make patterns on my bum?" I wriggle the piece of my anatomy under discussion, in the hope he'll take the hint.

"It reduces wind resistance, means I can hit harder with it. Not that I made use of that design feature this time. I went really easy on you, Molly girl, this being your first paddling."

"It didn't feel like it. Do you mean it can hurt more than that?"

"Oh, yes. I'll give you a demonstration now if you don't stop squirming about."

I go still as he slides his fingers through my dripping folds. I shift my knees further apart, opening as wide as I can for him.

Jared rams three fingers inside me, the sudden penetration causing me to cry out in surprise.

"Did I hurt you?"

"No, sir."

"Thought not. Feel free to squeal as much as you like." He withdraws his fingers, then spears them deep inside my pussy again. He twists his wrist so as to make contact with my G-spot, which he rubs mercilessly as I pant my joy.

"I'm going to come."

"Not yet." His tone is implacable.

"I can't help it. Please."

"Not unless you want another six strokes with the paddle. Remember that design feature, Molly."

I squeeze my inner muscles around his fingers in an attempt to quell my burgeoning response. It works, briefly, but he soon overrides my flimsy resistance and I'm hurtling toward climax again.

"Sir," I wail, despairing, my bottom clenching in anticipation of the paddling I know I can't avoid.

He takes pity on me and withdraws his fingers, only to replace them with the length of his cock. He drives it balls-deep inside me, my sensitive inner walls convulsing as the blessed friction sends waves of pure, exquisite sensation coursing through my nervous system. I let out a scream.

"Liking that, Molly?"

"Yes, sir." My pussy is spasming, contracting around his wide cock. He's slides out, slowly this time, then thrusts back in. He's huge, stretching me more than I imagined possible, but it feels like bliss. I know I can't suppress my response, however many strokes of that bloody paddle it might earn me. "I'm going to come. I'm sorry—"

"Feel free." He delivers another long, slow stroke, and my resistance shatters.

My orgasm seizes me, whirls me around and spits me out. I'm floating, weightless, my senses humming as my muscles spasm and contract. I lower my forehead onto the mattress as Jared continues to drive his erection in and out of my pussy, savouring the aftershocks as my body relaxes again. Jared takes that as a signal to reach around under me to caress my swollen clit. In moments I am coming again, gasping as he teases not one but two more climaxes from me.

Jared slows, the pressure on my clit lessening as I writhe under him, my breathing ragged. He releases the quivering bundle of nerve endings to place both his palms on my smarting buttocks then presses his fingers into my punished flesh. I whimper; it hurts. Perversely though, rather than seeking relief I push my bottom back to increase the sensation. I'm fast realising that pain is the flip side of pleasure, and I'm finding it harder and harder to separate the two.

Jared eases my buttocks apart and slides his fingers into the groove between them. He circles my arsehole with his fingertip, pressing the ring of muscle.

"Let me in, Molly."

His command is delivered in a soft tone. I know he won't force me, or press the point if I'm unwilling. In this moment though, there is nothing I wouldn't allow Jared North to do.

I nod, and will my body to relax as Jared pushes his finger through the tight rosette. He's gentle but firm, and my body capitulates readily. The first knuckle, then the second. Soon his finger is fully inside my arse. He withdraws then buries it again as he slides his cock from my cunt. As he thrusts his cock back in he pulls his finger out, alternating the strokes with artful skill.

Somehow, I have no idea how he does it, he slides his free hand under me again to reconnect with my clit. He flicks, rubs, and I orgasm again.

This is the most powerful release yet, and seems to go on forever as Jared plays my body like a finely tuned instrument, teasing the tune he desires from me. I tremble, shiver, clench, and convulse as wave after wave of sensation pulses through me, until I drop limp onto the mattress.

Jared follows me down, his cock still pumping in and out of my pussy until with a grunt of pleasure he drives it deep and stops. His erection jerks hard inside me as he comes, then he slumps onto the bed beside me. If his weight against my buttocks causes me any pain, I'm way beyond caring. His cock is still inside me as I reach to trail my fingers down his cheek.

"Thank you, sir," I murmur. "I think I could manage that coffee now."

CHAPTER EIGHT

I come awake slowly, my mood a curious blend of elation and sadness. Why? What's happened? What's different?

Molly. Molly is the difference. She's here, hence my high, but she leaves today, which accounts for my dampened mood. Still, she'll be back. Never one to brood, I reach for her.

And come up with nothing. The bed beside me is empty, not quite cold but getting that way. She's been gone for a while.

I leap out of bed and check the en suite. Nothing. I go out onto the landing and call her name, but I don't need the answering emptiness to tell me that I'm alone in the house.

Shit! What the fuck went wrong?

I rack my brain but come up with nothing. We were fine. Better than fine. There's no reason for her to run out on me without a word.

I give myself a calming lecture as I throw on jeans, a sweater, and a pair of decent trainers. She probably fancied a breath of fresh air. I'll find her outside, admiring the views or some such thing. Molly's a city dweller and they do tend to wax a bit lyrical over the rugged moorland landscape.

Downstairs I find Molly's weekend bag where she left it in the hallway. Her coat's gone though, and so is her phone, which she plugged into my charger last night. I check my patio and cobbled forecourt, but she isn't there. I scan the further horizons and my heart sinks. A dark grey mist is rolling in from the northwest. Although the southern views remain bathed in bright early morning sunshine, that happy state of affairs won't last long. The weather can change in minutes out here, and it looks as though it's about to.

I try calling her but without much optimism. Vodafone does their best, but it'll be a while if ever before we get a half-decent signal out here. Sure enough, the call goes to voicemail.

Seriously worried now, I rummage around in my kitchen drawer and find a small pair of binoculars. I charge back upstairs and up the second flight of steps into my studio, silently offering up thanks for the three hundred and sixty degree views from up there. If she's taken a walk there's a possibility I might be able to spot her, provided she hasn't got too far and isn't already enveloped in mist.

My luck's in, and hers too. I spot her. She's due north of the house, I'd guess about a mile and a half away and heading home. She's obviously spotted the mist approaching and has had the sense to realise she needs to get back here before it reaches her. She's trying to outpace the gathering clouds, but she's not going to make it. Once the fog surrounds her, she'll be hopelessly disoriented, unable to pick out any landmarks or find her way back.

I know this landscape, I probably would be able to reach home in those conditions, but not Molly. I change my shoes quickly in favour of a pair of sturdy hiking boots, grab an extra layer of fleece from my wardrobe, and pack a spare in a rucksack for Molly. A waterproof over the top completes my preparations and I'm out of there in less than two minutes.

I spot Molly a mile or so uphill as I stride out across the rough heather. She sees me, waves, and picks up her pace.

Shit, that's a sure way to twist an ankle. I find an extra gear and plough on fast.

Mercifully she doesn't meet with any disaster before I reach her, though through no fault of her own. The fog is swirling around the pair of us as I hug her and sweep the damp hair back from her face.

"Thank God you're all right."

Her usual smile is somewhat forced as she gazes up at me. "I thought I was going to get lost. Come on, we need to hurry, before—"

"What the fuck were you thinking, coming up here on your own?" Anxiety and relief probably make my tone more brusque than I intended. There again, perhaps not.

"It was such a lovely morning. I was awake early, and I didn't want to disturb you…"

"Lone hiking's one thing, but you should always tell someone where you're going. Christ, if I hadn't spotted you…"

"I know. And, thank you for coming to find me. Can we go home now?"

"Too fucking right we can. Here, put this on." I hand her the warm fleece from my rucksack and wait until she tugs it on over her own flimsy jacket. While I'm at it I assess her totally unsuitable footwear too. Her lace-up canvas shoes are neither waterproof nor tough enough for this terrain.

Molly has a hard lesson coming her way about taking care of her personal safety, and I intend to make sure she learns it well.

I hold out my hand, and with the other I turn on my phone. Vodafone may be a non-starter out here, but the GPS signal is solid enough.

"Come on, let's get you home. You need some breakfast and a hard, bare-bottom spanking—though not necessarily in that order."

Molly is silent most of the way back. Wise girl. I use the relative peace and quiet to get my own anxiety under control. I would never lay a hand on a sub while I'm still upset myself so I need to calm down, and concentrate on what needs to be done to ensure she never pulls a stunt like this again.

We enter the house by the back door and troop into the kitchen. Molly removes the borrowed fleece and her jacket then reaches for my waterproof.

"I'll put these away. Would you like for me to wait upstairs, sir?"

At least she's under no illusions about what's coming, and appears to accept the prospect of discipline. She's made no attempt to talk her way out of it. I suspect I may shatter that mood. Up to now her 'punishments' have had an element of play about them. This one won't.

"No. Strip, and bend over the table."

"Here? Sir?"

I don't dignify that with an answer, and Molly accepts my raised eyebrow as sufficient incentive not to question me further. To her credit, she undresses as quickly as I've ever seen her do it, folds her clothes neatly, and places them on a chair.

She adopts the position I instructed, stretching up onto her toes to lift her gorgeous bottom for me. Perhaps she thinks I'll go easy on her if she impresses me with her perfect obedience. Not happening. She scared me half to death. This morning's little escapade could have ended very differently.

Despite her compliance I can tell she's nervous. Well, she might be. Her face is turned toward me and her lip is quivering. She's on the verge of tears but putting a brave face on it. I school my features into a stern expression and begin to check my emails on my phone. In her current state of scared anticipation it'll do her no harm to wait, and I intend to give her every opportunity to reflect on the foolishness of her actions.

A few minutes pass. I continue to tap away on the screen of my phone while Molly shifts her weight from one foot to the other. Her upturned bottom makes a beautiful sight, and will be lovelier still with a few stripes from my belt to decorate that pale, delicate-looking skin.

She's apprehensive, and confused too at my delay. She clenches those pretty cheeks hard. I watch with what I hope passes for detached interest at the play of the muscles in her taut buttocks. Molly's arse is firm and toned, but I know from experience that the flesh will flatten and then spring back perkily when I spank her. She was built for this.

"Sir, I… I'm ready." From which I read, 'please, can we get this over with?'

"Good." I continue to scroll through Facebook posts in which I have not the slightest interest.

"Sir, how long before…?"

"Problem, Molly? You're not cold, are you?"

"No, sir, but I was wondering if we could just… I mean…"

"You'll wait until I'm ready. In silence."

Her eyes widen, but she has the good sense to keep her mouth shut. I give it two more minutes before I push myself away from the counter I've been leaning on and walk up behind her. I swear, she almost goes into orbit when I lay my palm against her quivering backside.

"Settle down, Molly. I expect you to keep still when I touch you." I punctuate my commands with heavy, massaging caresses to both her buttocks.

"Yes, sir," she murmurs, widening her stance though I haven't asked her to.

I part her butt cheeks and can see clearly the moisture that glistens on the lips of her pussy. One of life's eternal mysteries, it never fails to fascinate me that a submissive can be scared to death of what's happening to her, but still be hopelessly turned on by it.

I slide my palm across her damp slit, and she lets out a groan.

"You're wet, Molly. I do hope you're taking this seriously."

"Yes, sir. I am, I swear." The vehemence in her tone might be amusing in other circumstances, but Molly's not the only one who needs to be aware of the gravity of this situation.

"Okay. So, tell me, why is this happening to you?"

"Because I went out alone this morning. I should have asked you first."

"Close, but not quite." I continue to stroke her wet pussy as I speak. "You don't need my permission to leave the house, Molly."

"No, sir. I meant, tell you. I should have told you I was going out."

"Yes, exactly. Why is that, Molly?"

"Because it's dangerous. It was foggy, and I would have gotten lost if you hadn't come to find me. I'm sorry, sir. I know I put you to a lot of trouble."

"No, you didn't, Molly. I don't consider you to be a nuisance and coming to help you was no trouble at all. I care about you and I'd do anything I needed to do to make sure you're safe. Do you understand that?"

"Yes, sir."

"So?"

"So you're going to spank me, sir. To make sure I don't do that again."

"Spot on, Molly. And because you're being so forthcoming I'm going to give you a choice now. You can stay where you are, or if you prefer you can lie across my lap for your spanking. Which is it to be?"

"Your lap, sir. Please."

Her reply doesn't surprise me, and I confess I prefer the connectedness, the intimacy of laying a sub across my knee. I can get a better swing with her in the position she's already adopted, bent over the table, but I doubt she realises that. Maybe she just wants me to hold her while she's being spanked. I hope so.

I unbuckle my leather belt and slide it through the loops on my jeans, then I drop it onto the table next to her. I pull out a chair and sit down.

"Okay, assume the position. You know the drill."

Molly wastes no time at all in getting up from the table only to drop face down over my lap. She grips my ankle tight, as though afraid she might slither to the floor. She won't. I have no intention of letting her fall. I pull her in close with my left hand, hard up against my straining, erect cock. With my right hand I reach for the belt.

"You can count if you like, but there's no fixed number. I'll stop when I'm sure you've learned what you need to know, and that the lesson has sunk in."

She mumbles something which I take to be a muffled attempt at 'yes, sir.'

"Ready?"

There's another indistinct sound from Molly. Her entire body stiffens as she braces for the first stroke.

I caress her bottom again and wait for her to soften. It takes the best part of a minute, but I'm patient. As soon as I achieve my goal, I lay the first strike across both buttocks.

Molly jerks hard, but makes no sound. I continue to stripe her arse, alternating the strokes, first one side, then the other. After the first half dozen or so she is whimpering, and becoming more vocal with every blow. She squeals, lets out several yelps as I pepper her now flame-red bottom with the leather, then she starts to scream with each new spank.

I shift my focus to the backs of her thighs, and in a particular that sweet sit spot just below the lower curve of her arse. Molly is crying out, sobbing noisily, wriggling, squirming against my lap, but she's going nowhere. When she forgets herself and reaches back in a vain attempt to protect her sore bottom, I just fold her hands into the small of her back and I hold them there.

She stops struggling at last, and as the final vestiges of resistance are spanked out of her she allows her body to go limp, draping herself across my thighs and accepting whatever I choose to do to her.

That's good enough for me, and it's the reason I prefer

not to set a limit for a punishment spanking. If I can bring my sub to this stage of acceptance before I meet the promised target, any remaining spanks are just unnecessary and cruel. Similarly, if I set the target too low, the punishment fails to have the desired effect. But this way requires honesty, and trust.

I stop and allow the belt to drop onto the floor. Molly is quite still, crying, but nothing to alarm me. She's contrite, and very sore I daresay, but she's okay. Or she will be.

I ease her up to stand on her own feet, holding her elbows to steady her as I stand up. I sweep her up into my arms and carry her from the kitchen and into my living room. Once there I arrange the pair of us on the sofa, me propped in the corner and Molly snuggled up against me, on her side to give her bottom the relief she needs. I grab a soft throw from the back of the sofa and wrap it around her, then I hold her, saying nothing, until her sobs subside and there is silence again.

"I'm sorry." Her voice is small, still breathy from her crying.

"I know. It's done. Over."

"Can I…? I mean, will you still want me to come back here again?"

"Of course. I'm counting on it." I drop a kiss on the top of her head to emphasise my point.

"Are you still angry?" She peers up at me, her expression puzzled.

"I was never angry, just scared. For you. I don't want to lose you, Molly, and I intend to keep you safe."

"You kept me safe that other time too. At Armley."

"Well, not entirely. It was my fault you got caught up in all that in the first place. I'm trying to do better now."

"I always feel safe, when I'm with you."

I heave a sigh of relief, and of thanks probably. It seems I'm getting some of this right.

• • • • • • •

Three hours later I stand on the platform at Leeds City Station and watch the red and grey livery of the Virgin East Coast inter-city express snake along the track, eventually curving away out of sight. Molly's gone, at least for a little while. After two days spent for the most part tied to my bed, and following that interlude over my lap, she's heading back to London. My new little subbie has things to do, matters to settle.

So do I, starting with the unwelcome text I received first thing this morning and have yet to deal with. I pull out my phone to reread it.

U have Brad's address?

The message is from my old partner in crime, quite literally. Stevie Horrocks was the moron who brought down the ceiling of that post office when he emptied two barrels into it and got the whole lot of us locked up. He got ten years to my five, because he was the one who fired the shots, but I have to assume justice has been served. He's out now it would seem, and keen to pick up where he left off. I couldn't be less interested.

I consider just deleting the text. It's not as though I'm in touch with Brad anyway, not since he and Rachel went their separate ways. Stevie's a persistent sod though, I do remember that much about him. And he's too stupid to come up with an alternative strategy now that he's somehow managed to track down my number. He'll only keep on texting me. I sigh and tap in my reply.

How would I know?

A couple of minutes later, as I approach my car in the short stay car park, my phone starts to ring. I check the screen, though I know exactly who this will be.

"Stevie." My greeting is curt to say the least.

"J, how's it going?"

I shudder at the old nickname. No one has used that in years. "Fine. Look, I'm busy so if you could—"

"I need Brad. Where's he hanging out these days?"

"I told you, I've no idea."

"Fuck that, you and him were always tight. I know he's out again."

Out? I didn't even know he'd been back inside. "You know more than I do then. Look, I can't help you."

"No? Well I'll just have to call round and see Rachel then. She'll know where her old man is. I'll give her your regards."

Shit! That's the last thing I want, Stevie Horrocks turning up at The Eagle to harass Rachel and the kids. I need to steer the bastard way from there.

"Okay, I'll phone round and see if anyone knows where he is. Give me a day or two and I'll get back to you."

"You've until tomorrow, then I start making house calls. I always did have a soft spot for little Rachel, maybe I'll just nip round there anyway."

"Do that, and you'll fucking regret it. You've no idea how unpleasant I can be if you piss me off. Got that?"

"Hey, no sweat, old buddy. Just get me Brad's address, right." He chuckles down the phone as though we really are old friends. "I don't suppose you'd be interested in a spot of work? A good earner, this one."

"Fuck off. Last time I worked with you it earned me a five stretch."

"Shit happens, mate. This is a cert. Petrol station over the other side of Leeds. Your cut would be a grand, just for driving."

"Not interested." I end the call and throw the phone onto the passenger seat of my car. Christ, no wonder so many ex-cons end up back inside—it just never goes away.

• • • • • • •

It goes against the grain to help Stevie, but rather than allow Rachel to become embroiled in this I make a couple of calls and soon manage to locate my ex-brother-in-law. I may be out of the armed robbery business these days, but I still have my old contacts. Stevie's information is good. Brad's apparently just completed an eighteen-month stretch in Belmarsh prison for receiving stolen goods but he's back in Yorkshire now, living in Bradford and doing casual work as a bouncer at one of the seedier nightclubs. I suppose it's a living. I text the details of the club to Stevie and hope that's the last I hear from him.

No such luck. By the time I arrive back at my converted barn Stevie has phoned me twice more. I'm driving so I don't pick up, but the phone rings again the moment I get inside.

"I told you, I'm not interested."

"And I told you we need a wheel man, fuck head."

"Not me. I'm not in the trade these days."

"No, you ponse about taking pretty pictures according to Brad. I don't give a fuck what business you think you're in. You're on my fucking team so when I tell you I need a driver, you fucking do it."

Is this moron for real? "Stevie, you're starting to bore me. Is there some part of no that you don't understand? You were never the sharpest knife in the drawer, but even you should grasp that."

"Right, two grand then. Cash."

"Fuck you." I hang up, and turn off the phone.

I switch it back on again a few hours later. There have been seven missed calls, all from Stevie. He's a persistent bastard, I'll give him that, but he hasn't phoned me now for almost two hours so perhaps he's got the message.

There's another text as well though, and this one is more welcome. Molly got back to London okay, and has already made an appointment with a solicitor. Her legal status makes no difference to me; it's clear her marriage is dead in the water, but it seems to matter to her. It's a loose end to be tied off, and I can relate to that. I hit Molly's tiny picture in my speed dial.

"Hi there." She sounds breathless, as though she's been running.

"Hi yourself. Good journey?"

"Yes. I just got back from my mum's."

"Oh. Nice visit?"

"Not really. I told her I was divorcing Andy. She doesn't think it's a great idea." Her voice sounds strained. I guess the discussion was a difficult one.

"Ah. The new driveway?"

"Among other things. My mum always thought Andy was a good catch. You know the sort of thing—nice, steady job, doesn't smoke, and reasonably sober."

"She should marry him herself then. Once the divorce is absolute, of course."

Molly giggles. I'm pleased to be able to lift her mood a little. "I'll suggest that to her."

"When are you seeing the lawyer?"

"The day after tomorrow. The same day you fly to Paris."

"Why don't you fly out too, after you've finished your legal stuff? I can arrange a ticket for you to pick up at Heathrow."

She pauses; I can tell she's tempted. Then, "I can't, really. I have to work."

"That's a pity." I can think of worse things than spending a few days playing at being tourists with Molly—getting caught up in Stevie Horrocks' little escapades being right up there at the top of the list. "Another time, perhaps."

"I'd like that." She hesitates.

I know there's something else she wants to say. I wait, silent.

"When can I come back?"

I smile to myself. "Whenever you like, though after tomorrow I'm away until the weekend. I'll phone you when I'm back in the UK."

"Right, okay. I'll wait to hear from you then."

She thinks that was a brush-off. I'm not having that. I need her to trust me. "Molly, I told you, you can call me any time. I meant it."

"I know. It's just—"

"Any time, Molly. Remember that."

"I will." She pauses, as though considering whether or not to believe me. Then, "I should go. I need to catch up with some orders, and get my invoices in order."

Fair enough, she does have a lot to think about. "Okay. We'll talk soon, right?"

"Yes, sir. Soon."

"Good night then." I hang up, wondering what I need to do to convince her I'm sincere and going nowhere. My train of thought is shattered when the phone rings again. I decline the call, but it's followed straight away by a text.

FUCKING ANSWER THE PHONE, DOG SHITE

He doesn't scare me, never did, but I think of Rachel and take his call a couple of minutes later.

"Like I said we need a wheel man, and it's you. Thursday. I'll be in touch."

"Don't bother."

"Thursday."

"Fuck off." I end the call and switch the phone off again. This is fast degenerating into a farce. I amend Stevie's ID in my phone to read *Dickhead. Do Not Answer*. I've done enough for him already by tracking down Brad. I don't need to read his texts or take his calls, and there's no way on God's green earth I'm going on a bloody job with him.

Fucking loser.

• • • • • • •

Heathrow is manic. It's just turned two on Sunday afternoon when I emerge from customs into the bright, bustling chaos of the arrivals hall. Thousands of weary travellers are milling around, many with phones pressed to their ears as they seek to negotiate their onward journey. I switch on my own phone and wait until the network reconnects as it comes out of flight mode, though I don't need to call a taxi or minibus firm. I find Molly on speed dial and hit call.

"Jared? Hi. I… I wondered where you got to. Is everything all right?" She sounds anxious. I don't blame her, I suppose. I *am* two days late.

"Yeah. Ran into some problems with the weather so the shoot took longer than we anticipated. It's done now though."

"Are you back then? In the UK?"

"I am."

"I was thinking, I might come up to Yorkshire next week. If that suits you, obviously. I mean, I know you said any time, but—"

"I said it and I meant it."

"Yes, of course. Would Wednesday be okay? I have some stuff to complete, and… I thought I might bring some work with me and my laptop. Then I wouldn't need to rush back."

Yes! I grin to myself. Molly MacBride makes for very pleasant company.

"Wednesday's fine. Bring whatever you like." I drag my small suitcase on wheels out through the massive plate glass doors of the airport onto the flagged forecourt teeming with passengers scurrying to be away. The chill of an autumnal afternoon in England hits me, the contrast sharp after the dry air-conditioned atmosphere of international arrivals. I shift my phone to my other hand and hail a cruising taxi.

"Jared? Are you still there?"

"Yes. Sorry, just got distracted. What are you doing right now, Molly?"

"I was just going to have a shower actually, then I thought I might nip out and do some supermarket shopping. On second thought though, if I'm not going to be here—"

"Are you up for a visitor?"

"What? Who?"

"Me. Who else? I can be there in under an hour."

"I thought you were two hundred miles away."

"I'm at Heathrow, and the cab driver needs an address to dump me at. So…?"

"But, I wasn't expecting… I mean, I—"

"Say no if you want, and I'll see you on Wednesday." Having me suddenly pitch up on her home turf might not appeal. At least when she comes to my place, Molly can leave whenever she decides she's had enough. I won't press her on this. But I cross my fingers anyway.

"Yes. Yes, I'd like that. Do you have my address?"

"You told me it before you left. Wait for me, we can shower together. Oh, and I have a present for you. Well, a couple of presents, in fact." The nipple clamps and clit clip caused a raised eyebrow when the female security officer spotted them in the plastic tray as I came through Charles De Gaulle airport, but she offered no comment, just smirked and nodded me past. The toys are now tucked away in my jacket pocket, and I can't wait to see them glistening on Molly's curvy little body. I hope she's going to find them as entertaining as I know I will—eventually.

"There's no need to bring me presents. I mean, it's not as though…"

I sigh, knowing what she's thinking. My agenda is, I am beginning to realise, somewhat more complex than Molly's, but I'll start from where we are. "I know, just sex, right. But wait until you see what I brought you before you say any more. An hour then?"

She hesitates, then, "An hour. Yes, sir. Bye then."

"Bye, Molly." I end the call and lean back in the rear seat of the cab. The driver regards me in the mirror.

"Where to, mate?"

"Wandsworth," I reply. "Can you get me there in less

than an hour?"

"No problem, guv'nor." He signals and pulls into the lane headed for the M4 and inner London. I settle in for the ride.

• • • • • • •

Exactly fifty-seven minutes later I press the doorbell for entry into Molly's building. Hers is the basement flat in a converted terrace house, complete with three square yards of garden and a window box sporting the bedraggled remains of summer bedding plants now succumbing to the seasonal chill. The neighbourhood is not exactly salubrious, but I've seen worse in inner East Leeds.

Molly's disembodied voice from the intercom invites me to push the outer door and come straight in. Her door is immediately inside, on the left. I do as I'm told, to find Molly awaiting me in her tiny entrance hall.

She looks utterly delicious. Her hair is shorter, cropped back into the sleek, sassy style I recall. It's much more her. She's barefoot, wearing faded black jeans and a loose-fitting tunic-style top in a rich shade of blue that complements her eyes to a tee. Unless I miss my guess she isn't wearing a bra. I lean on the door jamb and watch as her nipples pucker and harden under my scrutiny. Oh, yes, clamps will be perfect— an inspired choice. The clit clip was an impulse buy at the adult store just off the Champs Élysées but if I can convince Molly to experiment with it the toy will send our level of intimacy soaring. Maybe I will need to be just a little more forceful...

"Sir, I... It's good to see you." She steps back to allow me to pass her. "Come in. Please."

She ushers me into the compact space that doubles as sitting room and bedroom, her three-quarter-sized bed nestling in a small alcove at the far end of the studio flat. A cluttered worktable is the only other furniture, unless you count the bookcase, the tiny portable television balancing on an upturned milk crate, and the single chair. I suppose the bed must serve as seating as well as a place to sleep. Two doors lead off the main room, one to a kitchenette where I can just make out the corner of a sink, and the other I assume must lead to the shower and toilet. The place is minuscule and rekindles unwelcome memories of my cell at Armley. All we're missing is two farting, snoring cellmates and a solid steel door.

I force this notion to one side, Molly is a far cry from my previous roomies. Apart from the table the place is neat enough. From what I know of London property prices, this studio flat with just about enough space to swing one very modest-sized cat is no doubt costing her an arm and a leg.

"It's not much, but I haven't been here long. I do have a garden though." She offers me an apologetic little shrug. "I'm looking for somewhere a bit further out."

How about two hundred miles out? I keep that notion to myself for now. Molly has family in London although I get the impression that despite the geography they may not be that close. She chooses to live here for her own reasons, I suppose, and this thing between us is just sex. Or so she thinks.

I dump my overnight case beside her table and turn to face her. A two-handed finger-wiggling summons is all it takes to bring her into my arms. I hug her and bury my nose in the soft, freshly clipped ebony-coloured locks and inhale the fruity fragrance of her hair. Apples, perhaps and a hint of vanilla. Very apt. I run my fingers through it.

"Nice. Much better."

"I got it cut yesterday. I... I had a Brazilian wax too."

Jesus, Mary, and the fucking donkey! My cock springs to attention.

"For me?" I manage to keep my tone level. More or less.

She nods within the circle of my arms. "I read somewhere that in the BDSM lifestyle it was sort of expected. So I thought, maybe—"

I tilt her face up so she has no option but to meet my

gaze. There's to be no hiding. "I would have asked you to do it soon enough. I prefer my subs truly naked."

"Is that what I am then? Your sub?" Her features are flushed, her expression uncertain.

"That's a choice only you can make. If it's truly what you want though, I'd be honoured if you'd put yourself in my hands."

"That *is* what I want. I was hoping, wondering…" She breaks off, chewing on that full lower lip again, one of her infallible tells. I bend my neck to lower my lips to hers and brush a soft kiss over her mouth.

"What were you hoping and wondering, Molly? If it's in your head, tell me. If you have questions, ask me. This is as much about honesty between us as it is pleasure and pain. Did your kinky reading not tell you that too?"

She nods. "I read a lot about trust too. I do trust you, sir."

"I'm starting to trust you as well. And myself. It'll build, over time."

Her brow furrows. "Why do you need to trust me? You're the one with the whips and paddles?"

I smile. "Ah, Molly, you have a lot more to learn. I need to trust you to tell me what's happening, for you. How you're feeling, what you like me to do to you. And I need to trust myself to listen, to watch, to take notice and to take care of you."

"I see." Her expression suggests otherwise.

"Do you? I wonder. But you will, I promise you that." I wink at her. Enough of the intense navel gazing, it's time for some kinky fun. "So, did you wait for me, for that shower?"

"Of course. Do you want me to wash your back?"

"Maybe. After you've sucked my cock, on your knees, naked, as water streams over the pair of us."

Her eyes widen, the tip of her tongue pokes between her lips. She bows her head, her posture that of the perfect, obedient little submissive.

"I'd love that, sir."

She's not alone. "Get naked, Molly. Now. Oh, and for future reference, next time I arrive here I expect to find you kneeling at the foot of your bed, nude and ready for whatever I decide to do by way of a greeting. Is that clear?"

"Yes, sir, perfectly clear." She steps back one pace and tugs the tunic over her head.

Her beautiful breasts are bared for me, pert and firm, her dark pink nipples pearling and swelling. That reminds me…"Ah, yes, your present." I open my jacket to retrieve the clamps and drop them onto the corner of her work table.

They're the tweezer sort, decorated with small, azure beads that dangle from each one, a delicate chain linking the two clamps. I could attach a weight to the chain, but I think not this time. I drop the clit clip next to the nipple clamps and wait for her to ask the question writ large across her pretty features.

To her credit, she unfastens her jeans first and shoves them down, her underwear too, and steps out of the clothes to stand before me naked.

"Nipple clamps, sir?" *Did she just wince?*

"Yes. They'll look very pretty."

"Will they hurt?"

"Yes."

"And the other thing? Where does that go?"

"It's a clit clip."

"Oh." Her face pales. I decide to put her out of her misery.

"That doesn't hurt, but you'll have to trust me on that."

"Do I need to put it on? I'm not sure I know how."

"No. I'll handle all of that. You just need to lie still with your legs spread wide for me. Can you manage that, do you think?"

More lip chewing, then, "I believe I can, sir." She manages a nervous little smile. "Shall I help you to get undressed?"

"No. You go on and get in the shower. I'll be there in a moment."

Delightfully obedient, she steps past me and through the door. A few seconds pass, then I hear the sound of running water. I'm naked in less than ten seconds and I follow her into the bathroom.

Correction, there's no room in here for a bath. A toilet, a tiny wall-mounted washbasin, and the shower cubicle fill the space. The frosted glass doors are already steaming up, but Molly's silhouette is still clearly visible. I pause to admire her for a moment, then I slide the door open and step in with her.

Molly moves back out of the spray to make room for me, then she drops to her knees.

Christ, what a find. I arrange myself against the tiles opposite her, my shoulders resting on the cool white surface. The water streams over my chest, stomach, thighs, the flow powerful and comfortably warm. Thank God for decent water pressure. I glance up and note that the showerhead is the sort that you can adjust to create a narrow, concentrated spray. I have plans for that later.

I turn my attention to the lovely Molly, kneeling at my feet. She looks up at me, her wet hair in dark spikes around her face, the residual spray from my body trickling down her breasts and belly in gentle rivulets. My cock has been rock-solid since the moment I heard her low tone through the door entry system but now I take my erection in my fist and pump hard.

"Open your mouth, girl," I command.

Molly inches forward and parts her lips. I place the head of my cock against her lower lip and allow her to widen and accept it. She shuffles closer, taking the whole of the head and a couple of inches of my shaft into her hot, wet cavern.

"Ah, Molly, that feels good." I comb my fingers through her dripping locks, tightening my grip at the back of her head. I don't force her head forward, but I hold her fast, leaving her in no doubt who's in control here.

Molly laps at my cock, pressing her tongue against the sensitive area at the base of the head, then running the tip around the rim. She bobs back and forth, hollowing her cheeks to create suction.

Jesus, yes!

"Use your hands too. Cup my balls."

She does as she's told, squeezing and lifting, caressing my scrotum with her left hand as she wraps her right fist around the base of my shaft, the part she can't quite manage with her mouth. She runs her hand up and down, the hot, wet friction sending my senses reeling.

"Harder," I rasp. "Faster."

She complies, increasing the pace of her rhythm. Her teeth scrape across the head of my dick, creating an additional edge of excitement. My balls draw up and contract. This won't take long, though I suppose I could spin it out if I wanted. I decide not to. It's been the best part of a week since she left my house in Yorkshire. I could have jerked myself off, I usually would, but I haven't felt so inclined. I want Molly and she's worth the wait but now I have an increasingly urgent need to shoot my load.

"Swallow it. All of it. Understood?" My voice is low, little more than a growl. I glance down. Molly's eyes are wide, meeting mine, her gorgeous lips stretched around my cock as she nods her acceptance. Her hands find an additional gear as she speeds up her ministrations. She sucks harder, swirling her tongue over my cock and massaging my nuts to generate the last frisson of stimulation that tips me over the edge. My balls clench and twist, sending the surge of jizz up and out. I visualise my cum hitting the back of her throat in warm, viscous ribbons. A few drops spill from the corner of her mouth but she uses her fingertip to swipe them back between her lips.

My semen continues to flow, filling her mouth again as her throat works fast to clear her airway. I twist my fingers in her hair to the point I know I have to be hurting her, but she makes no protest, just continues to suck, to lick, to swallow until at last I'm spent.

I release my grip and relax back against the tiles as Molly eases my cock from her mouth. She holds it in both hands, using her tongue to clean the head thoroughly before finally looking up at me.

"Was that okay, sir? I haven't had much practice."

My eyes are closed, my head tilted back as the world rights itself again. "It was fucking wonderful. And believe me, practice won't be an issue."

She remains on her knees until I extend my hand to help her up. She reaches for the soap but I shake my head. "Turn around, Molly. Lean on the tiles and shove your bottom out. Spread your legs as wide as you can."

As soon as she's in position I dislodge the showerhead from its cradle and adjust the spray. The powerful, concentrated flow causes the shower to press back into the palm of my hand. Fucking perfect.

I reach between her legs and stroke her pussy. Molly sighs and arches her back. I use my fingers to part the lips surrounding her clit and drop to my knees behind her.

"Sir? What are you—Oh!"

The jet of water hits her clit. She jerks, would probably leap out of range but for my growled command to not move a fucking muscle.

I angle the spray, first one side, then the other, then I aim straight at the tip. It's intense, I know that, but I don't let up.

"Sir, I can't. Please…"

"You have my permission to come, Molly."

"Thank you, sir," she mutters, the relief evident in her low moan, right before the first convulsion seizes her quivering frame.

I continue to play the water across her sensitive core, drawing out every last shiver and tremble before I finally let up. I have my reasons. Her first experience of a clit clip is likely to prove problematic if I attempt to fit it while she's on the verge of orgasm. This will take the edge off enough for me to be able to manage her.

Satisfied she has no more to offer me right now, I stand and replace the showerhead. Taking the soap from the dish on the wall of the cubicle I start to massage it into her shoulders, her back, her bottom, then down the backs of her thighs. I even pick up each of her feet and soap up the soles before ordering her to turn around. I work the lather into her breasts, across her stomach, her smooth mound, her still swollen pussy and clit, then I crouch before her to wash her legs.

When there is not an inch of her body not lathered and cleaned I stand and grab her shampoo. It only takes only a few moments to work a thick lather through her cropped hair but I take my time massaging her scalp, loving the way she relaxes under my fingers. I reach for the shower again, adjust the flow to a more moderate setting, and proceed to rinse her hair. It squeaks as I run my fingers through it. A small squirt of conditioner comes next, and more massaging followed by rinsing. At last I take the showerhead again and start to swill the soap away. Molly is compliant and obedient throughout, turning on command, lifting her arms, her feet, spreading her legs. The soapy lather disappears down the plughole and the water runs clear.

"That was nice. Thank you. Shall I do you now, sir?" Her eyes are languorous, the pupils already dilating. Perfect for what's to come next.

"No, I can manage. Grab a towel and wait for me on your bed."

She blinks up at me as though not entirely comprehending. I turn off the shower and slide open the cubicle door to reach for one of two fluffy yellow towels dangling from a hook on the back of the door. I wrap it around her and tuck the ends in between her breasts, then I kiss the end of her nose.

"Wait for me. I won't be long."

She nods and pads away. I might have insisted on a 'Yes, sir,' but decide to let that go on this occasion. The door closes behind her and I turn the lever to start the shower again, then step back under the spray. I turn the temperature down and direct the water right onto my stiffening cock. Every little bit helps.

Molly is curled up on her bed when I exit the shower room, the pillows propped behind her. The towel remains tightly wrapped around her damp body, its twin now draped around my hips. The nipple clamps and clit clip remain on the table just where I left them. I pick them up as I pass and drop them onto the duvet by her feet.

"You ready?"

She smiles but can't quite conceal her nervousness, her features betraying a delectable blend of apprehension and curiosity. And lust. "I think so, sir. Should I take this off now?" She loosens the towel.

I nod and hold out my hand to take it from her.

Naked again, and delightfully unselfconscious, Molly kneels up on the bed. I pick up the clamps.

"Put your hands behind your back, cup each elbow with the opposite hand if you can, please."

She obeys at once, the posture thrusting her shoulders back and her breasts forward. Her rose-tinted nipples are already pebbling but I need them even harder, stiffer, longer. I perch beside her, one hip on the mattress, and place my hand under the lower curve of her left breast. I lift it, testing the weight, caressing the firm mound for several seconds before I slide my hand up to take the nipple between my finger and thumb. I roll it, gentle at first, then more firmly. I watch her carefully, searching her expressive eyes for the first glimmer of discomfort. I have it, and I pause, not releasing the pressure but not ramping it up either.

She lowers her gaze, so I give her tight peak a hard squeeze. "Look at me. Don't look away. I need to see exactly how much this is hurting you."

"It is, sir. Aagh!"

"I know. It's the point just before it becomes unbearable

that I want to hit though. I want that moment, right before you say your safeword."

Her eyes are glittering as tears gather, then start to spill. I twist the engorged nub, eliciting another startled squeal.

"Are we there yet, Molly?"

She shakes her head, her lips flattened into a tortured grimace. It would have been easy for her to nod, to tell me it was enough. She could whimper her safeword 'cooler' or even 'jailbird,' but she doesn't. Despite her lack of experience my little Molly is a refreshingly transparent sub, even when honesty is not in her best interest. I store that away for future reference and apply just a fraction more pressure.

She opens her mouth, but I know it even before she gasps her safeword. I slacken my grip just a little, and slide the first tweezer over the pebbled peak. The sliding bead adjusts and I use it to apply just the same amount of pressure as my fingers, then I tilt my head to appreciate the result. The pretty little blue beads are suspended from her nipple, twinkling as they catch the light. Molly continues to gaze at me, never once wavering.

"Nice. Now, the other one." I twirl my finger in the air to I indicate I need her to turn around so I can reach. She does so, though her fear is evident in her expression, and the sharp hiss of alarm as I start to roll the vulnerable nub between my finger and thumb.

"You know how this works now. Use your safeword when it gets too much." I tug and twist and squeeze, all the while holding her gaze as the pain builds, blooms, and eventually reaches the point where it's about to mushroom out of control.

"Cooler," she gasps.

I stop and slide the other clamp into place. "You can move your hands now."

She does, though still kneeling on the bed. She looks thoroughly miserable. I cup her jaw in my palm. "Breathe in through your nose, hold the breath for a few seconds, then out slowly. The pain will lessen as you get used to it."

She does as I suggest, and after a few seconds her expression clears. I would not go so far as to describe her as comfortable exactly, but she's certainly coping. I lean in to kiss her.

"You're doing so well, sweetheart. Are you okay to continue?"

She frowns, but nods.

"Say it, love."

"I want to continue, sir."

"Good. Lie down then, on your stomach."

"But, that'll hurt. Sir."

"Pain adds to the pleasure though, wouldn't you agree? You need to be fucked, hard and deep, and fast, and I want to take you from behind this time, just to remind you who calls the shots here." I pause, hold her gaze, then, deliberately hardening my voice I clinch it. "Do as you're told, or accept the spanking. It'll be no fun going over my knee with your nipples clamped. Last chance."

Molly gets the point and wriggles onto her stomach without further ado, squirming as her clamped nipples press against the mattress. I'm pleased to see that the bed's headboard is made of metal, with handy-looking vertical bars. I didn't bring any cuffs with me, but resolve to be better equipped next time.

"Take hold of the bed head and hang on." I grab a couple of pillows and shove them under her hips to elevate her bum a little, though not enough to relieve the pressure on her clamped nipples. Then I drop the towel still covering my lower body and extract a couple of condoms from my jacket pocket.

Despite my sternness earlier, when I enter her I do so gently. My intention is to test Molly's pain threshold, nothing more. She's done as I asked, allowed me to clamp her and I know full well that this is a big deal to her. I want her to enjoy what comes next.

Molly is wet—delightfully, enticingly dripping, her cunt

tight and hot and so very ready. I stroke in and out, careful to hit her inner sweet spot with each pass. She gasps and moans, writhing under me. I can only assume the clamps are forgotten for now, or at least no longer the foremost thing on her mind. I slide my hand around to make contact with her clit, still swollen and moist from her arousal earlier, in the shower. She groans and arches her back to lift her bottom up even further.

"Feeling good, Molly?"

"Yes, sir," she breathes. "Very good."

"Not too sore?"

"Sore?"

I slip my spare hand under our bodies to brush against her distended nubs. Molly lets out a yelp.

"Sore," I affirm. "I'll remove these soon. Now, I want you to come for me."

I draw my cock back and deliver a sharp, deep thrust, followed by several shallower strokes. Molly goes wild, her inner walls quivering around my cock as she starts to climax. She gyrates her hips and clenches her lower muscles hard. I deliver a quick slap to her buttock, and that's enough to drive her over the edge. She screams her release, her body racked by a series of hard shudders as she convulses under me. I pick up a hard, rapid pace again, and in just a few seconds my nuts clench in readiness to eject more semen. I spear deep into her, the head of my cock bumping her cervix as I hold still, my erection twitching madly as the semen surges from my swollen balls to fill the condom.

I drop forward, my weight momentarily resting on her, then I roll to the side. I pull her in and wrap my arms around her soft, warm body.

"We need to get those clamps off. Get your breath back, Molly girl. You'll need it."

CHAPTER NINE

I roll onto my back and meet Jared's gaze. He is leaning over me, propped up on one elbow, handsome as sin and looking decidedly pleased with himself. He takes hold of the dainty little length of chain between my throbbing nipples and tugs on it.

"Sir. Sir!" I gasp as the gentle ache peaks sharply.

Jared's grin is wicked and unrepentant. "I think that's enough for your first time. Put your hands behind your head and hold still, girl."

I link my fingers at the base of my skull and close my eyes, waiting for the relief which will come as the clamps are released. Jared's fingers brush my swollen peak as he loosens the right hand clamp.

"Aagh! Christ, sir..." I scream as a wave of agony brings me up off the mattress. Jared presses me back down as he latches onto my nipple with his mouth. He sucks hard and presses the tortured peak with his tongue, squeezing it against the roof of his mouth. The unexpected pain dissipates in seconds, and my cries dwindle to whimpers.

Jared releases my nipple. "Okay now?"

I nod, glaring at him. "You should have told me it would hurt. Can you be more gentle next time?" I'm oddly disappointed that he took me by surprise in this way.

He frowns at me, then nods. "You're right. My apologies. But I *am* being gentle, and I'll help with the next one too. Ready?"

"I suppose, but don't expect me to keep still."

His eyes harden, just a fraction, but enough. "I expect you to do exactly as you're told, Molly, or accept the consequences." He waits, holding my gaze.

Long moments pass, then my brief flirtation with mutiny evaporates. "Yes, sir," I concede. "I'm ready now."

Forewarned is forearmed. I manage to remain still, my hands clasped behind my head, as Jared slips the second clamp off then sucks my nipple hard. The explosion of pain is horrible but over in seconds. As Jared releases my nipple I remember my manners and murmur my thanks.

"You're welcome, Molly. So, did you like my present so far?"

I shake my head. "Not much, sir. Do we have to use them in future?"

"You can say no at any time, I told you that. But I like them and I enjoy seeing your pretty nipples clamped and throbbing for me."

I consider his comment for a few seconds, then, "In that case I'm happy to do it, for you, sir."

A smile illuminates his handsome face. "Thank you, Molly. I appreciate that. So, shall we try your other present?"

My heart sinks. He said the clit clip wouldn't hurt, but my sensitivities are scraped raw right now and I already have a lot to process. "Must we?"

It takes just one raised eyebrow to answer that. Of course we must, he has said so. This is not negotiable, not really. Either I use my safeword, or I obey. Simple.

"What would you like me to do, sir?"

He rolls from the bed and saunters over to the table for the remaining item. He returns and hands it to me to look at. The toy is tiny, very light as it lies in the palm of my hand. It looks innocuous enough, resembling a pair of tweezers with silicone caps on the ends. The sliding ring is proof that it can be made very tight, but however improbable I have no option but to trust Jared when he says they won't hurt.

"You look doubtful, Molly. Tell me." His command is delivered in a low tone, but he means it. He takes the clit clip from me and places it on the pillow.

I look up at him. "Will you do the same as you did with the nipple clamps? Squeeze and twist and—"

He shakes his head. "No, Molly. You will."

"Me?" I squeak.

"You. Come on, I'll show you. Wriggle to the edge of the bed and spread your legs wide."

Despite my doubts I do as he asks. Jared stands beside the bed to watch as I open for him. He grabs the pillows I laid on earlier and shoves them back under my hips, tilting my pelvis up for a better view.

"That's good. So tell me, Molly, how do you like me to touch your clit?"

"I like it very much, sir."

He chuckles. "How reassuring, but don't be evasive. You're close to a spanking now, which might spoil the mood a little. What I meant was, what sort of touch arouses you the most? Do you like it when I circle your clit like this…?"

He demonstrates, tracing a pattern around the base of my clit with his fingertip. I thrust my pelvis forward and let out a soft moan.

"Obviously that works. And this…?"

Next he flicks the pad of his middle finger from side to side, stroking the very tip of my clit with each pass. It feels sublime.

He pauses. "Which did you like best?"

"The second one, sir. But the first was fabulous too."

"Okay. Noted. What about this?" He takes the swelling bud between his finger and thumb and strokes up to the tip, his touch gentle as I writhe and squirm.

"I'm going to come."

"No, you are not, greedy girl. You've had two orgasms already, you can wait now. So, is this better than the first two? Or not?"

"I… I like the second thing you did. That's best, sir."

"Okay. So now, I'll part the lips of your pussy so your clit is exposed, and I want you to stroke it in the way you like best. Show me exactly what a dirty little slut you can be."

"Sir…?"

He smiles at me and winks. "*My* dirty little slut, remember?" Kneeling beside the bed now, he uses his fingers to peel back my inner lips, then leans forward to blow on my exposed clit. "Come on, Molly. Do as I ask, please."

I'm embarrassed, but already hopelessly aroused. My inhibitions are fighting a losing battle and any modesty I might have still had is in shreds. I reach between my spread thighs and stroke my slick pussy to coat my fingers in the moisture. Then I go to work on my clit, exactly the way I love it the best.

"Ah, so hot, Molly mine. You have the most beautiful cunt. So pink and tight. Do you want me to fuck you again?"

"Yes, sir," I breathe, flicking the taut bundle of nerves even faster, then taking it between my fingers and pressing. "I want you to fuck me. Hard."

"So I shall. Later." He trails the fingers of one hand down, over the entrance to my pussy, then on to my tight arsehole. "I want to fuck you here." He presses a finger inside. I jerk, surprised at the intrusion and a little intrigued. I've read of anal sex, but never tried it. Never saw the point until this moment.

As he eases his finger deeper into me, every sensation I am evoking in my clit is heightened, every stroke more intense, each scrape of my fingernail across the distended nub sending shivers of acute need to tease every nerve ending.

"Oh, God. Sir, that feels so good…"

"Mmm, let's see what we can do to make it even better then. I think you're ready to try our new toy. Use your fingers to hold the lips apart, just like I did."

I'm past caring if it might be painful. Carried on an unstoppable wave of greedy lust, I place my fingers on either side of my clit and spread the delicate lips. Still with one finger embedded inside me Jared reaches past me to retrieve the clip from the pillow. He adjusts the ring to open the arms wide, then slips it over my clit, one tweezer arm on either side. He slides the ring back along until the tension starts to bite. I gasp, and he stops.

"Enough?"

I should nod, but I don't. Instead I shake my head, craving more. More of what I'm not exactly certain, but Jared seems to comprehend and he tightens the clip a little further. Then more still, until I whimper, "Enough, sir."

He stops there, and resumes his intimate probing inside my arsehole. My entrance has slackened shamelessly to allow him in, and now he slides his finger back and forth as the clip exerts a gentle, constant pressure on my clit. It's a feeling like nothing I have ever experienced, and all for me. Everything that's happening now is for my pleasure, my fulfilment.

It won't last long. It can't. The feeling is so intense, so focused, so demanding. My orgasm surges from within my core, my inner muscles clenching, spasming.

Jared ceases his gentle stroking, though his finger remains inside me.

"Be still for a moment, Molly. Settle down again. I don't want you to come just yet."

"No, sir." I'm not convinced I have any say in the matter, but I want to please him. It's the least I can do when he's doing so much to pleasure me.

"Two fingers in your arse, then three. Then my cock."

Oh. Oh! I shiver, beyond coherent thought. He's going to put his huge cock inside my arse, and I can't even bring myself to protest. My voice comes from somewhere far away. "Yes, sir."

He starts to thrust again, but it's tighter now, my entrance stretched and burning. Two fingers. Without thinking I bring my knees up toward my chest, offering him better access to my helpless, vulnerable arse.

He squeezes a third finger into me, and I cry out. He pauses, waits until I'm quiet again, then he resumes his relentless thrusting.

"Stroke your clit again, baby. But keep it light, soft. You're very close and I want you to come with my cock inside you, not before."

I manage a feeble nod as I reach for my clit again. I brush my fingers across the clamped, swollen bud, the blood trapped there by the clip, but even that feather-like caress sends waves of sensation pulsing through me. I'm on the point of being swept away by the most powerful climax yet. It curls deep inside, unfurling, readying itself for the moment when—

"Hold it. Wait, and settle." The low command is compelling. I obey, offering up prayers that my traitorous body might behave, and not betray me by succumbing to a reckless, out of control orgasm. Jared doesn't want that, and I couldn't bear to disappoint him.

I sob with relief when the climax recedes, if only slightly. I have a few more seconds, a few more sweet, desperate moments to savour this delight. Jared drives his fingers deep again, twisting and curling them inside my tight rear channel. I rest my middle finger on the tip of my clit, applying just the most gossamer-like touch, but it feels like so much more. The clip grips me, holding my clit erect and plump, sensitised to the merest whisper of pressure.

Jared pulls his fingers out. I lie still, not daring to move, barely daring to breathe for fear of unleashing the volcano within. Jared positions his cock at my entrance and pushes. My arse resists, denying him entry. He is more insistent, his thumbs easing my entrance open as he forces his cock past the tight ring of muscle. Suddenly, he is in. My body capitulates. It hurts, burns…

"Rub your clit, Molly. As hard as you like."

"Sir?"

"Don't fight it, love. Let me in."

He pushes again, the pressure firm, unrelenting, and his cock surges forward until he's buried balls-deep inside me. At the same time I increase the friction on my engorged clitoris. One hard rub, then another. That's all it takes, and I'm spiralling into the most intense climax I have ever imagined. No, this is beyond imagining, beyond anything I have dreamed or read about, or ever come close to experiencing. My whole body convulses as Jared leans forward to trap my knees between his chest and mine. He withdraws, then slides his cock back into me, impaling me as my orgasm seizes the pair of us. I quiver and clench around him, his solid, wide presence within me amplifying every sensation.

As my orgasm recedes I lie still, limp and spent, but aware of every deep, demanding thrust of his thick erection filling my body in the most intimate way possible. He fucks me, his strokes long and slow, the inner friction a curious blend of pleasure and pain, hurting in the most delicious manner, terrible in its erotic beauty. I'm greedy, needy, wanting more. And more still.

He's right, I *am* a slut. A sloppy little fuck-slut, and I care not a jot as long as he doesn't stop.

Jared drives his cock into me, the stroke hard, almost savage. He grunts and holds still as his erection lurches and jerks within me, the movement wild now and beyond even his iron control. I let out a squeal as the heat of his semen fills the condom, and his arms give way. He drapes his boneless body over mine like a blanket. I wrap my arms around his waist, and I hang on.

• • • • • • •

"How long can you stay? Overnight?"

"I've a meeting tomorrow, in Leeds, but not until early afternoon. I could leave first thing. Are you offering to share your bed, Molly?"

I snuggle against him, my duvet drawn up around the pair of us, and I gesture around at the extent of my domain. "I don't even have a sofa for you to sleep on, so yes, I guess that is the offer."

"Suits me. So, limited choice in sleeping arrangements but you can make it up to me. Do you feed your guests, Molly? I'm starving."

"Oh. Oh, shit, I never got to the supermarket." I make to scramble from the bed, though I know without ever getting as far as my tiny kitchen that the pickings there will be sparse. "I might be able to cobble together an omelette."

Jared tightens his grip and hauls me back into bed. "No problem. I spotted a Pizza Hut takeaway on the corner as I got out of the taxi. I'll go and grab us a stuffed crust. Soon."

"But that costs a fortune. I'll need my spare cash for the train fare next week."

Jared gives a snort and rolls me beneath him again trapping me between his elbows, which are planted on either side of my shoulders. He cradles my face in his hands and rubs the tip of my nose with his own. "Dinner's on me. And the train fare. Since you're clearly bothered about getting value for money, perhaps we should work up a bit more of an appetite. Any ideas?"

I spread my thighs. His swelling cock nudges my entrance and I wrap my legs around his waist.

"So enthusiastic. I like that. We have a problem though."
"Oh?"

"Condoms. I don't suppose you…?"

I shake my head, disappointed. "I'm on the Pill," I offer hopefully.

"Good to know, but old habits die hard. Where's the nearest pharmacy?"

"Not that close. There's a Tesco Express though, just round the corner. I think they sell that sort of stuff. Shall

146

I—?"

"I'll go. You keep the bed warm." He kisses me then gets out of bed. He drags on his jeans, then sits on my one and only chair to pull on his socks and trainers. "What toppings do you like?"

"Hawaiian? Or spicy chicken. You choose."

"One Hawaiian coming up."

"With coleslaw? And spicy wedges. Oh, and I like those chicken dipper things…"

"I see, no expense spared now that I'm paying. And here I was thinking you're a cheap date." He's grinning, and I know he's not exactly short of cash. Even so, I feel uncomfortable and wish I'd kept my mouth shut about the coleslaw. He shrugs into his jacket. "All the trimmings then. See you in about half an hour."

The flat is deafeningly silent as his footsteps fade. I pull the duvet up around my throat and stare at the door which just closed behind him. How has Jared North come to fill my world so completely? I've yet to come up with an answer to that when the quiet is pierced by a shrill ringing. My own ring tone is twittering birds. Jared must have forgotten to take his phone with him.

I get out of bed and follow the sound of the phone. I find it, under the bed, and can only assume it fell from one of his pockets when he dumped his clothes. The screen is lit up, the words on the display clear.

Dickhead. Do not answer.

I stare at the device, bemused. But I take the hint and let it ring out. As soon as voicemail kicks in the caller hangs up.

Ten minutes pass, and it rings again. The screen tells the same story, so once more I leave the phone to go to voicemail. By the time Jared returns, a large flat box and several smaller ones balanced in his arms, there have been five missed calls from the dickhead.

I throw on a loose wrap and grab plates from one of my

147

cupboards as Jared deposits our supper in my kitchenette. We are curled up on my bed for a picnic when the phone rings again.

"That'll be the dickhead. He's keen to talk to you."

"What?" Jared pauses, a forkful of coleslaw halfway to his mouth.

I gesture to the phone, which I left on the corner of my table. "You left your mobile here. He's been ringing every five minutes."

Jared reaches for the device and rejects the call. He resumes his meal.

"Who is he?"

"Just someone I know. I don't want to talk to him."

"I guessed. He's persistent though. Perhaps it's important."

"It's total fucking crap. Forget it." His expression is closed, cold. I'm suddenly reminded of the man I met when I first started working at Armley jail, the surly, embittered prisoner on G wing. This is a new side to Jared. Or should that be old side, re-emerging?

"Jared? Is something wrong?"

He shakes his head and his smile is forced. "Yes, but it doesn't concern you. Us. I'll phone him back later and tell him to piss off."

"Who is he? What does he want?"

His body stiffens, withdraws from me. "Just drop it, Molly. Please."

"But maybe I can help."

"Christ, are you not listening to me? You can help by minding your own fucking business."

I sit bolt upright, my appetite vanishing. "What are you talking about? There's no need to speak to me like that."

He shakes his head. "No, I know. I'm sorry. It's just—complicated."

"I want to help. Perhaps I could—"

"Look, this isn't working. It's better if I go."

"Go?" I gape at him, stupidly. "Go where?"

"A hotel. The station. Anywhere I won't get interrogated like a bloody convict. We're not back in fucking Armley now. I don't have to tell you anything." He slams the pizza lid closed and stands up. "You finish that, I'll get something later."

"Jared, I didn't mean—" I bite back my apology. Jared's features have hardened, his expression now a vicious glower. I shrink back, afraid of him for the first time I can recall. Even when I was his jailer and he had every reason to resent me, he never made me feel this way.

I swallow, then tilt up my chin. I may be a submissive, but he's way out of line and I have my pride. Lots of it. "Yes, you're right. It *is* best if you leave."

He's already halfway to the door, pausing only long enough to collect his small case from the corner of my room. He glances back at me, his hand on the doorknob. "It was nice meeting up with you again, Molly."

I don't reply. I can't. I have no words. I'm reeling, baffled by the sudden storm that erupted from nowhere and engulfed us. Jared offers me a brief nod, then he is through the door. He closes it behind him, and he is gone.

CHAPTER TEN

By the time the cab drops me at the entrance to Kings Cross station my temper has cooled and I'm calling myself all sorts of an ignorant, abusive arsehole. I scared Molly, I could tell that much, and I loathe that about myself. I'm no stranger to violence, though not in recent years, but even when I lived as a career criminal I never threatened a woman. Until tonight.

Fucking Stevie Horrocks! Even from two hundred miles away he taints anything he touches.

I briefly consider telling the cabbie to turn round and take me back to Wandsworth. It'll take some grovelling—a fuck of a lot of grovelling in fact—but maybe I can convince Molly to give me another chance. I dismiss that. She won't listen to me, at least not tonight, and I can't blame her. If I turn up in person, that might just intimidate her more and make everything worse. I'll make it up to her when she comes to Yorkshire later in the week.

I get out of the cab and pay the driver, then I stride into the station. My luck's in. It's almost nine o'clock in the evening but there's one last train due to depart for York in just under three minutes' time. I pick up my case and sprint for platform three.

The first class carriage is almost empty as I recline back in my plush seat, a large latte on the table in front of me. I extract my phone from my jacket intending to phone Molly. During my headlong dash to catch this bloody train the realisation hit me that unless I can convince her I'm suitably contrite there's no way Molly's going to come to my home on Wednesday. Why would she? I pretty much told her we were over.

It was nice meeting up with you again. Shit! What a stupid thing to say. Fucking crass. And her face—she looked so hurt. I couldn't have wounded her more if I'd slapped her across the cheek. I was only just starting to get to know her, understand her kink, her needs and desires, and I went and fucking blew it big style.

What is it about Stevie that brings out the worst in me? It always did. He's only been out a matter of weeks and already he's screwing up my life again. It's probably only the fact that he got a much longer stretch than I did that's kept me out of trouble this long. So much for talent and being a reformed character. Stevie Horrocks is both stupid and vicious. I can't stand the man but he's dragging me back down to his level without even trying.

I need to limit the damage, at least try to rebuild my bridges with Molly. I find her in my speed dial and hit call. To my relief she answers after a few seconds.

"Jared? Where are you?"

"On the train. I just managed to catch the last one."

"Oh, good. That's all right then, I had visions of you sleeping on the platform."

I don't bother to mention the Great Northern hotel, five-star luxury, adjacent to Kings Cross station. That would have been my fall-back but I'm pleased she cares. That's a promising sign. Slightly heartened, I press on.

"Look, Molly, I'm sorry—"

"Jared, I—"

We both go silent. I'm the first to speak again. "Molly, I owe you an apology. That was unforgivable of me."

"It was, yes." Her tone is quiet, but no less convincing for that. My heart sinks.

"But even so, *will* you forgive me?"

"You frightened me."

"I know. But I'd never harm you, you must believe that."

"I did believe that, before. But… I hardly know you, do I? Not really."

"You know me well enough. And you trust me, you said that."

"I saw a different side to you tonight, a side I can't live with. If I'm going to allow a man to do the sorts of things we were doing, I need to know that he's nice. I need him to be kind, gentle, calm. I need to know he likes me, that I'm safe with him, and that I can trust him. It seemed as though you didn't like me earlier, when you were swearing at me, when you just got up and left with hardly a word. I certainly didn't like you, and I didn't feel safe."

I cringe inside. Every word she says is spot on. I deserve her anger, though what I'm hearing sounds more like disappointment, which is worse if anything.

"I know that, Molly. If I could turn the clock back, I would. I was angry, but not with you."

"Who else was there?"

"It was him, the dickhead."

"You took it out on me. That's not acceptable."

"I know. Molly, let me make it up to you. I was a prize pillock, a total jerk, I know that, but it won't happen again. Come up to my barn on Wednesday, like you planned. Stay a few days, or as long as you like. We'll scene if you want to, or not. Let me convince you I *am* that nice guy you need."

"I'm not sure. I won't let a man push me around or put me down. Or take out his bad temper on me. Andy did enough of that and I'm not going there again."

"I hear you, Molly, and I swear it won't be like that. I screwed up earlier. It won't happen again. Come to Yorkshire next week. Please."

"You said we'd scene, or not. I thought this was just

about sex, this thing between us. You agreed to help me explore my submissive nature. What will we do if we don't scene?"

An excellent question. "Molly, a D/s relationship is about much more than screaming orgasms."

"I like the screaming orgasms though."

"Me too. Am I to understand you *will* want to scene?"

"I haven't even decided to come back to your house yet."

"Please do, Molly. Or if you prefer I'll come back to London to talk to you. I can stay in a hotel."

"What's wrong with my place? Too poky for your taste?"

"No, your flat's fantastic, I wish I was still there, with you. Shall I get the first train back in the morning?"

She laughs, the sound the most precious I have heard in a long time. "No, you don't need to do that. You have a meeting, anyway, in Leeds."

"Fuck that. I could—"

"I'll see you on Wednesday."

"You will?"

"Yes. I'll text you to let you know what time my train gets in."

"I'll pick you up from the station."

"You don't have to, I can manage."

"I'll meet you. I'm a nice guy, remember, and that starts with me carrying your luggage for you."

"You're a dom, you're not supposed to pamper me."

"Ah, but I am. That's exactly what I'm supposed to do. Pleasure, pain, pampering. And screaming orgasms. I have a lot to prove. Thank you for giving me the chance, Molly."

"You're welcome, sir. But, about what happened earlier, please don't speak to me like that again."

"Agreed, we'll put temper tantrums from me on the hard limits list. Non-negotiable."

"And if I want to ask questions, is that allowed?"

"Christ, yes. Of course it is." I'm mortified that she would think otherwise, though I really can't blame her. I acted like a total shit.

"And if I ask about the dickhead?"

I hesitate. "I'd prefer it if you didn't…"

"Because it's private, a sensitive subject, and you want me to respect that?"

Exactly. "Yes, pretty much."

"Okay. You had only to say so."

"Got that." I opt to quit while I'm ahead. There's always a danger I might open my mouth and stick my fucking boot right in it again. "Text me. Every day."

"Until Wednesday then. Goodnight, sir."

"Goodnight, Molly."

I end the call and lean back, smiling. That went well, better than I hoped. I wish I could be as optimistic about my next conversation.

As though conjured up by my thoughts, my phone rings again. I know it's Stevie, even without the announcement on the screen. I sigh and hit the green key to take the call.

"Where the fuck have you been?"

No preamble, no pleasantries. Stevie Horrocks can always be relied upon to be objectionable.

"France." I can be equally abrupt.

"What were you doing in fucking France?"

"Working."

"You were supposed to be working here. I had a job for you. I told you to be there."

"And I told you no. Is there a problem with your hearing, or maybe you're just plain dense? Come to think of it, you always were."

"You're just plain dead." Stevie announces my apparent demise with deadpan calm, then goes on to elaborate. "Syko fucked up. The fucking motor he nicked for the job turned out to be a dud. The police had been tipped off and he got lifted, Barry and Lofty too. Me and Brad got away, managed to slip out the back and leg it across the fields while the wooden tops were chasing Syko, but we were lucky." He pauses for a moment. I can hear his heavy breathing on the end of the phone as he relives his mad dash for freedom over the Yorkshire countryside. "It was you told the screws."

"Was it fuck!" I'm oddly indignant at the accusation. "I didn't even know where the job was, so how could I? And who's bloody Syko?"

"Alec Sykes. Came recommended but he's a nutter. Turned up at the garage with bloody Corsa as the getaway motor. Who the fuck robs petrol stations with a fucking Vauxhall Corsa?"

Who indeed? I would never have turned out with anything less than a Cortina.

Stevie continues to vent his anger, as though this whole bloody cock-up he seems to be embroiled in has something to do with me. Weird place, Planet Stevie.

"I texted you the time and place. You were supposed to be there, with a decent bloody motor. Instead I end up dragging bloody Syko in at the last moment, he fucks it all up, and the cops are waiting for us when we come out the petrol station."

"Fucking tough." I grimace; it would have suited me just fine if Stevie had gone down for another ten years, though I wouldn't wish that on Brad. My brother-in-law's never going straight, but he's likable enough in small doses and his kids miss him when he's away. I never even read the bloody texts so I truly didn't know the details of Stevie's ill-fated heist, but even if I had I wouldn't have dropped Brad in it.

It's not true what they say about honour among thieves.

"Are you saying it wasn't you who tipped the police off?"

"Ah, now we're getting somewhere." I make no attempt to conceal my sarcasm, which is probably lost on Stevie in any case.

"Are you sure?" Thought so, my sarcasm sailed right over his stupid head.

"Of course I'm fucking sure."

"Okay, I'll let you off. But you still owe me. We need a place to stay for a couple of nights, me and Brad.

Somewhere nice and quiet where the cops won't come poking around. I hear you got yourself a fancy place out in the middle of nowhere, sounds just right."

"Forget it."

"Two nights, tops."

"Not happening."

"Okay, just a thought. Brad reckons Rachel might be a bit more hospitable. We'll go there, then."

"You fucking won't. Rachel doesn't need the hassle."

"None of us do. But Rach understands loyalty, and family. She's a good lass, is our Rachel."

"She's not *your* anything. Or Brad's anymore. Leave her out of it."

"No can do. We've been on the run for three days and we need a place to lie low. It's either you or that swanky pub."

I swear, something particularly obscene. The woman sitting across the aisle from me glances my way and I mouth an apology. From the moment he brought my little sister into this I knew I had no real choice.

"Two nights, and you're gone. First thing Tuesday you're out, the pair of you."

"Sure. The heat'll have died off by then. And don't worry, we'll see you right. The job went tits up, but we still got a few grand out of it."

"All I want is to see the back of you. This is a one-off, right, and I don't want to know anything about the job. Not this one, not future ones. Not now, not ever."

"Your loss, bro. Right, you'll have to pick us up. We've got no transport and nicking another motor would just attract attention we could do without."

"Where are you?"

"Leeds. I'll text you the address. Half an hour, right?"

"You'll be fucking lucky. I'm on a train out of London, just passing Peterborough, then I'll have to drive across from York. It'll be three hours, maybe more."

Stevie treats me to a few choice epithets of his own, but

none of that makes any difference. He'll just have to sodding well wait. At last the penny drops and he hangs up, leaving me to enjoy the remainder of my journey in peace.

Fat chance of that.

• • • • • • •

"Right, you two need to be off. Now."

"But we're just getting comfortable."

"Now. We agreed Tuesday morning. It's Tuesday now, and after three in the afternoon. I want you gone." I glare at Stevie, reclining in my lounge, his stockinged feet up on my sofa, his grimy fist wrapped around a can of my lager. Christ, I loathe this individual.

"Aw, come on, mate. Another night or two won't hurt." Brad's wheedling tone from the depths of my favourite armchair is really starting to grate on my nerves. He's also making short work of my beer. Whatever made me think this man was a friend of mine?

He's wrong though. Another night *will* hurt. Another night brings us to Wednesday, and to Molly. No way am I letting her walk into this mess. Apart from anything else, she's sure to recognise Stevie from when he was locked up, God knows if there was ever any trouble he'd be at the heart of it. He was on report enough times, all the screws knew him. He may not remember her, but I'm not taking that risk. Stevie harbours no love whatsoever for the forces of law, order, and authority and Molly would be in a whole heap of danger if he knew she used to be a prison officer. Jesus, if she found me scary the other night…

"Now." I turn on my heel and march upstairs to the spare room they've been sharing, wrinkle my nose at the mess and pervasive odour of sweat and stale bodies, and start to rake their gear together into a pile. I shudder at the pair of used needles I spot on the window sill but leave them where they are. I can come back later with a dustpan and brush to shift those. I phone to order a taxi, which I'm assured will be here within fifteen minutes. That sorted, I cram all their crap into Brad's duffel bag and haul it downstairs to dump at Stevie's feet.

"You can finish your beer while you wait for the taxi. Outside."

He doesn't even look up at me, the cocky bastard. Instead, he takes another swig of my Carlsberg before he bothers to reply. "I don't think so. Chill, my man. Like Brad says, another day or two won't make any difference."

My last shreds of patience exhausted, I grab the front of his grubby T shirt and drag him off my couch. The lager slops everywhere, but I don't give a shit, it'll wipe up. I have worse filth to clear out. "You just don't fucking listen, do you? That was always your problem. I agreed to let you stay here for two days. Two fucking days. Not three, not four, not as long as you damned well please. You're out of here, both of you. Go dump your shit on someone else, but not me and not Rachel."

"Rachel'd be pleased to see us. So would the kids." Brad chimes in his contribution, and by the confident look on his sallow face I can only think he actually believes that rubbish. I'm ready for him this time though.

"Correction, Rachel's bar manager's ex-CID. She won't be pleased to see you, but he might."

"Fucking hell, what's she doing taking up with scum like that?" Brad's suddenly bewildered expression might be comical if I wasn't so pissed off. I wish I'd thought to mention the burly ex-copper earlier.

"She runs a decent pub, the kids are in decent schools, doing well. The last thing they need is you fucking up their lives again. I'll just wave the pair of you off, then I'll phone Rachel and warn her that you might show up. The bar manager lives in, I think. That'll be handy, just in case of unwelcome guests."

"For fuck's sake, man, you're crumpling my gear." Stevie wriggles away from me and makes a great production out of straightening the front of his T shirt. "Jesus, if you really want us to go, we're out of here."

Hallelujah! I pick up the duffel and toss it at Brad. "The taxi should be here in five minutes. You can wait at the bottom of the drive."

"What are we gonna use to pay? The cash from the job's still hot."

Stevie has a point, and the last thing I want is a curious police investigation tracking the notes from a recent robbery to a taxi pick up at my home. I pull fifty quid from my wallet and hand it to Stevie. "Don't bother paying me back, call it a parting gift. Now fuck off. I don't expect to ever clap eyes on either of you again. Are we clear?"

There's a great deal of muttering and complaining, but the pair of them seem to finally accept that the party's over as far as free board and lodgings at my barn is concerned. They amble out into my hallway and start peering around for their shoes. I'm ahead of them.

"Outside, on the porch." I open the door and herd the pair of them through. "Have a nice day." I slam the door behind them, and lock it. Good fucking riddance. Now I just need to phone Rachel and make sure she's not thinking of giving her new manager any time off over the next few days.

She picks up on the second ring. "Rachel?"

"No, it's Katie. Is that you, Uncle Jared?"

I can't help grinning at when I hear my step-niece's voice. She's a nice kid. "Yes, Trouble. How's the new school?" Katie just started at the local grammar school. The place is supposed to be one of the best in the area.

"I got an A in biology."

"Good stuff." Rachel's stepdaughter was always bright. I know my little sister harbours hopes of university for her. That'll be a first for our family, but I wouldn't be surprised if she pulls it off. At least we should be able to manage the tuition fees, as long as we don't let Brad screw everything up. "I'll be wanting to hear all about it later. Is Rachel about?"

"She's in the bar. I'll get her."

I hear the distant call of 'mum,' then a crackling as the phone is passed to Rachel. "It's Uncle Jared. I told him about my A."

"Is there anyone you haven't told?" Despite her words, I detect the pride in Rachel's tone. She took on Katie as a confused and difficult toddler. It wasn't always easy, but they've become close over the years. Since Rachel threw him out, Brad's shown no interest whatsoever in any of his children. Katie stayed with Rachel and she's as much a part of our family as the younger two. "Hey, how's things?" Rachel's voice comes on the line.

I don't sugar-coat it. "Brad's been here."

"What? Why? I thought you never had anything to do with him these days." She sounds shocked, scared even.

"It's not been for the want of trying. He's been up to some crap and needed a place to hide."

"Oh, no, you need to get rid of him. Now."

"I did. He stayed here for two nights, then I turfed him and his mate out."

"Stevie? Was it Stevie Horrocks who was with him?"

"Yeah, why? How did you know?"

"Don't you ever watch the news? Their faces have been all over the television since they shot that cashier last week. The girl's still in intensive care."

My blood runs cold. "What? They shot someone?"

"In the thigh. It might have been worse but Stevie never could aim straight."

"I never saw a gun."

"What? You were there? Please, Jared, tell me you're not involved." She sounds desperate, terrified. "The police have been here already looking for Brad. I told them I hadn't seen him in years. They never mentioned you. Jesus, that kid could have been killed."

I sink into the armchair so recently vacated by Brad and drop my head into my hands. The remote is on the floor by my feet so I switch on my television, then surf through channels until I find a news programme. I leave it on while I go back to my conversation with Rachel.

"No, I wasn't there. Bloody hell, of course I wasn't there. I was abroad last week, in Paris. Only got back on Sunday." *Thank God for a rock-solid alibi.* "So go on, tell me. What did they do?"

"As I understand it, they burst into a petrol station last week, Thursday I think it was, wearing clown masks and brandishing a shotgun. There was a girl in the kiosk, only nineteen, and they demanded she empty the till. She panicked, I suppose, and tried to phone the garage owner, so that mad sod opened fire. The glass shattered and she was hit in the leg. Most of the gang made a run for it out the front just as the police arrived but somehow Brad and Stevie ended up at the rear of the garage and they disappeared into the woods. The police had helicopters, tracker dogs, the lot, but they still managed to lose them. They've been combing the area for days trying to track them down. They've been round to all their old friends, family, contacts. I'm surprised you didn't get a visit."

So am I. And relieved. My parole would have been revoked in a heartbeat if two armed robbers on the run had been discovered holed up in my spare bedroom and I'd have been back inside. Still might be, if those two goons left any trace to lead the police back to me. Jesus, why didn't I ask more questions? Where else had they been before I picked them up? Who had they seen? Did they tell anyone they were coming here? I managed to avoid them for most of the time they spent at my barn, locking myself away in my studio upstairs. I didn't want to know anything about the job, just wanted rid of them.

"No one's been here looking, and in any case I threw them out. They've gone now. There's a chance they might show up at your place though, so you need to make sure your bar manager's around. Do you want me to come over?"

"No, I'll be fine. Jack can deal with them if they turn up

here, and the police are definitely watching this place. I can't see them getting within half a mile."

"Is the girl going to be okay? Jesus, I never saw a gun. They must have stashed it somewhere."

"She's out of danger, but still…"

Indeed. But still…

The least Brad and Stevie can hope for is a robbery charge, but attempted murder might be on the cards. That's going to carry a long stretch back inside. Fucking idiots.

And they just dragged me right back into it. I ponder the merits of phoning the police myself and turning them in. Christ, shooting a poor cashier, just a kid really, and all for a few lousy quid. Any honour among thieves—or ex-thieves in my case—evaporates. This is bloody serious; innocent people get killed when guns are involved.

"Look, I knew they'd robbed a garage, but I swear I never had any idea about the shooting. I was away, didn't see the news, still haven't. I let them stay here for two nights, and then only to keep them away from you and the kids. I threw them out just now, sent them off in a taxi. I've no idea where they went, but perhaps the police can trace them. I should report it."

"No. No, don't do that." Rachel sounds desperate, but no more so than I am. "Look, you could end up back inside as an accessory."

Don't I know it? Regardless of the fact that I knew nothing of the robbery, I doubt the police will be easy to convince. Still, a cast-iron alibi and a decent lawyer should help. That said, and logic apart, it still goes against the grain to inform on my old partners. Perhaps I'm not such a reformed character after all. Something in my DNA recoils from the prospect, even with the gun involved. Even so, the chances are I'm soon going to be on the police radar and I need to do what I still can to limit the damage.

"I don't see what else—"

"Just leave it. They'll be picked up eventually, sure to be, but even then they might not mention you. Jared, I don't want you to go to prison again. I thought all that was in the past."

"Me too. But if I explain, and I can prove I had no part in the robbery, the police might accept that."

"And they might not. You can't take the risk, Jared. Please, promise me you won't contact them. We'll just stay out of it, keep our heads down and wait until this passes."

I consider Rachel's plan, but can't really see it coming off. Old loyalties be damned, I should cut my losses now, do what I can to limit the damage. "Rachel, I—"

"Please, for me, Jared…" She's on the verge of tears, I can hear the catch in her voice.

I weaken, though I've an uneasy feeling I'll come to regret this later. "Okay, we'll see what happens over the next few days. But I'm going to contact Charles and have a word with him. If he advises me to talk to the police, then I will. Agreed?"

Charles Manners is the solicitor who handles all our family business. It can do no harm to seek his advice. Rachel reluctantly agrees. "Okay, talk to Charles, but don't do anything without talking to me again first. Promise me that."

"I promise. And if Brad shows up there you're to call me, okay?"

Rachel agrees, and I hang up just in time to catch the latest bulletin on TV. I watch with fatalistic fascination as the report outlines the continuing search for two dangerous armed robbers on the run in the Yorkshire area following the vicious raid on a filling station that left a nineteen-year-old woman fighting for her life. The public are advised not to approach the suspects, who may still be armed. There have been various sightings, though none remotely close to where I live.

There might be a glimmer of hope after all.

CHAPTER ELEVEN

I spot him, beyond the barriers. Jared is here, waiting for me, as he promised he would be.

My bag is heavy, I packed enough for a stay of several days, though I wasn't really sure how wise that might be. For all I know I could find myself hopping on the next train back to London. Jared really shocked me, shattered my growing trust in him and confidence in myself. I was actually scared of him for a few moments, and angry too. I resented that he would treat me that way. It was not so much what he said—that was little enough, on reflection—but more his callous dismissal of my desire to be supportive.

He fucked me in the most intimate way I can imagine, then because I spoke out of turn he snapped at me, wished me a nice life, and just walked out.

I was humiliated, but it was more than that. I felt stupid, naïve, and vaguely as though I'd been used. It was not a good feeling, not good at all. I never want to feel like that again

I'd thought we had something. Our relationship was fragile, embryonic, but precious and filled with potential. Maybe it still is, but I'm less certain of that now. There's so much at stake here for me. Dare I trust Jared with my emotions and more besides?

I draw in a deep breath and start to drag my hold-all along the platform toward the ticket barrier. I may have my doubts now but there's only one way to find out what's really going on between us—just sex as we agreed, or perhaps a little more than that.

Jared promised me that what happened on Sunday won't happen again and if I didn't at least try to give him the benefit of the doubt I could well spend the rest of my life wondering about what might have been. I set my bag down and shove my ticket into the slot at the barrier and the gates open. Before I can grasp my bag again Jared has leaned in to take it from me. He hoists it onto his shoulder, then wraps the other arm around me.

"Thank you for coming." He cocks his head to one side, questioning.

I reach up on tiptoe to kiss him on the mouth. I'm here, and I didn't come all this way to sulk.

Jared returns my kiss, his tongue spearing into my mouth as I cling to him. I so want this to work.

He breaks the kiss to nuzzle my neck. "It's good to see you, Molly mine."

"You too, sir," I whisper. And I mean it.

● ● ● ● ● ● ●

"Should I undress?" I ask the question as soon as we arrive back at Jared's lovely converted barn. I'd almost forgotten how stunning this place is, rugged, isolated, windswept, but once inside with the doors closed his home is cosy and comfortable too. And spacious. We're surrounded on all sides by wild, rolling hills dotted with weird, towering rock configurations. I got my first proper look at the unearthly but beautiful Brimham Rocks landscape as we drove up to the house, and I hope we'll find time to go out and explore while I'm here. First things first though. I peer up at Jared expectantly as I wait for my next instruction.

"An attractive offer, and usually I'd say yes, that is what I expect as soon as we're alone. But I wonder if we need to talk first."

"Talk, sir?" I meet his gaze. Jared appears troubled, uncertain. It's not a look I like on him. I hope he isn't having second thoughts about me, about this thing we're doing together. "I thought we settled our argument. I promised not to pry."

"Sweetheart, I don't mean that. I thought perhaps you might have things you need to say to me, things to ask me?"

I shake my head. "No, sir. I just want to put all that behind us and move on."

He steps forward to cradle my face between his hands. "You know I meant it, don't you? What happened at your flat was out of character. I promise not to behave like that around you again."

"I know that, sir."

"As your dom, I will be displeased with you sometimes, and I'll punish you. But not for asking questions. Disrespect, disobedience, not being honest with me—all of those will earn you a spanking, but curiosity won't."

"I don't mind the spanking, sir. That was what I liked about you in the first place, if you recall, back at Armley. I was having a bad day, but as an officer I could have—should have—been more sympathetic to your needs. Afterwards I felt bad about your gym session, guilty for letting you down, and you made it all go away when you spanked me."

He smiles. "I do indeed recall. And I loved the way you responded to a decent spanking. Who would have known what was hiding beneath that uniform of yours?"

"You knew."

"Maybe, yes. I suppose I guessed. And now, do you still feel the same way? Are you ready to trust me again?"

"You scared me on Sunday, but it's over now and I do know you wouldn't harm me. But…" I hesitate. *Can I, should I, share with him what hurt me the most?*

"Molly? Tell me." His tone is gentle, but I know he expects the truth, all of it.

"I hated that you left. You just said it had been nice meeting me again, then you left me. That really hurt. I missed you." His handsome face shimmers before my eyes as tears start to form.

"Baby, I know that. I saw it, then, but I was too much of a bastard to put it right straight away. Let me make amends now."

"It's over, and you did come back, sort of. You phoned me."

"I regretted it, almost before I got to the end of your road. You have my word, however much you might piss me off, I'll never walk out on you. We talk, and we carry on talking until it's sorted."

"Or you could just spank me."

"I could. That'd work for me."

"And me. That's what I want now, sir. It's what I need from you."

"I was the one in the wrong."

"I don't want to spank you, sir."

He grins, his expression lightening now. "Thank God for that, because it's not happening."

"So, shall I undress now?"

He releases me and steps back, his warm smile fading to be replaced by his stern dom persona. Something clenches and twists deep in my abdomen.

"Please do, Molly. Upstairs, in my bedroom."

I almost skip up the stairs. This is going to be fine, I just know it.

Jared follows me, and closes the bedroom door behind us. He leans back on it to watch as I remove my clothes.

"I'd like you to fold all your things neatly and place them out of the way. Then, when you're ready, bend over the foot of the bed." He leans against the door to watch as I obey his instructions. "Put a couple of pillows under you as well, to lift your bum up a little more. I'm thinking a decent hand spanking to get you in the mood, then perhaps a few strokes with a crop. I have one that's nice and stingy, should leave some very pretty stripes."

My pussy clenches. That sounds wonderful. I grab three pillows from the head of Jared's bed and arrange them at the bottom, then drape my nude body over them. I look back over my shoulder as Jared eases himself off the door and comes forward. He caresses my upturned buttocks as he passes me to open his box of kinky toys.

The crop he selects is made of brown leather, plaited along most of the length, with a short tail at the tip. He flexes it between his hands then lays it beside me on the bed.

"We'll get to that later. First things first. You ready, Molly?"

"Yes, sir." I'm already sinking into that pleasant, hazy place that only Jared seems able to find for me, and he has yet to properly touch me.

He stands behind me and caresses my bottom again, rubbing large, lazy circles across my quivering skin. I lift up to press my buttocks into his palm, and it's all I can do not to purr.

The first slap is sharp, landing on my right buttock, the sound reverberating around the quiet room. He follows it by palming my tingling cheek, stroking the pain away. Soon the discomfort dissipates and I squirm under his sensual caress.

The next slap falls on my left cheek, and he repeats the soothing caress. He continues to slap then stroke, alternating between pain and pleasure until I can no longer separate the two. The spanks are getting harder, enough to bring me up onto my toes, but I crave more. I lift up my bottom, offering a better target, and I spread my thighs hopefully.

"Getting wet, Molly?" He swipes his open palm over the length of my pussy then examines his damp hand. "Oh, I see you are. By the way you're opening for me and drooling all over my pillows I think perhaps you're hoping I might finger-fuck you before we finish your spanking. Is that right?"

"No, sir. I mean… yes, if you like." I'm stammering, almost incoherent with lust.

"If *I* like? I was asking what you want."

"I want you to finger-fuck me, please." I open my thighs a little wider.

"Reach back, pull your arse cheeks apart for me."

"Oh!"

"Do it, Molly. I will finger-fuck you, since you've asked me so politely, but I prefer your arse right now. Show me your pretty little arsehole and invite me to fill it with my fingers."

When he puts it like that, I see no serious objections. I grasp my smarting buttocks in my palms and pull them apart to expose my tight pucker.

"How many fingers do you want?"

"Could I have three, sir?"

"Ambitious, Molly. We'll work up to three though, if you like."

He steps away for a moment to get a tube of lubricant from his box of tricks, then I gasp as he squirts some directly onto my arsehole. He places his fingertip at my entrance, works it around for a few seconds, then he pushes. The pressure is firm enough to gain entry, and as instinct kicks in, I push back against him to take the length of his finger inside me.

"Oh, God, that feels so good," I moan, gyrating my hips around his invading digit.

He twists his hand to swirl his finger inside me, then slides another in alongside it. I can feel the tension, the stretching of my entrance, but the sensation is one of intimate arousal, not discomfort. He pulls back, then thrusts his fingers in again, filling me. He scissors them to rub against my inner walls, the friction sending me into a writhing, squirming state of ecstasy.

"I need to come, sir."

"Do you?"

"Sir…" I can hear the pleading in my tone, hope that he'll take pity.

He does. His other hand connects with my clit, his finger flicking the swollen nub at the same time he sinks his thumb into my wet cunt. My orgasm is instant, my pussy and arse convulsing around his fingers. He thrusts, strokes, teases, and presses as my climax turns my muscles to liquid. I sag onto the pillows, moaning and gasping as my body shudders under the onslaught of pleasure.

As the tremors subside and my head clears a little, Jared withdraws his fingers from my body. "Was that good, little sub?"

"Yes, sir. Thank you," I murmur.

"Good. So, back to your spanking, I think."

I nod my assent, still quivering as the last pulses of delight shimmer through my boneless limbs.

"Words, please, Molly. And you can move your hands now. Tuck them underneath you, out of the way."

I'm still gripping my buttocks, though I have no idea how when the rest of my body seems to have dissolved into a slushy mess. I do as he tells me and fold my hands under my chin. "Yes, sir, I still want the spanking." I plant my feet on the carpet as best I can and raise up my bottom in confirmation.

Jared chuckles and picks up the crop.

I hear the soft whistle an instant before the leather connects with my right buttock. I yelp and kick up my heels as the pain ricochets through me. It was more than I anticipated; sharper, hotter, much more intense than his hand.

"Be still, Molly. You can shriek if you like, there's no one to hear you except me, but I expect you not to move. If it's too much you can use your safeword."

"I'm sorry, sir."

"You want to continue?"

"Oh, yes, yes I do. It was just a bit of a shock."

"If you think you'll be a wriggler, just tell me and I can use restraints to help you. It's important that you remain very still though. For one thing it demonstrates your submission and I want to see that, to know you're allowing me to do this to you of your own free will. And for another I wouldn't want to injure you by accident. A spanking crop isn't especially dangerous, but if I was using a cane things would be different."

"A cane?"

"Maybe. Another time, if you want to. So, do I need to find some cuffs for your ankles?"

"No, sir. I won't move, I promise." I stiffen my body, bracing for the next stroke and determined not to get this wrong again.

"You've gone rigid, Molly. Are you sure you're all right with this?"

"Yes, sir. It's just so new, that's all. I do want to carry on."

"I'm going to use restraints so you don't have to concentrate on anything but the spanking, okay? It's best, this time."

"But sir, I want to do this." I turn my head to face him, expecting to encounter disappointment or exasperation in his face, but all I find there is concern and compassion.

He crouches beside me, his face now inches from mine. "I know that, love, and it's my responsibility to make sure it works out well for you. I want you to relax and enjoy what I'm able to offer, not spend the entire scene tensing up in case you make a mistake. So you'll let me help you? Yes?"

"Are you sure?"

"I'm sure. And I do know best."

"Okay then. Just to keep my feet still…"

He nods then stands and returns to his chest to select ankle cuffs. He crouches behind me and quickly secures a leather band around each ankle, then attaches them to a rail at the bottom of the bed close to the floor. I try an experimental kick and find my feet won't move at all. So far so good. I turn to face him again.

"I wonder, would you fasten my hands too? Just in case."

"Of course." He smiles at me again. "It's good that you asked me, shows you're learning to trust me, and yourself. Stretch your arms out to the sides."

I do as he tells me while Jared finds a set of smaller cuffs for my wrists. In moments they too are buckled into the warm leather bands, which Jared clips to rings set into the sides of the bed. I'm stretched out, spread-eagled face down on the bed, ready for whatever comes my way.

Jared picks up the crop and takes up his position behind me. He waits, saying nothing, but allowing me the moments I need to collect my thoughts and settle. The breathy swish of shifting air heralds the next stroke.

"Aagh!" I scream and jerk in my restraints. Pain sears my bottom, but I am soaring, exalted by the heady impact, pain and pleasure blended together in a rich, seductive cocktail of sensation.

"Okay?" Jared waits again, unhurried.

"Yes, sir. More, please." I'm trembling, quivering with need, anticipation, lust.

"More coming up. Remember, 'cooler' is your slow down safeword, 'jailbird' means I'll stop."

"I know. I'm all right though, really. I love this, sir."

"Good to know. Just checking."

The next few strokes send me flying again. Pain envelops me, pleasure wraps around my senses, confusing, sharpening, muting. I scream and jolt with each one, secure that he has me, that Jared is in control. My vision blurs, I can hear Jared's voice, soft and low, but as though it's reaching me from a distance. His words are hard to make out, but nothing of that matters to me as long as he doesn't stop.

The crop carries on its glorious work, each stroke an exquisite caress, branding my tender skin. I writhe and moan, turning my hips to better catch each stripe. The spanking may have slowed. I'm uncertain, struggling to separate one stroke from another. I can still feel, but it's all merging, blending until everything coalesces into one sensual hum.

I'm aware, dimly, that Jared has stopped using the crop. His hands are on me now, but not spanking. He's stroking my inflamed buttocks, rubbing in the pain as though to massage it right into my muscles and flesh. It sinks in, then transforms into a different sensation, something light and tingly, tantalising yet incredibly satisfying too. He caresses away the discomfort to create a rich, warm languor. I stretch my bound limbs, sinking into a sated, contented haze.

"I want you to fuck me, sir. I need you inside me." The words are mine, but I wonder I can find the energy to express my needs.

"I need to be inside you. You'll come on my cock, my sweet slut."

"Yes, sir. Anything…"

He pushes my thighs apart, and I realise he must have freed my ankles. My wrists are still secured to the bed. Jared lifts one of my knees and places it on the mattress, opening me more fully. The punished skin on my buttocks stretches, the discomfort a sharp reminder of the spanking. I wriggle, seeking more of that, as Jared lifts my other knee. His fingers are inside me, testing my readiness. The sounds of hot, wet pussy are unmistakable. I squeeze my inner walls around his fingers, but what I really need is his cock.

Seconds later, he's there, poised at my entrance, then he drives forward to bury his erection in my channel. I let out a deep, satisfied moan and rotate my hips in silent thanks. Jared pulls back, then thrusts again, the angle allowing him to fill me utterly. I'm panting, bobbing my hips up and down as I seek more friction, greater penetration, an intensity I crave more than air to breathe. Jared seems to know, setting up a fast, demanding rhythm as he fucks me hard, then harder still.

My orgasm grips me. I should seek permission, but I

can't find words. It happens anyway, and Jared seems content with it, reaching around me to stroke my clit as my pussy convulses around his thick length. Seconds later he drives deep again, then holds still as his cock jerks violently inside me. He swears under his breath, something wonderfully obscene as he comes too. I'm still shaking when he reaches to free my wrists, first the right, then the left, then he rolls to the side taking me with him, his cock still embedded within my clinging channel.

I'm very, very glad I decided to give my sexy dom another chance.

"Could we go out? I mean, I know it'll be dark in a couple of hours, but I'd like a walk." I roll over in Jared's arms to nuzzle his bare chest. At some stage in the proceedings he lost his clothes, and now we're curled up together in his huge bed.

"Sure you can manage that sort of exertion? You must be pretty sore." He kisses my hair and reaches down to pat my smarting bottom.

"Ouch! Yes, but it's a nice sort of sore." I tip my face up to look at him. "Please, I want to climb on those rocks."

"Okay, but we'll need to be quick. It gets dangerous after dark, especially if you don't know the terrain. Did you bring sensible shoes with you?"

"Of course. I brought my hiking boots, just in case."

"Right. Just let me get a quick shower, then I'm all yours."

If only. I shove that unexpected yearning to one side and wriggle into a sitting position. "Feel like sharing? I'll wash your back this time."

He rolls from the bed and extends his hand to me. "I'll hold you to that. Come on."

An hour later we're striding through the thick gorse toward the nearest of the rock clusters, a pile of huge flat stones stacked one on top of the other, getting larger the higher they are in the pile. The overall effect is that of a giant mushroom, the whole crazy structure defying gravity.

"Are they natural?" I ask as we circle the rocks at the base. "They look as though they could just topple over, like a giant game of Jenga."

"Yes, they're natural. They've stood like this for thousands of years. I doubt they're going anywhere any time soon."

"How did they come to be like this?"

"I wondered that so I checked it out on Wikipedia. I gather the stone is millstone grit and it's been eroded over the last few thousand years to carve out these weird shapes. Wind, rain, glaciers, and probably the odd spotty kid with a penknife. A lot of the formations have names, but you need to use a bit of imagination to understand them. It helps to get the right viewing angle too." He stops and points to a huge tower about half a mile away. "That one's called the Camel, and over there's the Turtle. My favourite's the Dancing Bear but you can't see that one from here."

"How far is it? The Dancing Bear?"

"Another twenty minutes or so. Maybe more—it's uphill, and steep."

"Do we have time? I'd like to see it."

He laughs. "Ah, so eager. I do love an enthusiastic little sub. Come on." He holds out his hand and I take it as we stride out through the crisp bracken blanketing the hillside.

CHAPTER TWELVE

Molly laughs almost all the way up the steep incline as we scramble through the rock-strewn landscape. She's a game little thing, I grant her that. Despite the discomfort she must be feeling—I wasn't especially gentle with her earlier—she is undeterred as we climb. I like to think I keep myself pretty fit, but I'm panting hard by the time we crest a rise in the hillside and the Dancing Bear comes into view. Molly is barely out of breath as I point it out to her. She grabs my hand again and drags me forward. I fall into step behind her. With luck we can reach the gnarled lump of stone by nightfall, but we'll need to pick our way back with care. Lucky I remembered to shove a couple of torches in my pocket before we left.

"This place has been used as a film set. There were some kids' TV shows filmed here I think, and it was featured in a Bee Gees video." I dredge up the trivia from somewhere at the back of my mind. I can be a mine of useless information when it suits me.

Molly glances at me, her eyes bright. "We should come here sometime, when there's no one about, and make our own film. Or better still, you could take photographs. You could tie me to the rocks and record it all for posterity. Do you think the pictures would sell?"

I laugh out loud. "Oh, yes, I reckon they would. I'd produce them in monochrome, very trendy. We could probably display them in the National Trust shop. The tourists would go wild for them."

"I'd want a percentage, obviously."

"Goes without saying."

"What's the going rate for nude modelling?"

"Nude, did you say?"

"Yes, and in kinky poses, like those pictures in your studio. That must be worth a fair bit."

"Priceless, Molly. Absolutely fucking priceless." I grab her and kiss her on the mouth before picking her up and swinging her around. Her booted feet fly out behind her as she whoops and wraps her arms around my neck. We roll onto the springy grass surrounding the rocks and I can't recall ever feeling quite so at home in my own skin.

Just sex, my arse.

• • • • • • •

It's dusk by the time we start back, and darkness falls quickly in this part of the world. I lead the way, using my torch to pick out the safe places to walk. "Keep close, and watch where you put your feet. It's easy to break an ankle in a rabbit hole."

She moves in close, gripping my hand in one of hers, brandishing her own torch in the other. Our progress is slow, but eventually the outline of Cote House Barn looms out of the murky distance. "Home sweet home," I murmur. I'm more than ready for a slug of good, reviving caffeine.

Inside I set the percolator going while Molly sits on the bench in my back porch to drag off her muddy boots.

"We should have waited before having that shower," she calls after me. "I'm filthy again."

"Feel free. You know where everything is. Do you like fish?"

"Fish?" She pads into the kitchen in her stockinged feet.

"Rainbow trout to be exact, in a nice lemon sauce."

Molly grins. "Sounds delicious. Can I help?"

"No need, I've got it covered." I open the fridge and pull out the fish I bought earlier, on my way to pick Molly up from the station, right after I took a call from Charles Manning.

I phoned my lawyer's office straight after speaking to Rachel yesterday, but he was with another client. I left a message, and he returned my call as I drove to the station. His advice pretty much confirmed my own assessment, namely the police might well try to tie me in to the offence as an accessory but I can put together a decent defence. The chances of being charged myself will drop dramatically if I help them with their enquiries, and that's exactly what he advises I should do.

I'll have to swallow my distaste and make that call. There's no way I can keep it from Molly once the police become involved, but I prefer to explain it to her myself first. Over a nice dinner will do, which is where my visit to the fishmonger's came in. Two beautiful, fragrant trout, their eyes glassy, peer up at us from the wrapper.

"Oh, real fish. From the sea," Molly exclaims. "Are you going to cook it?"

"I just said so, didn't I? In lemon sauce."

"I thought you meant something you'd stick in the microwave—not real fish, fish that looks like it might swim off if you chucked a bucket of water over it." She peers suspiciously at the trout as though expecting them to start flapping about at any moment.

I laugh. "These bad boys are going nowhere. There's nothing wrong with microwave food if you're in a rush but I prefer the real thing. And I like to cook. So, are you up for a spot of only-just-dead trout?"

She laughs. "I'll get fat if I stay with you too long."

"No chance of that, Molly. I intend to work you hard. Do you know how many calories you can work off in one orgasm?"

That drags her attention from the fish. She gazes up at me, wide-eyed. "I've no idea."

"A hundred and fifty, maybe more." That's another snippet of trivia dragged up from I know not which corner of my brain, but Molly looks impressed. I put the trout back in the fridge until I'm ready to cook it. "Come to think of it, I'll need to feed you well, Molly mine, to keep you from fading away to nothing."

"Promises, promises." She makes to dart past me, but I manage to grab a tea towel and flick it across her lush arse. Molly squeals and dives for the door to the stairs.

• • • • • • •

My trout is a triumph—succulent, tender, just the right burst of tang from the sauce but not so much that it might overpower the delicate flavours of the fish. I toss in some baby new potatoes and green beans, steamed al dente, and the meal is complete. Molly, still clad in just my oversized towelling robe, clears her plate with lots of oohing and aahing, then licks her fingers to capture the last drops of sauce. My cock leaps to attention and I postpone the serious conversation we need to have. Instead, I'm pondering the merits of ordering her to lose the wrap and drop to her knees right here in the dining room. I could put that nimble tongue of hers to good use. I turn that delightful prospect over in my mind as Molly stands to clear the table.

My train of thought is interrupted by a loud banging on my door. Molly drops the stack of plates she's holding, her startled expression telling its own story as the hammering continues.

"What? Who's that?" She clutches her chest in alarm.

I can't say I blame her. I have a pretty good idea who's out there and I'm already kicking myself for ever letting her become embroiled in this car crash. Christ, why didn't I at least tell her what was happening instead of letting myself be led by my dick? It's too fucking late now.

"Don't move, you might cut yourself on the broken plates." The shattered remains of the crockery surround her bare feet. "I'll get rid of them, then I'll find a brush." Already I'm striding for the door, determined to leave Stevie and Brad in no doubt as to the lack of welcome here.

"I'll go get dressed," says Molly, ignoring my warning as she picks her way through the shards of broken flatware and follows me out into the hall. She darts for the stairs as I head toward the front door. The thumping is getting louder, and is now accompanied by shouting from outside.

"Open your fucking door." It's Brad's dulcet tone. I entertain the hopeful notion that he might be alone.

"Brad? Is that you?"

"Of course it's fucking me. Open up, I'm freezing my nuts off."

Shit! Shit, shit, *shit*.

"Not this time. I want nothing more to do with it, whatever pile of crap you've got yourself into." I'm still playing dumb about the shooting at the petrol station, as much for Molly's benefit as anything else. I've no doubt she's hearing all of this.

"There's a grand in it for you. Let us in, you twat." He punctuates his request by booting my door. The thud reverberates around the house. It's only the knowledge that Molly is upstairs and probably terrified by all this bloody racket that propels me down the hallway.

"All right. For fuck's sake, stop making all that noise."

"Get a move on then. We're fucking dying here."

We? I stop, my hand on the lock. "Who's we?"

"Me, Mikey, and Stevie."

My heart sinks lower. Apart from getting me locked up eight years ago, Stevie was also one of the idiots who started the riot on G wing and brought my previous encounter with Molly to such an untimely end. There's every chance he'll remember her.

"Jared, who is it?"

I spin around. Molly is right behind me, wearing a loose T shirt of mine and a pair of jeans. She frowns as the thumping starts up again.

"I looked out and saw a van in your driveway. Who's out there? Are you going to let them in?" She turns and heads back toward the stairs. "Maybe I'll just gather up my things then I can be off and leave you to it. I don't suppose you'd call me a cab to the nearest station, would you?"

"No!" I rake my fingers through my hair. "I mean, stay. Please. I'll get rid of them." *I hope.*

She looks doubtful, but offers me a brief nod. "I'll wait upstairs."

That sounds like a decent plan at least. I resort to yelling at Brad through the closed door.

"There's someone else here. It's not a good time."

"We heard. We'll stay out of your way. You and your little lady won't even know we're here."

"Yeah? Well you can stay out of my way by going somewhere else. I'm telling you, Brad, just fuck off."

"No, you fuck off." A new voice takes up the quarrel. Stevie. "You've got five seconds before I blast this fucking door off its hinges."

For fuck's sake! This is all I need. "Have you come up here with bloody guns? Brad, what are you thinking of?"

"We're thinking you've pissed around long enough. Stand back from the door unless you want a face full of this as well." It's Stevie again, and I have no doubt at all that he means it. The man's a card-carrying lunatic.

I twist the lock and pull the door open. "You can have five minutes, no more. In the kitchen."

The three men troop past me, each one toting a rucksack. Brad treats me to an apologetic grin and a shrug. Stevie's expression is positively beatific. I recall he always appears that way when he has a double barrel shotgun in his hands, as he does now. He enjoys the sense of power a firearm gives him, but his intellectual capacity is not far up from an amoeba, so he has zero chance of harnessing that potency or of channelling it anywhere useful. Stevie might be more lethal if he had a few brain cells to rub together, but he's dangerous enough as it is. My third unwelcome visitor, Mikey, is just plain stupid. He's harmless enough on his own, just a lumbering heap of muscle and brawn really, who does as he's told. Paired up with Stevie the psychopath, he's a disaster waiting to happen.

The three of them fill my kitchen. No one comments on the debris littering the floor. Stevie lays the gun down on the table, then plonks himself in the chair closest to it. The others make themselves comfortable too, all three peering at me with varying degrees of expectation.

"Coffee smells good. Is there anything to eat?" Brad stands and heads in the direction of my fridge.

I ignore him for now. I have more pressing concerns. "Give me the gun. There's no need for that in here."

"Do you think I'm fucking stupid?" Stevie reaches for the shotgun and pulls it closer to him.

I decline to answer his question and instead pray that Molly has the sense to stay upstairs out of the way, just until I can send them on their way again.

"So, what do you need now? Cash?"

"We got money. We got loads of money." This from Mikey, who hauls his rucksack from his shoulder and upends it onto my table. A shower of banknotes scatters everywhere, in various denominations, and all look to be used.

"Fucking hell! What have you done? Where did that come from?" I gape at the pile in front of me and wonder how such a perfect day went to absolute shite so fast.

"Tesco. Or should I say the back of the security van after it left Tesco." Brad leans out around my fridge door to smirk at me. "Like I said, a grand's yours just for the bother of putting us up for another day or two. Just until the fuss dies down."

"You robbed a security van? On top of everything else? Where? When?"

"Just this side of Harrogate. About an hour ago." Brad's a mine of useful information, imparting a stack of facts I have no desire at all to hear. He emerges from the fridge with a loaf of sliced wholemeal, a tub of butter, and some halloumi cheese. "Anyone want a sandwich?"

"You came straight here? Are you mad? The police will be about five minutes behind." I'm horrified. The terms of my parole were perfectly clear. As if things weren't already precarious enough this is a cluster fuck of epic proportions. "You're leaving. Now. Take your fucking cash and bugger off."

"Don't be like that, J. Mikey, count out his share." Brad dumps the food on the table between the shotgun and the stolen loot as though this sort of conversation is quite normal as we wait for the coffee to percolate. I suppose he's right. It always used to be in our circles, but I move in different company now.

"Mikey, don't bother. Keep it and go." I reach for the nearest bundle of notes, intending to start shoving it back where it came from.

Stevie shrugs. "Please yourself, dickhead. It's all the more for us. No one's going anywhere for a while though. Which reminds me, we need to say hello to your little lady friend. Give her a shout, there's a good lad."

Bastard. I itch to plant one right in the middle of his smug face but he's too near to that bloody gun for my liking. I shake my head. "Leave her out of it."

Brad does at least have the grace to appear regretful as he slaps butter onto slices of bread, though I'm not convinced it's just Molly he's thinking of as he leaves greasy smears all over my table top. "No can do, mate. For all we know she might be phoning the rozzers right now. Best to get her down here with us, where we can keep an eye on her."

"You go get her, or I will," snarls Stevie, reaching for the gun.

I make up my mind, and head back out into the hallway.

Molly is halfway down the stairs, rooted to the spot, her eyes like saucers. It's obvious she's been listening to the conversation from the kitchen. I offer up thanks that she did at least get dressed as soon as the din started, because I know full well that Stevie would have hauled her down here naked if she hadn't been. I can't help thinking these disastrous conclusions to our scenes are getting to be a habit.

"Jared? Is that…?" She looks bewildered. And scared.

I nod, my expression grim. "An old acquaintance of mine." I have my back to the men in my kitchen so I mouth the rest to her. *Don't let on you know them.*

Still out of sight to all but me, Molly nods her understanding. She knows as well as I do the likely outcome if they realise she's an ex-officer.

"Molly, some friends of mine have dropped in. They'd like to meet you." At least I can be certain they won't know her first name. Molly was always Miss MacBride to the inmates of G wing. I extend my hand to her, then wrap my arm around her shoulders, squeezing for good measure. She's shaking as she appears in the kitchen doorway to face the three thugs, who each regard her with varying degrees of curiosity, speculation, and undisguised lust.

"Stevie, Brad, Mikey, this is Molly, my girlfriend."

Mikey's leering gaze is riveted on Molly's breasts. Brad is somewhat less obvious, managing a smile that would pass for friendly in most circumstances. Stevie just scowls at her, his brow furrowing in concentration.

"Molly, did you say? I don't remember a Molly."

"You wouldn't. We've not been together that long."

"You never said nothing about no Molly." Stevie looks increasingly dubious about my explanation.

"I'm not about to discuss my love life with you, dickhead." No point at all beating about the bush, and if Stevie detects so much as a whiff of fear from me he'll be all over it like a fucking rash. Belligerence is the best strategy with him.

"Yeah, well, can she cook? We've not eaten since you chucked us out yesterday."

I catch Molly's start of alarm as she realises this latest visit isn't an isolated occurrence and I tighten my grip on her to keep her quiet. The less she says the better.

"Molly's more decorative than functional. Best we just send her on her way and we can sort out our business here." I dig my car keys from my jeans pocket and hand them to her. "Sweetheart, you can take my car. I'll collect it later."

She turns her head to look up at me, confused. I kiss her forehead. "I'll be in touch soon. I promise."

"But—"

"We're busy here, love. Make yourself scarce, eh? There's a good girl." I start to usher her back out into the hallway, desperately hoping Stevie will accept the story and agree to let Molly go. His zero respect for women is working in my favour here as he seems not to question my patronising dismissal of my girlfriend. In Stevie's usual circles it's quite normal to send a woman out into the night to make her own way home when she becomes inconvenient.

We might have made it, but for a sudden and uncharacteristic flash of insight from Brad. "I remember Molly. How are you doing, love?" He beams at the pair of us from his station by the kitchen table, my bread knife in his meaty paw. "Are you still at Armley?"

Stevie comes bolt upright. "Armley? What do you mean, fucking Armley?"

"This is Molly. Miss MacBride as was. From G wing. You look different out of uniform, I almost didn't recognise you."

"Uniform? You mean this slag was a fucking officer." Stevie gets to his feet and grabs the shotgun. He stalks toward us, chin jutting forward as he glares at Molly. His next words are aimed at me. "Are you fucking mad or just plain desperate? You're bedding a bleeding screw!" The biting contempt in his tone would be laughable if our situation was not so dire.

"Brad's dreaming, as usual. Molly makes jewellery." Short of other strategies I still try to brazen it out, though I'm far from optimistic at this recent turn of events.

Brad shakes his head as he butters another slice of wholemeal. "Never forget a face, me. I'm known for it. She was at Armley all right, used to bring the breakfast trays round."

Apparently that's proof enough for Stevie. "You, sit down over there." He brandishes the barrel of the shotgun in Molly's face. "You too." He prods me in the stomach with the weapon. We do as he says.

"Mikey, you tie these two up. I need to think what to do about her." Stevie is pacing, confused and far from happy. Molly and I exchange a glance, our expressions in perfect harmony. An agitated idiot with a loaded gun, such a bad combination.

"Is she still a screw?" Stevie leans on the table, glaring at Molly.

I answer for her, abandoning our ill-fated cover story. "No, not for years. You know that."

"How would I fucking know?"

"You'd have seen her. You're only just out, yes?"

He narrows his eyes and nods. "Right, so how do you two know each other then?"

"We met recently, by chance. She *is* my girlfriend."

"Fucking whore." Stevie quirks his lip in a vicious snarl. "All of them, fucking slags."

"Nah, she was always nice enough." Brad starts carving up my halloumi. "Sit down and leave the lass alone."

Stevie responds with another obscene observation to the world at large but does at least resume his seat. He continues to regard both Molly and me with unrelenting loathing as he caresses the barrel of his shotgun. Meanwhile Mikey has managed to procure a length of what appears to be washing line from somewhere and he proceeds to secure Molly's wrists at the back of her chair. I weigh up the likelihood of that gun being loaded or not as he turns to tie me up too. If I'm to make a move it has to be now.

I can't risk it. I sit quietly while Mikey wraps the rope around my wrists as well.

CHAPTER THIRTEEN

I remember Brad and Stevie too. I recognised the pair of them as soon as I entered the kitchen. The third man, Mikey, is a stranger to me.

There's a lull in proceedings as the three intruders help themselves to food from Jared's fridge. They have little to say to one another, at least not until their stomachs are full, so I have a respite in which to process what seems to be going on.

These men were here yesterday, that much is clear. And they're on the run. The pile of cash on the table is the proceeds of some robbery that took place today, but I get the impression there's more to all this, something I don't know about, something else that happened before today's raid and was the reason for their earlier visit. Jared clearly doesn't want them in his home but that might be just because of me, of what I might see and hear. I can tell there's no love lost between him and this lot, but he's involved somehow. They knew of this place and clearly expected to find sanctuary here.

I was convinced Jared was no longer involved in anything even vaguely criminal. I absolutely believed that. Why would he? He has so much to lose—a new, successful career, wealth, a family. His freedom. None of this makes sense. I might have decided to trust Jared with my submission, but what if he's not after all the man I thought he was? The tang of disappointment and betrayal is bitter. I swallow down my dismay and will myself to remain calm.

Someone will come, they have to. These men just robbed a security van, for Christ's sake, the police must be right behind them. It's only a matter of time.

The dangerous one is Stevie Horrocks. He was always volatile, a tiny intellect driven by arrogance and resentment, a sense that the world owed him something and the usual rules didn't apply to him. He spent most of the time I knew him on basic, only getting transferred onto the relative luxury of G wing a few days before that riot which changed everything for me. And now he sits across from me, glowering and cradling a double barrel shotgun.

"I need a piss." Stevie gets to his feet and passes the gun to Mikey. "Keep an eye on those two. Any pratting about, you know what to do."

"Sure, mate," agrees Mikey, his companionable smile deceptively benign.

Stevie lumbers out into the hallway as Brad starts to arrange the heap of cash into neat piles. He shoves the remains of their meal aside to create the space he needs.

"If you untie me, I can clear this lot away and help you to count," offers Jared.

"Shut it, you. You heard what Stevie said." Mikey lowers his brows and regards Jared with suspicion. "Neither of you is to shift. I've got the gun, so you just do as Stevie said, right?"

Jared shrugs. "Fair enough, I was just offering. So, does anyone fancy a drink?"

Brad looks up from his task, his face brightening. "What have you got? Any beer left?"

"I can do better than that. Best Russian vodka, came off the back of a lorry. There are two cases in the garage."

I'm nervous enough as it is with just the shotgun and

three hardened criminals to worry about. Add a few bottles of dodgy vodka to the mix and someone's sure to get hurt. I turn to the man tied up beside me. "Jared, I don't think—"

"It's okay, sweetheart, we've got plenty." He returns his attention to the huge man with the gun. "I know you like a drop, Mikey. Do you want me to go get it, or shall I just tell you where it is?"

"Stevie said—"

"Stevie's probably having his own party and decided not to share with you. Go on, where's the harm?"

"Well, I don't know… good stuff did you say? Genuine Russian?"

"From Putin's private collection." Jared smiles broadly at the man, who is clearly tempted if somewhat puzzled.

"Whose collection?"

"Never mind, believe me, it's the good stuff. Come on, I'll show you. You can bring the gun along. Stevie won't mind if we both go, and Brad can keep an eye on Molly. You'll be okay here, won't you, Brad?"

"Sure, no problem. Me and Molly can get reacquainted."

Jared catches my gaze and offers me a reassuring smile. "He's harmless," he mouths, for my attention alone.

I'm nowhere close to being convinced, but Mikey is already loosening the rope fastening Jared to his chair. As soon as Jared is free Mikey picks up the shotgun and jabs it in the direction of the door. "Right, hurry up, you. We need to get back in here before Stevie comes back."

It seems to have escaped his thinking that Stevie will cotton to what's happened the moment he catches sight of the vodka. Jared grins at him and leads the way.

"So, what are you doing these days?" Brad seems to consider it incumbent on him to make small talk with the woman tied up beside him. He continues to gather the crumpled notes into neat little bundles as he speaks.

"I make jewellery. Jared told you."

"Oh, right. What, diamonds and all that shit?"

"No. Costume stuff, ethnic designs. I use a lot of copper, and leather. And beads."

He looks up from his task, clearly unimpressed. "Yeah? Right."

Happily that seems to be the extent of Brad's social repertoire. He resumes his counting and ignores me so we spend the next few minutes seated in silence. The peace is shattered when Stevie marches back in and spots Jared's empty chair.

"Where the fuck did North get to? I said he was to stay put. Where's Mikey?" He casts his gaze about the room as though the pair of them might be secreted behind a cupboard or under the table. He even looks in the fridge!

"Chill, man. They just went to get some booze. Look, there they are." Brad gestures to the door as Jared precedes Mikey back into the kitchen. Jared's carrying a box labelled in a language I assume to be Russian, whilst Mikey still totes the weapon.

"What the fuck's going on? What part of 'don't move' don't you fucking understand?" Stevie is nose to nose with Jared, so close he sprays him with spittle as he speaks.

Jared is commendably unruffled by the outburst or the unfortunate spittle shower. "Hey, it's okay, mate. We just went to grab a few bottles. We might as well make a night of it. Plenty to celebrate, wouldn't you say?" He nods at the piles of cash. "You guys had a good day's work."

"I thought you wanted none of it. You chucked us out of here and told us not to fucking come back. If you think you're getting a cut now—"

Jared grins and waves away his protests. "No, mate, you earned it. I just wanted to be a bit more sociable, help you to celebrate." Jared dumps the vodka on a spare corner of the table and heads off to a cupboard to collect five glasses. He puts them on the table too.

Stevie peers at the glasses, mouthing the number as he counts them. Then he looks round the room, assessing the company assembled, and at last works it out. "She's not havin' none. I'm not drinking with no screw, especially a bent screw." Stevie jabs his finger in my direction, as though there might be some confusion over exactly who he means.

"I'm not bent." I should perhaps keep my mouth shut, but that accusation stings, not least because I'm not especially proud of my unprofessional behaviour in the past. But corrupt—never.

"No? How come you're fuckin' an ex-con then? And it's not even normal fucking…" Stevie turns to include his companions in his accusations. "I've been having a look around, and there's all sorts of porn on the walls in the attic. These two are into all that kinky stuff—whips and leather, all that." He turns back to me, his leer nauseating. "I bet you even kept your own special handcuffs, brought 'em with you from Armley, didn't you, slag?"

Brad shrugs. "Each to their own. I don't mind a spot of the old pervy stuff myself. Rachel always liked to—"

"Shut it, or the next time you see your teeth you'll be shitting them out your arse," Jared snarls at Brad, lunging for him, fists clenched.

Brad clearly sees the error of his ways and backs off, his hands raised. "Hey, sorry, man. No offence meant. You know I always thought a lot of your Rachel and even though we're not together anymore, well… I meant nothing."

"Just leave my sister out of this, arsehole. It beggars belief that she ever married a slug like you, but at least she saw sense eventually." Jared is still glowering at Brad, but seems less inclined to punch him in the mouth. Marginally.

"Pack it in, all of you." Stevie seeks to regain control. "You, sit down." He jabs his finger at Jared. "And you…" he turns to Brad, now moving to retake his seat at the table, "you finish sharing that lot out. Half's mine, you and Mikey split the rest."

"Hey," Mikey's the one taking issue now, his resolve perhaps fortified by the generous shot of vodka he has just poured and downed while the others were arguing over my and Rachel's sexual preferences. "How come you get most?

We never agreed that. It's equal shares."

"Is it fuck equal shares," sneers Stevie. "Since when did you do the thinking in this fucking team? I come up with the ideas, you just do as you're told and you can think yourself lucky to get a pay day at all."

"Yeah? Well if you're so smart, how come we're holed up here? We could all end up back inside, and it'll be your fucking fault." Mikey grabs the gun and waves it at Stevie. "We get fair shares, or I'm out of here."

"You're going nowhere till I say so. Half the North Yorkshire rozzers are out there looking for us and I'm not having you screwing it all up for me by getting yourself lifted. You're just a fucking half-wit, you couldn't wipe your own fucking arse without me to help."

"Who are you calling half-wit? You'll get the same as that bitch in the garage if you don't shut your fucking mouth." Mikey levels the gun at Stevie, peering at him down the barrels.

"Fucking moron. It's not me you should be worrying about, it's her." Stevie points at me and he advances toward Mikey. "She's the bent copper who'll grass all of us up given half a chance, her and this soft pussy she's fucking with the fancy house and ponsy car. The one who thinks he's too good for his old mates, but has plenty of time for a skank like this one."

Mikey lowers the gun, but only so he can take another swig of the vodka. Jared advances toward him, his expression grim, but Mikey points the gun right at his chest and cocks the trigger. Jared halts, standing stock still.

"Hey, now let's all just calm down." Jared's tone is low, intended to defuse the situation. "We don't want anyone getting hurt here, do we?"

"She's gonna get hurt," Stevie snarls. "I hate fucking screws and there's no way she's telling anyone about this."

"She won't say anything, I'll make sure of that. Just let me and Molly go, and you three can stay here as long as you need to."

Stevie gives a mirthless laugh. "Yeah, right. Do you think I'm fucking stupid? You'll be on the phone to the law before you get halfway down the drive. Not happening." He turns to glare at me. "We'll hang on to your little fuck-toy as long as she's useful. We might need a hostage and the police won't want to risk her getting hurt. She's one of theirs. Then when we're done, we waste her. You too, fancy boy. There'll be no one telling tales."

"Never mind all that, what about my share." Mikey's still quaffing vodka, and clearly having trouble shifting his focus from the subject most taxing him. "I want half. It was me who dealt with the guards, I did the most work and took all the risks. You just grabbed the cash and legged it."

Mikey still has the gun, and he raises it again. This time his target is Stevie. Jared shifts to the side, moving closer to me. I see alarm flare in his dark grey eyes.

"Either put the fucking gun down or give it to me. Shit, how fucking dense can you be?" Stevie makes to grab the firearm, then everything happens at once.

The gun goes off, the sound deafening in the enclosed space of the kitchen. There's a shriek, someone's screaming. It sounds like me.

Jared dives the remaining couple of yards to hit my chair sideways just as the sound of another shot deafens me momentarily. The pair of us topple to the floor. I'm winded, he's on top of me.

There's silence.

Total, deathly silence.

Long moments pass. No one moves. My heart is thumping, but that's a good sign, I'm alive at least. I try to move, but I'm still tied to the chair, though Jared has rolled from me and now lies face down on the floor. I wriggle, starting to panic. Something shifts. I'm free, sort of. The rail at the back of my chair was broken in the fall and I have some movement, enough at least for me to sit up and look around.

"Fuck! Fuck, man, what have you done? What the fuck

did you do that for?" Brad lurches past me to crouch beside the inert form that is Jared. He rolls him over to reveal the growing stain of brilliant crimson spreading across the front of Jared's T shirt. Mikey struggles to his feet to stand over Jared, his expression stunned, vacant.

I start to whimper, under no illusions that I'm not next. Neither man seems to notice me though, as they both turn to investigate the other body lying on the kitchen floor. Stevie's eyes are open, sightless, already glazing over. His expression in death reminds me, bizarrely, of the trout Jared showed me earlier.

"Come on, we need to be out of here."

"What about her? Stevie said—"

"Leave her. You emptied both cartridges anyway. Get the cash and we're gone." Brad's already tossing the bundles back into the rucksack. It's the work of moments to clear the table, then he sprints for the door without looking back. Mikey gazes around the room, helpless, utterly bewildered. He lumbers after his friend.

Seconds later an engine starting up outside penetrates my muddled thoughts. The sound grows as they accelerate down the drive, then dies away to nothing and silence blankets the scene again.

I have to get free. They killed Stevie, their friend, and for all I know they might return to murder me too. And I need to know if Jared's alive, though I don't see how he can be. He was shot at point blank range. Desperate, determined, I struggle and writhe on the kitchen floor, and manage to get one hand loose. It's enough. I drag myself, chair and all, over to the cutlery drawer and reach up to drag it out and onto the floor. I choose the sharpest knife I can see from those now scattered around me and saw at my remaining bonds. Seconds later I'm kneeling beside Jared, weeping.

I lay my fingers on his neck, feeling for a pulse. There's nothing. I can't accept that, it can't be true. I grab his shoulders, give him a shake, then try again.

There's a flutter, faint, but there's something. I'm sure I

felt something that time. I start to call his name, shaking him harder. After what seems like ages but must only be a few seconds, his eyelids flutter and he looks up at me. His lips are moving, he's saying something. I lean in to hear.

"Phone a fucking ambulance."

• • • • • • •

I crack my eyelids apart, only to have my retinas seared by bright, white light. For one fanciful moment I imagine I might be in heaven, but the rapid electronic beeping coming from somewhere close at hand eradicates that possibility, even if I had been a suitable candidate for eternal paradise.

No, hell on earth better describes my situation, evidenced primarily by the sharp, stabbing pain in my side. I shift, hissing in a sharp gasp as the discomfort spears upwards. It takes my breath away for a few moments.

I concentrate on lying still as a wave of nausea adds to my problems, washing over me then slowly dissipating. I try to think through it all, to make sense of whatever might be going on around me, though I've yet to summon up the fortitude to open my eyes and take a look.

What happened? Where am I? What's making that fucking awful noise?

And why do I feel like shit?

"Nurse, I think he moved."

I know that voice. I've heard it before, recently.

"He's coming round."

I rummage around among the tangle of chaotic images that seem to fill my memory right now and latch onto something. Someone.

Molly. That's Molly's voice. She's here, close to me, and that knowledge fills me with something akin to elation.

I fumble around, blindly reaching for her, only to have her cool, slender fingers suddenly encircle my own. I try to squeeze her hand, but again it is she who is the strong one now. She grips my feeble hand between both of hers and presses hard.

"Jared? Can you hear me? Nurse, look at that, his hand moved. It did, didn't it?"

"Aye, it did." A different voice now, a male, quite youthful, I think. "May I?"

Molly's welcome touch is replaced by another, equally gentle but more business-like. The nurse is taking my pulse. Next he shoves something cold against my chest, a stethoscope no doubt. Time to re-join the land of the living.

I apply my concentrated efforts to opening my eyes, forewarned this time about the bright lighting I'll encounter. Willing my eyelids to remain open I manage to squint around me, and make out Molly's silhouette against the backdrop of the harsh hospital illumination. I smile, I think, open my mouth to say something but all that emerges is a low croak. A movement catches my eye. I turn to see a male nurse scribbling notes on a clipboard, which he hangs on the foot of my bed. He looks up at me, his smile pleasant enough.

"Welcome back, Mr. North." He moves around the bed to lean over me. "How do you feel?"

"Fucking awful." Just about sums it up, I'd say.

"I see. Do you have any pain?"

I nod.

"Can you tell me where it hurts?"

"Everywhere." I grimace and shift in an attempt to bring Molly back into my sphere of vision, which sends more white-hot spears of agony shooting through me. "Fuck, what happened?"

"You were shot. In the side." Molly fills in the gap, though my own recollections are now starting to pour in. I remember being in my kitchen, Mikey holding the shotgun and arguing with Stevie. Mikey'd been drinking—my fault, I gave him vodka—but he was becoming belligerent and turning on Stevie. The situation was fast spiralling out of control.

Mikey shot Stevie. I recall that with startling clarity, and

I know that Stevie's dead. Then Mikey seemed to become disoriented, he didn't know what he was doing. Molly was there, too, tied to a chair. She screamed when the shooting started. Mikey turned to look at her, the weapon still in his hands. He was pointing it at her, and there was one barrel left.

I hurled myself at Molly to send her to the floor, but the gun went off before I made it. I took the shot in my ribs, and that's the last I remember until a few moments ago.

"I'll get the doctor to adjust your pain relief. We'll soon have you more comfortable, Mr. North. Would you like a drink of water?" The nurse's calm efficiency is reassuring. I might be writhing in agony, but he seems unconcerned and I suppose he's a better judge than I.

I nod again, testing my parched lips with the tip of my tongue. This time it's Molly who stands to attend to my needs. She pours fresh water into one of those invalid cups they use in hospitals, plastic beakers with a lid and a spout, then she puts it to my lips and tilts it.

Baby cup aside, the cool water feels wonderful as it slithers down my throat. I swallow, then suck in some more. Molly removes the cup and dabs at my lips with a piece of tissue.

"Do you want more?" she asks, her expression still apprehensive. Perhaps I'm not out of danger after all.

"Yes," I manage. My throat feels to be made of sandpaper.

Molly holds the cup to my mouth again, and this time I take several long draughts before finally twisting my face away, sated. I glance around the room to find the young nurse has left.

"He went to find the doctor. You're going to be okay though, they already said that."

I close my eyes, relieved. I hadn't been certain of anything, except for the fact that I didn't want it all to be over with Molly. I want her, I need her, and if I'm to have her I need time.

If she'll still have me. Christ, what must she think?

And what was I thinking of, ever allowing the situation to arise?

I open my eyes again to find her gazing at me. She's been crying, I notice, perhaps she still is.

"The police want to talk to you. They're outside. The doctor won't let them in just yet. Rachel's on her way, as soon as she can find someone to mind the kids. She said she's contacted someone called Charles and he's on his way too."

Ah, yes, good old Rachel. Trust her to phone my lawyer before anything else. The interview with the police is inevitable really, and there's not much point delaying it once my brief arrives, but first I want to get my head around the situation as it now stands.

"Where are Mikey and Brad?"

"In jail. They were picked up about two hours after they left, only got as far as Pateley Bridge. Apparently the van they stole had hardly any petrol in it, so they abandoned it about two miles down the road and ended up on foot. The police dogs did the rest."

I heave a sigh of relief. At least that danger is safely out of the way. "What about you? Were you hurt?"

Molly shakes her head. "Unless you count shattered eardrums. My head was ringing for hours after that gun went off." She pauses, then, "Thanks to you. He would have fired at me, he was going to. He did, but you…"

"Don't, Molly. It's over."

"You saved my life. And it almost got you killed."

"It was me who almost got you killed. I'm sorry, truly I am. I should never have let you come to the barn, not while that lot were still hanging around."

"But why were they there? That's what the police are wanting to know too. They asked me loads of questions, wanting to know how you were involved in the robberies."

"What did you tell them?"

"The truth, or as much of it as I know. I heard Stevie

199

and the others talking about robbing that security van and I saw Mikey fire at Stevie. But I gather they shot someone else too, a girl, last week."

"I know," I groan. Molly's shocked expression is almost more than I can bear. "I should have turned them in straight away."

"You knew? I don't understand. Why didn't you call the police? Was it because of Brad? I know he's your brother-in-law."

"Ex-brother-in-law. And no, it wasn't that. It's complicated."

"It must be, because I can't understand it at all and I'm usually fairly sharp. Why did you let them hide out at your barn if you knew what they'd done?" Her eyes glint, her temper starting to rise and replace the concern and anguish of just a few moments ago. "Jared, they were dangerous, desperate. Attempted murder. Robbery. I thought you'd put all that behind you."

"Me too." Another voice, Rachel this time. She glares at me from the open doorway. "I thought you were going to turn them in if Charles agreed. He told me that's what he advised you to do."

"You've been speaking to Charles?" A stupid question; it's clear she has. Typical reaction in my family; at the first sniff of police interest we consult our lawyer.

"Who's Charles?" demands Molly.

Rachel comes right into the room to position herself at the foot of my bed. "Our solicitor. The best criminal defence lawyer in Yorkshire. I'd have thought this moron might listen to him. He told you to contact the police, tell them what you knew about the robbery and Stevie and Brad's whereabouts. He said you had a cast-iron alibi and he could have pleaded a decent defence for the accessory after the fact problem. He reckoned he could have kept you out of jail."

"Jail? Why should Jared end up back inside? I don't understand." Molly's startled gaze swivels between the pair of us.

"It was in the terms of my parole, not to associate with previous criminal contacts. And I never did, not until a few days ago. Even then, they came looking for me. I wanted nothing to do with them and I slung them out after a couple of days. I swear though, I didn't know about the shooting at that garage until after they left and I phoned Rachel to warn her they might show up at hers. Then I intended to tell the police, but…"

"But?" Molly appears less than impressed with my excuses.

"But, Rachel persuaded me to hang fire. She was worried I might be implicated in the robbery, or be arrested as an accessory because I let them hide out at my place. I spoke to Charles just before I picked you up at the station and after hearing what he had to say I was confident that he could help me convince a court if it came to that. It wasn't that I was worried I might go down with them. My head knew it was the right thing to do, and I would have contacted the police that same day. I held back because I wanted to explain it to you before I got anyone else involved but events moved too fast and…"

"So you weren't expecting them to come back?"

"Hell, no!" *What the fuck?* "Christ, I'd never have let that happen, not with you there. It was a knocking bet at least one of them would remember you, and then… shit."

"They thought I was a bent officer. Maybe they were right. I mean, we did—"

"Officer? What's all this?" Now it's Rachel's turn to be confused. "What is it you're not telling me? Both if you?"

I gesture to the one spare chair in the clinical little room. "Sit down. This is going to take a while."

By the time Molly and Rachel are both fully in the picture, and the nurse has made good on his promise to sort out my meds and has succeeded in getting my pain down to manageable proportions, Charles has arrived. I'm ready to face the police interrogation.

Although my injuries aren't life-threatening, the consultant insists I have to remain in hospital for a few more days at least, so they have no option but to speak to me here. This is infinitely preferable to an interview room down at the local nick. I remember those places, not at all pleasant, though the tea is marginally better than that supplied on the NHS. Naturally, Charles is in attendance to work his customary magic, and by the time I've agreed to give evidence against Mikey and Brad in court the police appear content, though the final decision rests with the Crown Prosecution Service. My so-called heroic actions to protect Molly are going to stand me in good stead, though privately I suspect I shall never forgive myself for almost getting her killed.

The question is, will she forgive me?

CHAPTER FOURTEEN

"Are you sure you're up to this? We can always leave in a few more days." I peer at Jared from across the breakfast table. He's been out of hospital for over seven months now, but I know his injury is uncomfortable at times. The moorland hike we are contemplating will be taxing to say the least.

He grins at me over his coffee cup. "I'm fine. Good as new. But this weather won't last and by the weekend the whole area's going to be teeming with day trippers. If you want to do this with the sun on your back and without an interested audience, today's the day. Come to think of it, the audience would be a seriously bad idea. I can do without a public indecency charge on top of everything else." Jared gets up to deposit his empty mug in the sink then pulls the zip around on the case of expensive photographic equipment and hoists it over his shoulder. He holds out his hand to me. "Dancing Bear?"

I nod. "Yes. The Dancing Bear."

We make the trek up the rolling moorland hill in near silence. The late spring sunshine is warm and we're both glowing by the time we crest the first rise. We continue on through the swaying pale green of the ferns just now emerging from last year's bracken, and the patches of new heather that are yet to take on their vivid purple glow. Around us the sheep regard us with suspicion, keeping a safe distance as their lambs charge back and forth in rowdy gangs, bleating at the top of their just-born lungs.

I love it here. I can't even start to work out why I thought I might like to live in London. I tighten my grip on Jared's hand as we climb higher.

Eventually the Dancing Bear comes into sight. We pause, and I look up at Jared. His eyes are narrowed as he assesses the scene, glances skyward to evaluate the light quality, then down at me.

"Second thoughts?" He lifts one eyebrow.

"Are you sure no one's going to see us?" I turn to gaze back the way we came. The hillside is deserted but for the noisy lambs and their harried-looking mothers.

Jared shrugs. "I doubt it, but that's the risk you take for art."

"This isn't art. This is just kink."

"Philistine." He leers at me. "Come on, we need to get shifting before the light changes. I want to capture you silhouetted against the rock with the sun behind you."

We stride out again, and reach the Dancing Bear a few minutes later. Jared wastes no time in crouching to unpack the gear he intends to use. He selects his camera, a couple of tripods, various other bits and pieces with functions I'm not certain of, and a long length of rope.

"Get undressed, Molly. Apart from your shoes. You can keep those until we're ready to take the shots. Oh, and keep the pretty underwear for now." He straightens and leaves me to obey his commands as he heads off in the direction of the rock, the rope slung over his shoulder.

I slip off my snug hoodie, then my thick hiking top. Underneath I'm wearing a bright crimson bra, which I leave, as per my instructions. I have to take off my stout walking boots to get my jeans off. I peel off my socks too before shoving my feet back into the boots. I fold everything neatly then leave my clothes next to Jared's bag and follow him over to the rock.

By the time I get there Jared has the rope loosely circling the rock. He ties it in a slipknot and pulls the loop tight to form what looks almost like a rope belt around the bear's waist, about six feet from the ground.

"That should do. Now for you, Molly mine. Hold out your hands."

I do as I'm told, and Jared produces a pair of soft leather cuffs from his pocket. He fastens them around each of my wrists.

"Stand by the bear. Lean against the rock, your back to it and your arms above your head." His tone has lowered, his commands clipped and stern. Gone now is the playful, affectionate companion of just moments ago, his eyes glint with an intensity that demands my obedience. When he looks at me like this, speaks to me in that quiet, modulated tone, something flips over in the pit of my stomach. Already my pussy is becoming wet. Despite the spring sunshine I know that lump of rock will be cold against my naked skin but it never occurs to me to protest. Instead I pick my way over the remaining few yards of grass and rest my bare shoulders against it.

Jared nods. "That's good. Now lift your chin up, watch me."

Already he's looking at me through the camera, striding this way and that, clicking away, his expression intent as he captures various angles.

"Good. Turn to face the left, arm up higher. Great. Now the right. Chin up, tits out. Show me what's mine, girl."

I twist and turn, eager to obey, wanting to please him. He continues to take picture after picture, occasionally returning to his bag to select a different piece of equipment. I know better than to relax or move out of position.

Gooseflesh has sprung up all over my body and my nipples press against the fabric of my bra as they swell in response to the distinct chill in the air. I turn to face the rock when Jared twirls his finger to indicate that I should.

"Bend over and place your hands on the stone, push your bottom out for me." He's crouching behind me, angling a shot from below. My thong barely covers my pussy, but it's all I have right now. "Spread your legs. Wider. Wider still, girl." I move my feet as far apart as I can, sinking into a familiar haze of obedient acceptance, the perfect submissive.

"That's great." More clicking. "Now pull your thong to the side. Show me your pussy. I want to see how wet you are."

"I *am* wet, sir. And cold." As if any of that would make a difference.

"Good. Show me."

I lean on one hand as I use the other to draw the narrow strip of lace to the side, my pussy lips wet and swollen and now fully exposed for the camera.

"Ah, such a slut. Do you want me to fuck you?"

"Yes, sir. Always."

"Soon." I hear more clicking and I'm aware of Jared moving behind me. "You can stand up now and take everything off."

"Yes, sir." I straighten, relaxing my straining muscles for the few seconds it takes to unfasten my bra and slide my thong down my legs. I kick off my boots then step out.

"Pass your things to me."

I hand over my clothes and Jared takes them over to the pile I folded up earlier. He regards me under his lowered brows as he attaches a camera to the tripod and adjusts the angle to his liking. Apparently satisfied, he returns to me.

"Back against the rock, please."

I move into position and he takes each of my wrists in turn, then uses the cuffs he attached earlier to clip them to the rope he fastened around the standing stone. He stands back to peruse my nude form now lashed tight against the frigid surface of the rock.

"Fucking gorgeous. Are you still cold, Molly?" He idly

trials the backs of his knuckles over one pebbled nipple.

"Yes, sir."

"Thought so." He rolls the turgid nub between his finger and thumb, then squeezes until I let out a gasp. My pussy is spasming wildly as my arousal starts to spike.

Jared smiles at me, though without warmth. He releases my nipple and strides back to the tripod to make further adjustments. Then he sets up another smaller stand about a metre in front of my left foot. The camera he secures onto that stand is pointing up, and I know exactly where he will focus it.

"Lift your leg up and out to the side if you can. I want to get a good, clear shot here."

"You know what my pussy looks like. Why do you want a picture?"

"Maybe I'll keep a photo in my wallet."

"Yes, sir. If you want to."

He straightens and comes to stand in front of me. "Ready?"

I nod.

He leans in to kiss me. "Let's do this, then." He turns on his heel and returns first to the camera on the upright tripod, then to the one angled at my pussy. He triggers the timers on each, then comes back to plant his hands on either side of my head. He kisses me again as the cameras whir merrily behind him.

He reaches for my left knee and lifts it, higher than I could on my own. He pushes my knee out to expose my pussy to the camera, then uses his other hand to drive two fingers deep inside me.

"Oh, God," I moan, lifting my chin to expose my throat.

He nibbles and kisses his way down the length of my throat and down to my left breast, then takes that nipple between his lips. He sucks hard, all the while finger-fucking me as I squeeze around his hand.

I'm vaguely conscious of the rhythmic hum from the cameras as they take shot after shot, but far more focused on what he's doing to me. He drives his digits in and out, hard and fast. I start to climax, but a growled 'no' puts a stop to that.

"Sir?" Pleading never works, but I usually try it anyway.

"Make as much noise as you like, Molly. There's no one here but me. If you come without permission I'll clamp your nipples for the rest of the day."

The threat works. He knows I love spanking so he doesn't use that for discipline as a rule, but I really dislike being clamped, especially if he makes me continue about my daily routine with my nipples pressed between the clovers he usually keeps for punishment.

"I'm sorry, sir."

"I know." He drops to his knees in front of me and places my foot on his shoulder, angling his own body so as not to obstruct the camera's line of sight. His fingers are still inside me. With his free hand he peels back the hood shrouding my clit and blows on the sensitive bud.

"I'm going to lick your clit, then suck it. You'll remain calm and still for one minute, then you can come if you want to."

If?

"Yes, sir. Thank you."

He uses the flat of his tongue to press against my clit, licking from base to tip. I shiver, though no longer with the cold. He repeats the teasing torture, then flicks the tip several times from each side.

I grind my teeth together as the waves of sensation build, becoming more intense as he circles my helpless clit with his tongue. He scissors his fingers inside me, then twists his hand to press on my most vulnerable spot. He starts to rub, just light at first then increasing the pressure.

He slides his hand behind me to push my hips forward, then closes his lips around my clit. As the suction starts my knees give way. If he hadn't secured me to this rock I would crumple, boneless, to the ground among the ferns and heather.

I lose track of time. None of that matters anyway; he'll tell me when I can come. I'll wait, if I can. If he allows it. He has only to apply just a fraction more pressure, suck on my clit just that little bit harder, and I'll be gone.

I groan, my body coiling up to betray me. I tip my head back and gaze up at the blue of the sky, my mouth open as I drag in precious oxygen. It's all over. I'm past caring.

"Okay, Molly. Come when you like."

"Sir?" I whisper. "Is it…?"

"Yes. Time's up. You did well."

He returns his attention to my quivering clit and scrapes it with his teeth before pressing his tongue against the tip. He licks, long and slow, and I scream as my orgasm rips through me.

Long moments pass. My world spins. I convulse, shudder, and clamp my inner muscles around his fingers as he drags out my release as long as possible. The waiting is awful, always, but the reward is truly exquisite.

At last it's over. I'm trembling, dangling by my wrists from the rock, utterly sated. Jared kneels before me as I gaze at him through slitted eyes.

"Did I tell you how very photogenic you are, little slut?"

"No, sir. I don't believe you did."

"Remiss of me. Did I mention how fuckable you are? Surely I didn't forget to say that."

"I don't recall it if you did, sir."

He stands and takes my chin between his hands. "Liar." He kisses me. "But actions speak louder than words."

"True, sir. And you can't take photographs of words." The cameras are still whirring somewhere out of my sight.

"There is that." He opens his jeans to let his cock spring free, then lifts both my legs to wrap them around his waist. "Grit your teeth, Molly. This is going to be hard and fast."

He drives his cock into my wet pussy without further preamble, each stroke angling deep, each thrust plastering my body back against the rock face. His forearms are behind my neck, which prevents me from banging my head but other than that he gives no quarter as he pounds into me.

"Sir, I need to come."

"Me too, sweetheart."

"Sir, I love you."

He slows, though only marginally, and covers my mouth with his. The kiss is rough, demanding. He winds strands of my hair around his fingers to angle my face as he deepens the connection between us. He plunges his tongue into my mouth. My breasts are pressed against the thick linen of his shirt. His cock is buried deep inside me. Every part of me is his and he knows it. I know it, and I would have it no other way.

He breaks the kiss to rest his forehead against mine.

"I love you too, Molly MacBride."

"It's not just about the sex, is it?" I'm whispering, hoping.

"It never was."

My pussy clenches and he pulls back. He waits, his cock poised at my entrance.

I manage to lift my head and meet his intense grey gaze. "No, sir. It never was."

"Good answer, Molly." He sinks his cock deep into me again, and I convulse around him.

• • • • • • •

Jared helps me back into my clothes, then dismantles his equipment. As he unties the rope from around the Dancing Bear's waist we hear voices. Two hikers crest the hill, their faces red from the exertion of the climb up here. Undaunted by their efforts they march past us, offering a polite nod and the observation that it's a lovely day. That's the usual greeting around here, and Jared returns it automatically.

"That was close," I murmur, as they disappear from sight.

Jared shrugs. "It would have been worth it though. We got some great shots."

"What will you do with the pictures?"

"Well, there's always the National Trust shop…"

"Don't you dare!"

He grins at me as he coils the rope and shoves that back in the bag. "For my eyes only, then, Molly mine." He holds out his hand to me again. "Home?"

I nod and fall in beside him. "Yes, home."

EPILOGUE

"Will the foreperson of the jury please stand."

At the judge's calm command, the middle-aged woman closest to the bench rises briskly to her feet. She tilts up her chin to meet the stern gaze of the bewigged individual peering down at her, looking almost as nervous as I feel. Oddly, Jared appears to be the most relaxed person present as he regards proceedings from his vantage point in the dock.

"Have you reached a verdict upon which you are all agreed?"

"Yes." The response is clear, definite. The jury have taken just two and a half hours to deliberate and reach their conclusion. I have no idea if this is a good sign or not, but the brief non-verbal exchange between Charles Manners and the barrister engaged to defend Jared suggests they are confident of the outcome.

"On the first count in the indictment, that of conspiracy to commit robbery, do you find the defendant guilty or not guilty?"

"Not guilty, my lord."

I heave a sigh of relief. The conspiracy accusation was the most serious charge, the prosecution having tried to argue that Jared was aware of Stevie and Brad's intention to rob the security van and participated in the planning of the offence as well as harbouring the gang afterwards. Our barrister shredded that claim, and I would have been astonished if the verdict had gone any other way. Still, until it's over, it isn't.

The judge offers a brief nod and makes a note on the sheet before him. He peers down at the forewoman again.

"On the second count in the indictment, that of being an accessory after the fact, do you find the defendant guilty or not guilty?"

"Guilty, my lord."

Stunned, dismayed, I stare across the court at Jared, who stands perfectly still in the dock. Flanked by two security guards, he grips the rail in front of him then raises his eyes to look straight at me. He meets my gaze and offers the hint of a smile. It's an attempt to reassure me. It fails utterly.

"Thank you, ladies and gentlemen of the jury."

The forewoman retakes her seat as the judge shuffles the pile of documents before him. Long moments pass before he fixes Jared with a dispassionate, assessing gaze.

"Jared David North, you have been found guilty of a serious charge. As a result of your failure to alert the proper authorities once you became aware that a serious crime had been committed, the perpetrators remained at large and a further serious offence took place. Lives were placed at risk. Indeed, there is every reason to suppose that had he been apprehended at an earlier stage Stephen George Horrocks might not have died. However, your legal representatives have made known the considerable efforts you made to alleviate the danger to others, and indeed your intervention probably saved the life of Miss MacBride."

The judge pauses and consults his notes once more. "You have testified that you were unaware of the use of firearms in the earlier offence, and of the injuries caused to an employee at the filling stain. This is corroborated by the evidence given by both co-defendants, and goes some way toward mitigating the offence. Your actions in defence of Miss MacBride are also factors in your favour, as is the career you have built for yourself in the years since your release from prison. I am convinced that with the exception of the current charge, yours has been an exemplary example of reform and rehabilitation. I am minded to take these factors into account in sentencing you for the offence of which you have been found guilty, but I should caution you that a custodial sentence would be usual in such circumstances. I will retire to consider the sentence."

The judge casts his stern gaze around the rest of the court. "We shall adjourn for two hours. Please reassemble here at…" he glances up at the clock on the back wall, "three-thirty this afternoon. I will pass sentence at that time."

The guards escort Jared from the dock and down the stairs to wait out the two hours in the cells beneath the court. He raises his hand in a salute to me as he descends out of sight.

I make my way out into the crowded central lobby area, the space milling with people. The various courtrooms that make up the combined courts in the centre of Leeds seem to be all adjourning for lunch at the same time so the space is teeming with wigs, gowns, men and women in sober business attire. The rest of us, those not directly involved in the legal professions, pack the various seating areas. I can readily pick out the defendants, uncomfortable in their smartest clothes but doing what they must to gain favour with those who might determine their fate. There are witnesses too, waiting their turn to give evidence, and occupants of the public galleries who are here to observe proceedings. Justice being seen to be done.

Rachel is beside me, and together we edge our way into an alcove by a window.

"It'll be all right," asserts Rachel. "It has to be."

I nod, silently praying that she's right. "The judge said a custodial sentence though. That means Jared's going to jail.

It's so unfair."

"He'll survive. He did before." Despite her seemingly callous words, I catch the quiver of her lip. We both know that a return to prison is a fate Jared was determined to avoid, and he so nearly made it. But for that bastard Stevie…

My thoughts return to the man who, at least in my opinion, got exactly what he deserved out of all of this. Stevie Horrocks would have killed me in a heartbeat, and probably Jared too. Whatever the judge might think, I doubt the world is any worse off for no longer having that particular individual taking up oxygen.

Mikey too got his just deserts. He's starting a life sentence for murder with a recommendation that he serve no less than twenty-two years. Brad was sentenced to fifteen years' imprisonment for his part in the two robberies, though he was found not guilty of murder. Rachel and the children appear unmoved by the prospect of his prolonged absence; he hadn't been a part of their lives for years in any case.

Rachel peers around the corner into the milling throng. "It's rammed in here. Shall we go out and find a coffee shop, maybe grab a sandwich or something?"

"Might as well." I'm not hungry, but some fresh air would be welcome.

We shoulder our way back through the crowd and out the main doors into the pedestrian area at the front. Rachel leads the way to a small bistro-style eatery around the corner where we order coffees and paninis and settle in for the wait.

At twenty past three we are back in the public gallery, seated in the front row. Charles and our barrister sit huddled together, conversing in low tones down in the main court. I wonder if they are already plotting the appeal but I say nothing, fearing I might jinx Jared's chances. The prosecution team sip coffee from paper cups, looking smug. They have the verdict they wanted.

Just before half past there's a clattering of feet and Jared appears back in the dock, his two guards bringing up the rear. At once he seeks out Rachel and me, and lifts his hand again in silent acknowledgement before taking his seat. The two legal teams take up their positions on the rows of tables and seating facing the raised-up bench, and we all await the reappearance of the Honourable Mister Justice Withers-Benson.

He is right on time, emerging through his private entrance at the front of the court. The court bailiff shouts "All rise," and everyone stands. We remain on our feet as the judge takes his time getting settled and arranges his papers to his satisfaction, then at a nod from his honour we all sink back into our seats.

"The defendant will rise." Again the court bailiff's censorious tone rings out. Jared stands up to face the bench.

His honour places his rimless glasses on his nose and peers at Jared over the top of them. He consults his notes once more, then folds his hands in his lap. The court sits in silence as he delivers his final remarks.

The judge's summing up amounts to a damning indictment of Jared's nefarious past and the company he has elected to keep in the weeks leading up to the offences. His comments are fair enough, I suppose, but my heart sinks. This is not going well. It seems Jared is not to be allowed to move on, he will always be seen as the criminal he once was. And judged accordingly.

The Honourable Mister Justice Withers-Benson is not finished, however. He goes on to praise once more Jared's efforts to forge a new and exemplary life for himself, and to reiterate his gallant actions in coming between me and almost certain death. In moments it seems Jared is transformed in the judge's estimation from a menace to society to become an upright pillar of the community, and a hero to boot. Things are looking up.

"Notwithstanding the factors in your favour, North, there can be no escaping the severity of the offences of which you have been convicted, and I have no alternative but to impose a custodial penalty. The verdict of this court therefore is that you will serve a period of two years' imprisonment…"

A gasp flitters around the court. Rachel lets out a sob. I am stunned, silent. Jared bows his head, resigned to what's to come.

Two years? Two fucking years!

The judge clears his throat again, then, "…the sentence to be suspended for the period of five years. You are free to go."

My jaw drops. Did I hear correctly? I lean forward over the rail at the front of the gallery, looking for clues from our team. Charles is down there, grinning from ear to ear and pumping the hand of our barrister. Beside me Rachel gets to her feet. Tears are streaming down her features as she waves to Jared. I watch, disbelieving, as one of the guards unlocks the gate at the side of the dock and gestures for him to pass. Jared steps down into the body of the court. He stops to speak briefly to Charles and shakes hands with the barrister, then makes for the exit.

"Come on, we'll meet him outside." Rachel grabs my arm and drags me from my seat. I stumble after her, my knees weak with relief.

At last, it's over. We can go home.

· · · · · · ·

"Are you sure you don't want to come back to the barn with us?" Rachel has phoned for a taxi and we are all three now standing on the steps outside the Combined Courts building in Leeds city centre. She shakes her head and checks her watch.

"It's after four already. I need to get back. The kids will be back from school and they'll want to know how it went. Plus, I have a pub to run."

A cab pulls up alongside us. Rachel kisses first Jared, then me and she hops inside. She opens the window and leans out. "We'll see you at the weekend, for Katie's party. Don't be late."

"We'll be there," confirms Jared as the taxi pulls away. "Wouldn't miss it."

I link arms with him as we stroll across the city centre in the direction of the multi-storey car park. "For a while back there I didn't think you'd be coming home today. Christ, when the judge went on and on about your criminal record…"

Jared chuckles. "Yeah, he laid it on a bit thick. Still, a suspended sentence, that's not too bad. It means I have to stay on the straight and narrow for the next few years though."

I purse my lips. "Mmm, maybe I need to impose a curfew, make sure you don't drift back into bad company."

A sharp slap to my bum is Jared's response. "And maybe I need to apply a paddle to your arse to remind you of the proper and respectful way to talk to your dom."

My pussy creams, the familiar clenching a promise of delights yet to come. In the months leading up to the trial I never let myself contemplate how much I'd miss this part of our lives, if Jared wasn't around.

"Just a paddle, sir?"

"To start with. I need to teach you some manners."

"I'm glad you're still here. Cote House Barn wouldn't have been the same without you."

"You'd have stayed, though?"

I moved in with Jared as soon as he was released from the hospital, at first because he needed someone to fetch and carry for him. Then, after he was back on his feet, I stayed because I wanted to. I gave up my flat in London after a few weeks, and colonised one of his spare bedrooms for my jewellery business. Apart from worrying about the pending trial, I've never been happier. And now that black cloud has lifted, we can look forward to the future. Together.

"Yes, sir. I'd have waited for you. Apart from anything

else, someone has to feed that dog of yours."

He gives a derisive snort. "I seem to remember it was you who came home with a rescue puppy, and let it crap all over my kitchen."

"Marlow was a present for you."

Jared makes another sound in his throat, then announces, not for the first time, that he hates dogs. I know this not to be true; he adores the three-month-old German Shepherd/Labrador cross though the pup does still make a mess from time to time. Despite his grumbling, he allowed me to keep him, just in case I did end up on my own at Cote House Barn. I'm convinced there's every chance Marlow will make a fine guard dog, eventually, if he ever grows into his oversized paws and can manage to summon up some semblance of aggression. Until then, I suppose I'll make do with my ex-jailbird dom.

I tighten my grip on his elbow. Life could be worse. A whole lot worse.

"Let's go home," suggests Jared. "I have paddle with your name on it."

THE END

Made in the USA
Las Vegas, NV
05 November 2022

58842368R00125